Tom Benjamin grew up in the suburbs of north London and began his wor' g life as a journalist before becoming a spokesm: '- 'and .id. I Ie 'ne ec public health, v .ie develop Britain's fi ipaign against alcohol abuse, 1 v rour Limits, and led drugs awareness programme FRANK. He now lives in Bologna.

Requiem in La Rossa is the third novel in his Daniel Leicester crime series.

Find Tom on Instagram, Twitter and Facebook @tombenjaminsays.

Praise for Tom Benjamin

'Another thrilling crime novel from Tom Benjamin, with an intriguing and twisty mystery that unfolds within Benjamin's acutely-observed descriptions of Bologna, its history and its people. Elegant prose, immersive detail and a gripping plot make [it] a perfectly balanced crime read. I loved it!'

Philippa East

'This second novel in the Daniel Leicester series is just as atmospheric and gripping as the first'

Gregory Dowling

'Loved it – an engaging hero, sharp dialogue and an ingenious plot that grips from the start. It'll make you want to visit'

Philip Gwynne Jones

'A unique and

Emma Christie, autl

Also by Tom Benjamin

A Quiet Death in Italy
The Hunting Season

Requiem in La Rossa

Tom Benjamin

CONSTABLE

CONSTABLE

First published in Great Britain in 2021 by Constable

A CIP catalogue record for this book
is available from the British Library.

ISBN: 978-1-47213-162-1

Typeset in Adobe Garamond by Initial Typesetting Services, Edinburgh
Printed and bound in Great Britain by Clays Ltd, Elcograf S.p.A.

Papers used by Constable are from well-managed forests
and other responsible sources.

MIX
Paper from
responsible sources
FSC® C104740
FSC
www.fsc.org

Constable
An imprint of
Little, Brown Book Group
Carmelite House
50 Victoria Embankment
London EC4Y 0DZ

An Hachette UK Company
www.hachette.co.uk

www.littlebrown.co.uk

For Lea, and her first glimpse
of the Manhattan skyline

'Finally the episcopal auditor arrived with his many yeomen to put them to the test. The nuns immediately and with one accord climbed up high and, throwing down tiles and stones, forced his retreat out of range with his squadron. Then, as the bell sounded the alarm and the crowds flocked there, Donna Isabetta Vizzana, crucifix in hand and with her head veiled, made the convent's case so passionately that she moved her audience to pity and indignation.'

Gasparo Bombacci, 1640

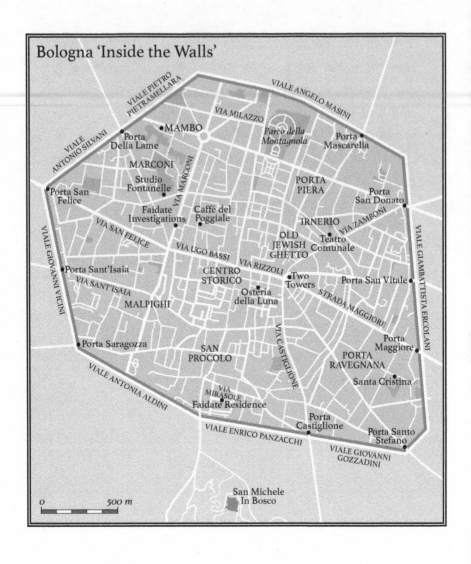

Bologna 'Inside the Walls'

VIALE PIETRO PIETRAMELLARA
VIALE ANGELO MASINI
VIA MILAZZO
VIALE ANTONIO SILVANI
MAMBO
Porta Della Lame
Parco della Montagnola
Porta Mascarella
MARCONI
VIA MARCONI
Studio Fontanelle
PORTA PIERA
Porta San Donato
Porta San Felice
Faidate Investigations
Caffè del Poggiale
IRNERIO
VIA ZAMBONI
Porta San Donato
VIA SAN FELICE
VIA UGO BASSI
OLD JEWISH GHETTO
Teatro Comunale
VIALE GIOVANNI VICINI
Porta Sant'Isaia
VIA SANT'ISAIA
CENTRO STORICO
VIA RIZZOLI
Two Towers
Porta San Vitale
VIALE GIAMBATTISTA ERCOLANI
MALPIGHI
Osteria della Luna
STRADA MAGGIORE
Porta Saragozza
VIA CASTIGLIONE
Porta Maggiore
SAN PROCOLO
PORTA RAVEGNANA
Santa Cristina
VIALE ANTONIA ALDINI
VIA MIRASOLE
Faidate Residence
Porta Castiglione
Porta Santo Stefano
VIALE ENRICO PANZACCHI
VIALE GIOVANNI GOZZADINI

0   500 m

San Michele In Bosco

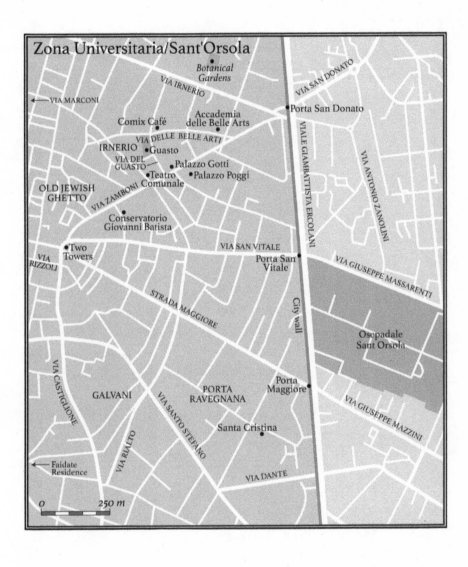

Zona Universitaria/Sant'Orsola

Chapter 1

'ONLY IN BOLOGNA' yelled the headline in the *Carlino*. It certainly seemed extraordinary for a respected university professor stepping out of the opera house on a balmy July night arm-in-arm with his wife to meet his death at the hands of one of the drug addicts who habitually shared the portico with concert-goers. But this was Bologna, and 'only' in Bologna, famous for reconciling the irreconcilable – Luxembourgish wealth and red politics, meat-rich cuisine and ethical dining, cultural highs with the very visible degradations of the heroin trade around Piazza Verdi – could an incident like this occur, according to the *Carlino*, at any rate, the tabloid's outrage-dial set to max.

I lowered the newspaper and watched my dog make his way methodically up the gravel path that led through the woods towards the church of San Michele in Bosco, moving between the trashcans like the Stations of the Cross, even though he and me both knew it was an act – woolly-haired, chocolate-coloured Lagotto Romagnolo, Rufus, an Italian breed prized for its truffle-hunting abilities, had no discernible sense of smell and was simply imitating the behaviour of other canines. Rufus may not have been able to sniff out prized fungi, but he damn well knew how to fake it.

Although there was currently no need for play-acting – it was barely seven in the morning and we were alone save for the saw of the cicadas and the heat that had settled like a blanket across the city and only been partly kicked away during the night. Inside what remained of its walls, Bologna's red brick was still warm to the touch, and as the sun continued its daily passage, an acrid edge would begin to emanate from the old buildings until, around dusk, it would seem like the only thing missing from the sighing streets was floating ash. But for the moment, following Rufus into the woods among the rosemary, mint and sage that had run wild since generations of monks had cultivated this hillside, I enjoyed the kind of fragrance people came to Italy on holiday for.

Magari, I said to myself – *I wish*. Lovely though it may have been, my Italy was not up here among the summer herbs, it was down there in the smouldering city.

At least, most mornings.

We emerged, the pair of us panting, onto the bare hillside beneath the ancient, rose bulk of San Michele, with Bologna, *La Rossa*, laid out below – a view that, were it not for the tubular, cream Kenzo Towers on the horizon marking the *Fiera* district, had remained unchanged in half a millennia.

I sat on the first bench along. I liked to picture myself as one of those old monks when I came up here, perhaps taking a pause from tending the vines they had once cultivated on this hillside, the mineral-rich soil of Emilia beneath my fingernails. But this morning, for all my proximity to history, the past felt hopelessly out of reach.

I took a swig of mineral water before removing Rufus's bowl from my daughter Rose's multi-coloured *Fedez* rucksack, which had now been handed down to the dog, and filling it up. Despite his summer haircut, Rufus fell upon the bowl as if it were a sparkling pool in an oasis. I checked my watch then produced my phone, initiating the appropriate app. As if on cue, I heard a dog barking, watched it race excitedly past.

Rufus raised his head from the bowl, his woolly jowls dripping, before turning uncannily human eyes upon me. 'No,' I said.

There was barking from the other side of the path. Sure enough, the first dog – a kind of fluffy, fawn-coloured Corgi breed – had met its playmate, a puppyish-looking German Shepherd. Together, they tore down the hill, then back up again.

Rufus gave me another look. 'Go on, then.' He went after them, creating a proper doggy posse. Meanwhile, the Corgi's owner, a sandy-haired woman with the lingering whiff of a little too much perfume, crossed to meet the German Shepherd's – a handsome, fit-looking older fellow free of any hint of grey – stood at a bench dead centre of the hill. They engaged in a prolonged, passionate kiss, before lowering down and continuing their embrace, more intensely, I had to say, than usual, but then this was probably *buona vacanza*. Although Pasquale Grande would be working in Bologna right up until August, Laura Guerrera had no option but to take the children to her late mother's old house in the countryside near La Spezia in case her husband became suspicious. In a sense, I was happy my firm, Faidate Investigations, had been hired by Pasquale's wife to spy on them rather than

Laura's husband, because I could see that although both, I supposed, were equally guilty of adultery, Laura had a lot more to lose. And while, as far as we knew, Laura had never strayed before, Pasquale had form. I vaguely hoped our client, Signora Grande, would keep Laura Guerrera out of it, but in any case, that was neither my problem nor responsibility. Harsh? Perhaps, but we all had to earn a living, even the dog here.

'Rufus!' By now all three were circling the lovers' bench like Apache in a Wild West movie, but Pasquale and Laura were oblivious. It was almost touching to see the middle-aged couple snog like teenagers, and really, I had enough material already, but for the absence of any doubt, I repeated: 'Stop that, and come here, right now.' Of course, I meant the dog, but the couple broke their clinch and looked up at me, again like teenagers – this time caught in the act. 'I'm sorry,' I said as Rufus came obediently to heel. 'He's always doing that.'

The sound of cicadas promptly ceased as if the insect army had paused to observe our exchange.

'No problem,' said Pasquale.

'Well,' I attached the dog's lead. 'I'll be off.' Pasquale gave me the wary nod of someone who was going to watch my every step until I was out of sight, when it happened.

It sounded like a gush of wind, but the trees remained perfectly still, the air dead, leaden even, with the gathering heat. The German Shepherd began to whine, Rufus pressed himself against me, but the sound kept building, seemingly rolling up from the red city through the very ground itself.

Of thousands of buildings, millions of roof tiles, shaking.

The ground shuddered. The chatter of the bench – Pasquale

and Laura instinctively grabbed hold of it – a child's scream from the foot of the hill.

The tremor stopped.

A moment of absolute silence, probably imagined, before a cacophony of car alarms. The sky, I realised, was crazy with birds. A dropping hit my shoulder, the bench, the bare ground around it.

'Aftershock,' said Pasquale. He looked at Laura. 'Nothing to worry about.'

'I'm not sure I'll ever get used to them,' I said.

The couple looked up at me as if to ask what I was still doing there. And they had a point – more than they could have conceivably imagined.

Rufus and I began to make our way down the hill. My phone rang. I was surprised – my girlfriend calling me this early in the morning. Stella Amore worked late and slept late.

'Is everything okay?'

'Yes,' she said, 'and no. In short – I'm trapped.'

Chapter 2

It had turned into a summer of tremors in the wake of 'the big one' that had struck the area around Modena, fifty kilo-metres northwest of Bologna, earlier that July, and which had caused some serious damage at its epicentre, including a dozen or so fatalities when a factory roof had collapsed. Since then, Bologna had rarely passed a day without experi-encing an aftershock, and what at the beginning had filled the streets and parks with hastily dressed Bolognese afraid to return home, now received about as much attention as a clap of thunder. Unless the ladder you were scaling slipped in the process and sent you flying, which was as much sense as I could get out of Stella Amore. I dropped Rufus at home and set off across the city for Via San Felice.

By the time I got there, the sun had risen sufficiently to banish that early morning cool and cast a sultry shadow even along the porticoes, percolating a layer of perspiration through my clothing and settling upon my brow like a fever.

The portico opened into a more ample colonnade outside Stella's place – a smart black door sandwiched between an upmarket florist and perfumery. Hers was the middle bell, although it wasn't her name, but *Lame*, on the buzzer.

'*Chi è?*' It was Stella's landlady, or 'patron', as she preferred to call her, Chiara.

'It's Daniel, Dan.'

'Oh, yes, yes. Come right up, come!' The door buzzed, once, twice, was still buzzing as I walked along the dim, cave-cold corridor and ascended the broad stone staircase.

Barking. Shuffling feet. Four drawn bolts, and, *eccola*, Signora Chiara Lame, instantly recognisable to anyone familiar with the Bolognese art-scene, as I – since I'd begun dating Stella – had become. In the winter, Chiara would materialise at openings in a silver fox fur coat and matching trainers, with perhaps a frilly flared skirt beneath – a striking ensemble for any woman, but especially a lady in her seventies. Now, in a pillar-box red sari, she greeted me, her French bulldogs Jules and Jim snuffling around my ankles

'Thank goodness!' she said. 'Stella's down there!'

'Down where?' But Chiara had already turned away. I followed her through a room that might have escaped renovation for two centuries, from the busy mosaic of its stone *Veneziana* floor to the Napoleonic-era frescoes, onto a windowed corridor running beside a series of similar rooms in the gallery-style typical of old *palazzi*. The rooms were crammed with furniture, their walls crowded with tar-dark ancestral paintings; sofas, chairs and tables piled with the precious (crockery, glass and silverware) and pointless (coils of string and ribbon, broken picture frames, shopping bags sprouting dusty old desk lamps or dead pot plants).

Stella was in the final room – or rather, beneath it: beside an assemblage of cane chairs, a stack of books, a corroded mirror and a box of yellowed photos, an old iron-strapped chest had been pushed aside to expose a square, pitch-black hole radiating coldness. Chiara nodded warily.

'She's *down there?*' I leaned over. '*Stella?*'

'Hey,' came a plaintive voice.

'What—' I took out my phone, switched on the light. Stella Amore looked up at me as pale as a prisoner, but otherwise apparently unperturbed. Dressed in her habitual black T-shirt and jeans, she was sat cross-legged about three metres below with a snapped wooden ladder across her legs, seemingly in the process of trying to lash it back together with some old curtain cord.

'It broke.'

I leaned further into the hole and swung my phone around. I could vaguely make out dim shapes in the darkness.

'What is this place?'

'It's . . .' She glanced at Chiara behind me. 'First things first – can you help get me out?'

I found a chair that seemed solid enough and lowered it through the hole. Stella climbed onto the seat then raised a foot onto its back. I grabbed hold of her arms and pulled. We fell back into the room like a pair of landed fish.

'Bravo!' Chiara clapped while Jules and Jim barked their appreciation. Stella and I got to our feet and pushed the chest back over the hole.

We declined an offer of coffee from Chiara, who wandered off chatting to her dogs, and I followed Stella back down the corridor towards the entrance. She swept open a gold velvet curtain that opened up to a huge room with four large windows looking onto a closed courtyard. The space had once served as a ballroom. It was now Stella's studio-cum-living space.

'It was for the exhibition.' She meant where I'd found her. It was quite a big deal – her inclusion in the Comune-sponsored 'multi-media event' *500 Anni di Resistenza*, '500 Years of Resistance', opening in a few days' time, where she was recreating a series of 'hidden spaces'.

'Your lucky day?' She meant the bird shit crusted on my shoulder. I stripped off my shirt and went to a basin crudely plumbed into a concoction of pipes excavated from the plaster, part of a kitchen knocked together by her artisan friends with a bare wood work surface, a small fridge and an old electric hob.

'What's this?' She held up a booklet that must have fallen from my back pocket snappily entitled: *Concessione della cittadinanza italiana per residenza sul territorio italiano ai sensi dell'art. 9 della legge n. 91 del 5/02/1992*

'Oh, Rose picked it up from the Comune. She's always badgering me about getting Italian citizenship, but take a look – it's a hell of a faff.'

'You wouldn't expect it to be easy.' Stella flicked through it. 'Demonstrating you can navigate the bureaucracy is a rite of passage. So they're finally going to kick you out, then, for being *extracomunitario*?' She used the term commonly employed for anyone outside the EU, but which had become a pejorative for illegal immigrant.

'Apparently that's what she's afraid of, but I keep explaining that since I settled here long before Brexit, there'll no getting rid of me.'

'Won't it be good, though, to get another passport? I mean, one that lets you travel in the rest of Europe.'

I smiled. 'I think the British one probably still works for that.'

'What I mean is – live, work in these other places.'

'I'm not planning on going anywhere.' I began to run the tap, heard her pull off her clothes. She came to stand naked beside me and turned on the shower – basically a pipe sticking out of the wall, curtained by transparent plastic sheeting. She stepped in. After I had wrung out my shirt, I went to join her.

'You heard about that prof killed coming out of the opera?' Stella returned to bed having closed the shutters against the sun and nestled beneath the crook of my arm.

'It was in today's paper.'

She lifted a leg over mine. My daughter's art tutor, we had been 'together' for a little over six months, although what that meant in practice I wasn't quite sure. I was in my mid-forties, Stella in her mid-thirties, but our relationship seemed to combine domestic intimacy with the open-endedness of a pair of twenty-something Interrailers.

Stella was svelte yet unapologetically visceral. Her forearms – one tattooed with a faded Chinese dragon – ended in fine-fingered hands which ended in broken nails painted absinthe-green. Her long legs were scratched and scabbed from hiking in the countryside, bruised from the physical labour involved in preparing her show.

When I *had* been in my twenties, Stella Amore would have been precisely the type of woman I fantasised being with. Instead, I had met my late wife, Lucia, who had kept me on the straight and narrow and, in the process, almost certainly saved me from. . . myself. Now I was all grown-up, I wondered if Lucia had done her work rather too well: looking down through Stella's mass of damp, shiny black curls to her prominent Roman nose, those chestnut brown, Sophia Loren eyes, I had the feeling of being vertiginously out of place.

Out of my depth?

Another tremor. The bed rattled, then stopped, but the chandelier continued to sway above us.

We shifted closer, staring it down until its lazy arc came to a halt. 'Vesuvio,' announced Stella. 'You know . . .'

'Your ex.'

'He was at La Luna.'

'He's always at the *osteria*, haven't you noticed? Since you took the late shift, he sees more of you than I do.'

'He wanted to know if you could look into it for him.'

'Into what, precisely?'

'Apparently the guy who's been arrested for killing this prof is a friend of his.'

'A thief?'

'I don't know anything about that. But he was cut up about it. He wants to see if there's anything he can do.'

'Rich people think throwing money at a problem can solve anything. He would be better off hiring a decent lawyer.'

Now Stella pulled herself on top of me. Her hair tumbled forward to enclose our faces. The tips of our noses touched.

'You're sure you're not jealous?' She rubbed her nose against mine. 'Not just a bit? I like a little jealousy in a lover. A touch of hot, Latin blood. It means,' she flattened her palm against my chest, 'there's a sign of life.'

'I've heard it said my Anglo-Saxon veins run with ice water.'

'Really?' She began to reach further down. 'Well now . . .' Her gaze softened. 'Perhaps you're not as English as you think.'

Chapter 3

Displaying characteristic modesty, Vesuvio had taken his name from the volcano that dominated Naples, the city of his birth. In Bologna, however, he maintained a lower profile. The address Stella had given me for his studio was in a relatively unprepossessing part of the city, actually not far from our office in Via Marconi – across the rather shabby, nondescript park September 11, 2001, among brick-built former light industrial units. You would also find MAMBO out here, Bologna's Museum for Modern Art, as well as university student residences and a weekend farmers' market.

I'd walked past 'Studio Fontanelle' twice before I noticed it – a single buzzer beside a typically graffiti-riddled door.

Vesuvio answered the intercom, his smoky rasp immediately recognisable as one of the regular *X-Factor* judges – the rocker who had been someone to the previous generation and wanted to resurrect his career with the next although, judging by my daughter Rose's reaction, he hadn't much hope of that.

'Come,' he said. 'I'll meet you in the courtyard.' The door clicked open and I entered a small reception area. Through a further set of smoked-glass doors I could see a stone-paved open space – what had once, presumably, been the factory loading bay – where a pair of black Range Rover SUVs were being packed with equipment cases by roadies.

'Daniel.' Vesuvio was dressed in torn black jeans and a Clash, *London Calling* T-shirt, with a silver key chain fashionably drooping from his pockets. His jet black hair was tied back and perfectly matched his black goatee, bordered by a couple of days' growth of grey bristles. He stood there as if I should have given him a round of applause or at the very least a hug just for being Vesuvio. Instead, I held out my hand. He looked a little crestfallen.

'Come through,' he said.

I followed him into the recording studio where he sat himself down on a high-backed ergonomic chair in front of an enormous slab of a mixing desk dusted with cigarette ash, presumably from long nights laying down tracks. He gestured for me to take the other chair.

I swivelled to face him, experiencing a sprinkle, albeit ever so slight, of stardust, despite myself. And possibly despite himself, Vesuvio appeared a little discomfited – good. I didn't want to waste my time on celebrity bullshit, and we weren't at an art opening where I might feel obliged to make an effort on behalf of my girlfriend. In truth, I could have done without being there, full stop, but I hadn't wanted to seem too sensitive about her ex, and neither could I afford to simply turn down the work, quite frankly. But as far as I was concerned, if we were going to do business, it would be English-style.

'You felt them, the tremors?' Vesuvio asked tentatively.

'Hard to ignore.'

'*La Rossa*'s especially restless this morning. You never get them in England?' I shook my head. 'Such a placid country.' He smiled as if recalling happier times.

The door opened. A woman – slim, blonde, with a serpent tattoo emerging from the top of her tight white T-shirt – stood with her hands on her hips.

'Last chance,' she said in American-accented English.

'Excuse me.' Vesuvio got up and went over, tried to take her in his arms but she wasn't having it.

'Fine!' She stalked out, slamming the door.

'Elvira's a little pissed.' Vesuvio sat back down. 'They don't have too many earthquakes in Holland, either.'

I scrolled to the story on my phone. 'Stella said you want us to look into the . . . individual who has been arrested for involvement in the death of Professor . . .'

'Bellario. I actually knew the guy, by sight – he'd just started teaching when I was in my final year at the conservatory, although by the looks of things he's moved on since then – I read he'd become head of musicology at the university.'

'Musicology,' I said. 'Sounds . . . theoretical.' Vesuvio nodded.

'The joke used to be that those who can't make a living with their music, teach. Those who can't teach music, teach musicology. But I'm sure there's more to it than that.'

'What makes you think we can help your friend . . . I'm sorry, I don't know his name.'

'Guido. Guido Delfillo.' He winced. 'It's a terrible thing . . .'

'What is?'

'That boy – he had such a gift. A multi-instrumentalist, he could make any instrument sing – you name it.'

'And you worked with him.'

'He was a session musician, and he came on tours. He wasn't cheap, either – I once got in a bidding war with Luca Carboni . . .'

'So how, then, do you think this came about? From hitting the stage with "Vesuvio" to mugging this prof outside the *Teatro Comunale*?'

Vesuvio looked at his hands. 'That's what I want you to find out.'

'They mentioned drugs,' I said. 'Was that always a problem for him?'

Vesuvio shrugged. 'Drugs . . . I mean, in our business . . . but . . .'

'What?'

'He was a nice kid, but you could tell, even when he was working with us – he should have been on the top of the world, but there was always this *tristezza* . . . sadness. Try and have a conversation? Don't bother! I asked one of the guys about the kid, like "what the fuck"? But no one could say.'

'Maybe he was an addict all along,' I said. 'Maybe he was harbouring this problem, trying to keep a lid on it.'

'He seemed the sober sort. Literally: didn't smoke, rarely even drank. No one said a word, there were no "whispers". Only this air of melancholy. I did wonder if he was seriously, you know, *medically* depressed . . . I don't know.' He hesitated.

'What?'

'We got rid of him.'

'What do you mean?'

'Like I said – we got rid of him.' A long sigh. 'All right, I did. The guy got me down. He was a downer. You go on tour, it's tough. People don't realise how tough it is, having to make every night a high. Every night that special night for the fans. At the end, you just don't need downers about. It affects you, it affects everybody.'

'So, you think this might have something to do with it? Why he turned to drugs. You feel responsible.'

Vesuvio spoke sadly. 'Such talent, this kid. You don't see talent like that often . . . To have ruined it . . . For it to have come to this . . .' He rubbed his hands together.

Damn it. I was almost beginning to warm to the guy. 'You can't feel responsible,' I said reluctantly, 'for whatever happened to . . .'

'Guido.'

'Guido. You can't take the blame for what happened to him when he was a kid, his chemicals or whatever.'

'Still . . .' Vesuvio shrugged. 'If there's something I can do – *you* can do – maybe it's not like the police, the papers say. Maybe there's something . . .'

'From what I've read it seems pretty open and shut. But there could be mitigating circumstances, a lack of witnesses or evidence, other suspects, issues around police procedure. We could look into the background, dig around a bit. But it would cost, and the outcome is likely to remain the same. Are you sure about this?'

There was a noise outside – gates opening, cars pulling out.

'I said I would meet Elvira there.'

'Where?'

'Grand Bahama.' Vesuvio shook his head. 'Screw the cost. I don't want to be sitting on a Caribbean beach thinking about that kid sweating in *La Dozza* because of something I've done . . . or haven't.' He gave me a meaningful look. 'Whatever some people might think.'

It was coming on for midday. The sun had reached its zenith and the Bolognese were ducking in and out of the porticoes as if evading enemy patrols. The temperature on one electric-green *Farmacia* sign read 42, although that was probably an exaggeration – Bologna didn't usually reach those highs, at least in the shade, until August.

My phone rang.

'You wanted to speak,' said Dolores.

'Meet me at the fish place.' She began to protest. '*Basta.* I'll pay.'

I checked my messages while I waited at *Banco*. I'd already put in a request to our contact at the Questura because, at least according to the press, Guido had been arrested by the Polizia di Stato, which was a pain because given our familial links most of our influence lay within the ranks of their rivals in law and order, the Carabinieri. But on this occasion I wasn't too fussed. Regardless of how much Vesuvio might want to salve his conscience, there was unlikely to be a *Miracolo al Teatro Comunale.* Even if Guido Delfillo hadn't meant to kill the professor (and that remained a bit vague) he was almost certainly involved in the attempted robbery that led to his death. If Vesuvio wanted to pay us to confirm that, then I wasn't going to have a guilt trip – I'd warned him.

'Anyway,' I said as Dolores took her seat, 'I don't understand why you're being so stingy – that's precisely what we

give you vouchers for.' It's common for Italian firms to provide staff with lunch vouchers as a 'perk' to avoid taxes. 'You
can't save them, you realise – they expire.'

'Oh, I don't. I use them.' Dolores looked cagey.

'You give them away, don't you.'

'I don't need them!'

Our twenty-five-year-old trainee investigator seemed
swamped by her cream silk blouse complete with shoulder
pads. She had taken to 'recycling' clothes from church sales,
which was at least an improvement on her former *punkabestia*
look when I had first come across her as part of an investigation into the local squatting scene.

Following the eviction of those squatters from the historic
buildings in the city centre, Bologna had moved on, at least
on the surface, and so had Dolores Pugliese, at least on the
surface: her blue Mohican had grown out and returned to
its natural fawn, making her look even younger and more
emaciated than usual, although I had to admit that when she
turned up wearing those mirrored Aviators (another charity
shop find) the sixteen-year-old boy in me had thought she
looked pretty cool.

'You're half-starved,' I said.

She glanced over the menu. 'I am extremely healthy. It's
you,' she frowned at my belly, 'who needs to lose a few kilos.
Middle-aged spread. Have you had a check-up? We also have
a health plan, don't we? Have you tried yoga? Pilates?'

I straightened up. 'I'm in perfect form.'

'At your age,' Dolores said brightly, 'people can drop dead
out of the blue. Stroke, heart attack. I bet they thought they
were in "perfect form", too.'

'Speaking of dying,' I said. 'This professor . . .'

'*Precisely.*'

'But he was old and *actually* overweight, I imagine.'

'Not according to this photo.' She held up her phone. A lean man in his early fifties with a mop of dark hair. He reminded me of a German soccer coach.

'Perhaps,' I said, 'he had an "underlying condition"?'

'Perhaps you do.'

I scowled. 'Well, something must have killed him – what do you have?'

'I've only had time to look online.'

'And?'

'Apparently he collapsed, which I suppose means he wasn't stabbed, and he died later in hospital.'

'Which?'

'Sant'Orsola.'

The *cameriera* arrived and took our order. Dolores asked for *Strigoli con pesto al basilico, fagiolini e patate* – strips of pasta with basilica pesto, beans and potatoes – while I went for the smoked swordfish salad. Dolores gave me an approving look.

'I was going to choose that anyway.'

'You could always join a gym,' she said. 'There's Performance right by our office . . .'

'Alba can speak to the hospital. I'll deal with the Polizia. You head down to Piazza Verdi, see what you can find out about Guido. I want to know about his background, how long he's been scoring, associates, sob stories, and if any of the druggies know anything about the night in question.' I thought about it. 'We'll pay for anything useful, fifty euros. A hundred if it's really special.'

'They'll spend it on smack.'

'There's nothing we can do about that.' Dolores bit her lip. 'We're not going to change them. You know that. But we might be able to help this Guido character. If you want to be *ethical*, maybe you can offer them your vouchers.' She looked down. '*All of them*? You've given them *all* away? To who?'

'There's an old man in my building. After his wife died he just started getting thinner. *He* was really losing weight. He can use them at a local restaurant.'

'Well,' I said uncomfortably, 'that's very nice. But we need this info, so do what you have to. Actually, before you speak to them, pop into the opera house itself. Ask to see the manager. Explain our company has been tasked to look into the background of the incident – they'll presume we've been hired by the family of the victim, so may be sympathetic – and ask to see any CCTV they have from the lobby or portico. I expect the police have already sequestered the stuff from the Guasto and, if they're any good, used it to track Professor Bellario all the way back there, but you never know.'

'What are we looking for?'

'I have absolutely no idea,' I said. 'Until we find it.'

Chapter 4

The lift to Faidate Investigations was finally back in service but I took the stairs, stung by Dolores' comments, and as a result arrived on the fourth floor panting and slick with sweat. I paused outside the entrance, trying to control my breathing and randomly tugging at the flesh around my hips. I hated those bellies of forty-something men that rose like sandbanks beneath their summer shirts, and loathed the idea of becoming one myself. Walking almost everywhere, and eating – obviously, due to the awfulness of the local Indian and Chinese food – only Italian, that is the fabled Mediterranean diet, I'd always considered myself in pretty good shape, but perhaps I was fooling myself. I might have been technically living in the Mediterranean, but meat-heavy Bolognese cuisine was infamously fatty, the 'Bolognese Liver', a thing of legend. *Tagliatelle al ragu* (which was not exactly a light pasta dish) aside, the city's signature *secondo* was *Cotoletta alla Bolognese* – fried veal, covered with prosciutto and smothered with melted Parmesan.

The lift arrived and the inner gate was drawn back. The Comandante – Giovanni Faidate – stepped out. The title was an honorific stemming from his days in the Carabinieri, which had followed him into civilian life to the extent it was commonly used by everyone in the family except my daughter – his granddaughter – to whom he was, and always would be, *Nonno*.

Despite the hot weather, the Comandante appeared as starched and unruffled as ever in dark slacks and a pale-blue, short-sleeved shirt.

'Are you all right, Daniel? The heat getting to you?'

'Just wanted a little exercise,' I muttered.

'Not in the summer, Daniel. Best to leave that to the cooler seasons.'

I followed my father-in-law into the marble-floored, air-conditioned reception. Venetian blinds shaded the afternoon sun.

'I was thinking,' said the Comandante. 'Given everything is winding down, perhaps we might close early, considering we now have the place in Cesenatico.' He meant the beach house on the 'Riviera Romagnola' he had recently invested in with some of his old cronies.

Alba, sat behind a Regency-style desk at the far end of the room, peered around her computer. 'You got the footage of Pasquale Grande?'

'Didn't Jacopo send it to you?'

'Jacopo!' Alba called her cousin.

'What?'

'Come out here!'

Jacopo emerged from the rear offices, looking like he had just woken up.

'Oh, hey, Dan.'

'Did you get the footage?' I asked. 'Of the adulterers?' He dug out his phone, held it up – there was the video of Pasquale and Laura caught in the act by the tiny Bluetooth-powered camera I had attached to my shirt.

'It's not at all bad,' he said, fiddling with his nose ring. While Dolores had apparently become less 'alternative' since joining us, Jacopo, the Comandante's son, had gone the other way with his expanding menagerie of tattoos and piercings; the habitual black T-shirt and camouflaged cargo shorts combo halfway down his hips. Although, as this was the standard summer uniform of Bolognese youth, I suppose in his way he could be said to be as much the conformist as his father.

'Now that's done,' Alba said excitedly, 'we can wrap up. We've completed this month's background checks – and of course everything else will be closing down so . . .'

'If you lot want to go to the beach, fine,' I said. 'But I've just got us a new job.' Alba's face fell. 'And before we go any-where,' I looked at the Comandante, 'your granddaughter will have to attend the *vernissage* for Stella's exhibition. It's all she talks about.'

'When is it?' he asked.

'End of the week.'

'What's this new job, then?' Alba asked grudgingly. As I explained, she began to perk up.

'Do you think that maybe next time you go to see him . . .'

'Would you like to come? You never mentioned you were a Vesuvio fan. You know *Stella*—'

'Yes, I know about Stella.' She looked back at her computer. 'Okay. Well. Sure. In fact, you know what: I've told

Vesuvio to expect a contract. How about I knock something together and you deliver it by hand? Just check he signs it with his legal name and not his autograph. Although I'm sure if you asked for one . . .'

She rolled her eyes. 'I'm not a teenager, Dan.' She clicked on something. 'But I'll try to pop it over if I have the time.'

'Thank you,' I said, trying not to laugh. 'That would be very helpful.'

I closed the door to my own office and went to stand by the blinds, looking down onto Via Marconi, as close to a 'business district' as Bologna had. The traffic was already thinning out in anticipation of the holidays.

As Alba had mentioned, almost all of Italy took the following month off – for good reason, given the average temperatures – and the school break lasted around three months. Which was all right for some: today Rose, together with Stefania, her best friend, was helping out at Stefi's mum's 'alternative therapy' summer school. Admittedly, I had my reservations about the amount of rubbish Rose spouted after spending time with Cristina, who filled the kids' heads with all the most fashionable conspiracy theories, but when you're a single father, you have to take your mother-figures where you can find them. Since my wife's death, her cousin, Alba, and Cristina, along with dashes of Dolores, and most recently Stella, had filled that gap, and I was ludicrously grateful to them all.

I looked at Lucia's photo on my desk, together with a six-year-old Rose. I had older photos, but preferred this, from the days without even a hint of death's shadow. I wasn't sure what Lucia would have thought about Stella – I suspected she might have laughed. Lucia had been political – an academic, campaigner, always at odds with her conservative, ex-Carabinieri father. She had certainly had it in her to be an artist – which was clearly where Rose got her ability to draw – but instead chose to channel her creative energy into changing the world.

I'd always presumed Rose took after Lucy one hundred per cent, but these days my fifteen-year-old seemed to be leaning more towards observing the world than transforming it, as demonstrated by her current obsession with creating comic strips, or 'graphic novels', as she rather more grandly called them, under Stella's tutelage. And the art of observation – that was certainly more my side of the equation.

This kid, Guido – another artist, albeit of the musical variety. Turned to drugs – every parent's nightmare, although given that many modern parents, myself included, had partaken in their youth, that was not the whole truth. More accurately, the fear was that their children would be among the unlucky ones – they wouldn't be able to handle it, that some demon would take over, an insatiable hunger that would draw everything into its gravity.

From what Vesuvio had told me, it sounded like Guido Delfillo had displayed the warning signs even when he hadn't, apparently, been using.

The old rocker shouldn't really have beaten himself up – the poor kid had been doomed. It was only a matter of time.

The landline chirped. 'Call for you,' said Alba. 'Avvocato Servi.' I was in luck: Filippo was one of the good ones.

'I hear you're interested in my boy,' he said.

'I've a client who would like to get him off. Do you think there's any hope?'

Silence, then: 'This client of yours must have deep pockets. Is it worth my trouble?' It wasn't what it sounded like – as the court-appointed lawyer, he wanted to know whether it was worth putting the effort in before he got replaced.

'I'll tell him you're one of the best, better than most of these private outfits. Maybe you can bill him for additional "expenses".'

'You flatter me, but then, words are cheap. I see your Italian continues to improve, Daniel. Do you know you're picking up a Bologna accent?'

'Now who's flattering? What can you tell me that I don't know already? He confronted this professor . . .'

'And his wife.'

'His wife – name?'

'Melodia di Battista.'

'*Melodia*? You're kidding.'

'Musical family.'

'Violence?'

'According to Signora di Battista, he flashed a knife. Didn't use it. They were halfway down the Guasto. Asking for trouble that time of the night.'

'And then . . .'

'There was some kind of altercation.'

'I bet there was.'

'What I mean was – an argument. Signor Delfillo fled . . .'

'The prof chased him.'

'No – the professor just collapsed. Massive heart attack. He was dead before the ambulance arrived, although officially pronounced at hospital.'

'How did they catch the kid?'

'He came back when Melodia began to scream. He claims he tried to help. When the police turned up – they were just around the corner in Piazza Verdi – she fingered him.'

'Not the brightest spark then, this Guido.'

'Are you suggesting he shouldn't have come to the professor's aid?'

'I don't know – is there some kind of mugger's code?'

'He knew him – the professor.'

'Oh? How?'

'Knew the wife, too. The pair had been students together.'

'So, was it a mugging at all?'

'He claims no.'

'What *is* he claiming?'

'Nothing – he just insists it wasn't a hold-up. After that he clams up.'

'But he *is* a drug addict.'

'He is. In fact I've just been trying to sort out his methadone.'

'Address?'

'He claims – No Fixed Abode.'

'That's ridiculous. If he studied here, he must have residency.'

'I've placed a request.'

'He doesn't sound very cooperative. He realises how bad this is?'

'I'm not sure if you could say he *realises*, precisely. He was in pretty bad shape – hence the methadone. But if he doesn't come up with something, he's going to be sent down. Attempted robbery resulting in the death of the victim – five years, minimum.'

'I'd like to speak to him, if I may.'

'Be my guest, although you might like to wait until he's out of the Questura and they've transferred him to *La Dozza*.'

'Why's that?'

'You'll be further out of the range of the investigating officer – Commissario Miranda.'

'*Shit.*'

Filippo chuckled. 'I thought you might say that.'

Chapter 5

In common with many other Bologna buildings, the *Teatro Comunale* could be accused of feigned modesty, her grandeur veiled by the line of porticoes that were an obligatory addition to any new build back in the day, and which she wears like a diva might a string of pearls.

Inaugurated in 1763, the *Teatro* sits on a piazza bordered by buildings dating from the Renaissance and is the second oldest opera house in Italy, the first publicly-built and owned anywhere in the world – the city's communal roots stretch far further back than the red politics of the twentieth century.

It was raised upon former public gardens known as *Il Guasto*, or 'the dump', the site where the vast *palazzo* of the Bentivoglio family had been torn down by an angry mob after *I Bentivoglio* became too big for their boots. In successive years, that rubble-strewn wasteland had become a dumping ground – hence *guasto* – before being transformed into a park, and finally the site of the *Teatro*.

A small parcel of the old park still existed behind it and, fittingly, retained the appellation – *dump* – not least thanks to a 1970s redesign apparently inspired by the creative use of concrete. It was between here and the rear of the *Teatro* that the confrontation between Professor Bellario and Guido had taken place.

'ONLY IN BOLOGNA', the *Carlino* had thundered, although I doubted you had to walk far from London's Royal Opera House before stepping around a homeless person. But anyone who knew Bologna knew what the *Carlino* was getting at – there was a peculiar brazenness and squalor around Piazza Verdi it would be difficult to replicate at the centre of other Italian cities. Well, perhaps Naples, but Naples was *Naples*, and we were in the north. Northern Italians commonly consider themselves separate from their southern counterparts. The north is industrious, wealthy, honest; comparatively *German* in its outlook. Northerners tend to view southerners as the world sees Italians as a whole.

So 'only in Bologna' would you find smackheads and drunks lounging between the columns of a venerable opera house beneath UNESCO-nominated porticoes in a square named after the composer who had made his name at the venue – Giuseppe Verdi. Only Bologna would create a 'zone of tolerance' at its historic heart – the piazza is mid-way along Via Zamboni, home to the majority of university buildings, and as such constitutes the social centre of 'UniBo'. Piazza Verdi was thus 'owned' by the students and invariably decorated with fiery murals and radical banners.

Judged by the slogans in the piazza, it was not hard to feel transported to a more revolutionary era, although in practice the politics were as antiquated as the *palazzi*. That train had left the station, carrying the revolutionaries with it. These were now the centre-left politicians who 'tolerated' the binge drinking in the square, the disco bars along nearby Via Petroni; the wealthy *professori* who accepted the graffiti and sit-ins, drunks and drug addicts. The times may have changed, but *radical chic* had never gone out of fashion in Bologna.

I sipped a Crodino on a table outside Il Piccolo e Sublime – a long name for a small bar opposite the *Teatro*.

Between the corroded metal tubs in front of me, from which sprung a trio of weary-looking trees, a down-and-out propped up his backpack and began to methodically strip as if he was alone in a hotel room, while from the side of the *Teatro* a couple of Polizia di Stato in berets and sunglasses stood smoking in front of their van.

Grateful, and not a little surprised, that the tramp had halted at his underpants before taking a bottle of water and pouring it over his long straggly hair, I gazed in the direction of Via del Guasto on the other side of the opera house.

The narrow road ran beside the *Teatro* then along what was left of the park before emerging onto Via delle Belle Arti – the 'street of fine arts', and home to the Accademia. It was a notorious spot, and even I would think twice about heading there after dark – the dingy lane was a byway for the druggies moving in and out of the piazza, and even the Comune had acknowledged the need to re-purpose the area, establishing pop-up bars during the summer. Perhaps this was why the professor had believed it safe to take the shortcut on his way home. But the encounter had happened in the stretch past the bars. Here there were still plenty of shadows and, as the residents of Via delle Belle Arti would undoubtedly tell you,

'Guasto Village' had not dampened down the drugs trade, it had simply moved it along.

The afternoon had entered its somnolent phase. Those of us unfortunate enough to be outside wore the heat around us like a cloak, and part of me envied the tramp his ablutions. He finished the bottle off by pouring the remainder across his tattooed shoulders, the water splashing onto those pale blue briefs, before he perched on one of the tubs, apparently oblivious to the people traversing the piazza – mainly students, some of whom were wearing the laurel crowns that marked their graduation, and ignored him, while parents and relatives in their entourage visiting the city for the *Laurea* festivities, gawped.

The tramp began waving in the direction of the *Teatro*. I thought he was signalling another derelict sitting further along the porch, but then I saw Dolores, her shades glinting in the low sunlight. She waved cheerfully back and stopped to chat until she spotted me and made her excuses. The tramp turned and gave me a convivial nod as if we were diners at some exclusive restaurant.

'As well-connected as ever,' I said. Dolores removed her sunglasses.

'One of my old professors.'

'You're kidding me.'

'Well, "associate" professor – he holds a doctorate in Minoan ceramics.'

'What happened?'

'They dropped him for an old buddy of the departmental head. After that, well, he had a bit of a breakdown. Honestly, he seems happier now. It's one of the reasons I never continued my studies – what's the point if they just give the jobs to their chums?'

'And I thought it was because you had a burning ambition to become a private detective.'

'Yeah, that too, obviously.'

'So, what have you got?'

Guido Delfillo was apparently well known by the crowd around the opera house – his musical talent meant he was able to serve his drugs habit by busking, and not just the usual Lucio Dalla covers, but real classical pieces, and on any string instrument that came to hand. Some members of the *Teatro's* orchestra had recognised him, it seemed, and even tried to help him out when he had first materialised beneath the portico, but after a succession of no-shows to gigs and auditions, this had tailed off. These days, aside from the odd guilty glance or tossed coin, his former advocates tended to avoid him.

None of the junkies and drunks believed Guido had tried to mug the prof although they were hardly character references. They had all suffered as a result of the incident because the dealers usually stationed at the corners of the piazza had melted away, at least for the time being. The last thing the pushers needed was trouble. It was bad for business.

'What about film from the *Teatro*?' I asked. 'CCTV?' Dolores pouted. 'No luck?'

'I couldn't even get past the ticket counter. You know what they're like.' The staff at the *Teatro's* box office were notoriously intransigent.

'You asked to see the manager?'

'They told me to get *my boss* to phone during office hours.'

I checked my watch. It was five. 'Aren't these office hours?'

'Eight to eleven, two to three-thirty.'

I sighed. 'So tell me, Dolores Pugliese, precisely why *did* you drag me out of the air-conditioning?'

She pulled out her notebook. 'I thought you'd like to check it out,' she said. 'I managed to discover Guido's address.'

'Third cardboard box on the left?'

'Not at all. He lives with his parents.'

'That explains it, then.'

'What?'

'Why he didn't want to say.'

Chapter 6

The parents lived nearby – a ten-minute walk down Via Petroni and onto San Vitale, one of the major arteries, or 'spokes', of the old city. The Delfillos' address was towards the end of the street, near the old stone gate that stood as a kind of monument to the former walls, although the fortifications continued to exist in the mental geography of the Bolognese – one either lived 'inside' or 'outside' of them.

I rang the bell.

'*Chi è?*'

'Signor Delfillo? My name is Daniel Leicester, I'm a private investigator working on behalf of your son. Can we speak?'

'My son? He can't afford a private eye!'

'What I mean is,' I looked at Dolores, 'he's been arrested, Signor Delfillo, but someone has employed us to try and get him out.'

A sigh blasted through the speaker. 'Why would anyone want to do that?'

'It's . . . complicated, signore. May we come in?'

Another blast. The intercom went dead. We stood looking at each other. The door clicked open.

Faced with a dark, narrow corridor, it was only as my eyes adjusted I saw him standing in the open *porta blindata*, or security door, mid-way down. A paunchy, grey-skinned man in need of a shave, he looked around seventy, but something told me – perhaps the creases across his forehead, those dark crescents beneath his eyes – this was premature. Judging by the age of his son, who was in his mid-twenties, he might only be a decade older than me.

'How do I know you are who you say you are?'

I showed him my ID, which he examined with care. Behind him, I heard a shuffle, glimpsed the pulled-back grey hair of a woman, presumably Signora Delfillo.

'Who are you actually working for?' Signor Delfillo's tired eyes narrowed. He had neither commented on my name nor my English accent (notwithstanding Avvocato Servi's compliment), which was the usual reaction when I introduced myself. But there was no idle curiosity about Signor Delfillo – he had clearly inspected too many IDs.

'My client is a musician – he worked with your son, read about what happened in the papers, wanted to help him.'

A woman's gasp. Signor Delfillo wearily shook his head. 'It's so bad it's been in the papers? We don't read them. What now?'

'He's been implicated in the death of a university professor. There was some kind of altercation.'

Signor Delfillo said flatly: 'He tried to rob him.'

'We're not sure about that. He claims not.'

Signor Delfillo rolled his shoulders as if to relieve them of the weight.

'You'd better come in,' he said.

It was a modest apartment, 'ill-appointed' as so many were within the walls, with little natural light due to the days when small windows were the standard means to repel the heat as well as the cold. But it was pleasant enough, the *soggiorno*'s white wooden shelves stacked with books, a closed piano in the corner, artfully-placed ambient lighting. Only, I quickly clocked the signs – that TV-sized gap in the middle of the shelves with a tell-tale black lead curled behind it; records and CDs but no player, turntable or speakers; no other obvious signs of electronics. Their son had even taken the silver picture frames, I noted, the wedding presents evident in every Italian household. I supposed Signora Delfillo – her mouth cast permanently downward – had long since bid *arrivederci* to her jewellery.

'Guido still lives here?' I asked.

'He doesn't have a key, if that's what you're thinking,' said Signor Delfillo. 'But yes,' he glanced at his wife rigid beside him on the sofa, 'he still lives here. So tell me – why would this musician . . . who is it?'

I wouldn't usually reveal the name of a client but, frankly, saw no point in beating around the bush.

'Vesuvio,' I said. His wife let out a sob. 'Is there something I should know?'

Signor Delfillo shook his head. 'Just memories, isn't that right, *amore*? When Vesuvio offered him a job we thought it meant light at the end of the tunnel.' Now the husband's eyes misted. 'But it wasn't to be.'

'Was Guido a drug addict before he began working for him?'

Signor Delfillo shook his head again. 'At least not as far as I know. But he was depressed, lethargic. Never happy. He never got over it.'

'Over what?'

'Rejection. That was why we moved here from Puglia – because it had the best music schools. "City of Music", all that.' I glanced at Dolores.

'Didn't you know? It's the UNESCO City of Music.'

'I thought that was the porticoes.'

'They've made an application, but it's already the City of Music.'

'He was a genius, my little Guido,' said his mother. 'He's like Mozart!' Her husband placed an arm around her.

'Well, that's what everyone used to say. But we were from a small town in the south, what did we know?'

'*It was true.*'

'So what happened?' I asked. 'What was this "rejection"?'

'When it came time for the conservatory, he couldn't cut it,' said Signor Delfillo.

'What do you mean?'

'He failed the admission exams. He couldn't get in.'

'Well,' I thought of my own patchy academic record, 'we all fail exams.'

'Not him,' said the wife. 'Never.'

'Like I was saying,' said Signor Delfillo, 'we were from the sticks . . . '

'He did well at the school here,' she insisted. 'He was their top student.'

'It was a private school – they'd say whatever you wanted to hear.'

'You never had faith in him, that's the truth!'

It was clearly an old argument, and I needed to get them back to the matter at hand. 'Excuse me – so, he failed this exam. Couldn't he have taken another one? Gone some-where else? Tried again?' Now they looked at each other, as I suspected they had looked at each other many times, with shared, helpless bewilderment. Signor Delfillo turned to me.

'We don't know what happened. After that, it was as if something snapped inside of him. Broke. We tried, but we couldn't fix it.'

'Doctors,' said his wife. 'Drugs . . . legal ones, I mean. Anti-depressants.'

'Did he mention a Professor Bellario?' They looked blank. 'No mention?'

'This is the guy who died?' asked Signor Delfillo. I nodded. 'Never heard of him.'

'But he didn't start taking *illegal* drugs immediately after the exam?' asked Dolores.

'No,' Signor Delfillo informed her. 'It was only after the second time, that second rejection – this Vesuvio. I mean . . .' He sighed. 'We don't blame the guy. We knew Guido had his . . . moods. We hoped the new job would . . . lift him up. But . . .'

I said to his mother: 'He's a sensitive boy.' She nodded, the tears now flowing freely.

'He's always been sensitive. *But he's an artist.*'

I stood up and went over to the bookshelves. There were plenty of photos, mostly now frameless. I examined one – a good-looking, dark-haired teenager draped around a cello and smiling at the camera. 'This is him?'

'He was fifteen – just before we left for Bologna,' said the signora.

I picked up a group photo – a dozen teenagers, perhaps a couple of years later. That boy again, but this time with wavy hair and a sort of cavalier-style beard. There was laughter in those eyes – the laughter of one who knows how good he is, who's going places.

'This is him, too, right?'

'The last one we have,' said his father. 'Before it all went wrong.'

'May I borrow it?' Signor Delfillo looked at his wife.

'Will it help him?' she asked.

'It might.'

We walked back along the portico of San Vitale.

'When you were using drugs,' I said to Dolores, 'did you—'

'I never stole anything.'

'But when we met, you said—'

'Yeah. But it was never as bad as that. I mean – I lost a year of university. . .' She shook her head. 'I was just looking for a purpose.'

'One thing I'll never get used to,' I said, 'is their sheer ubiquity in Bologna – in the whole of Italy, in fact.'

'Isn't it the same in England?'

'But here it's something else. You don't see people shooting-up or smoking heroin in the open in Britain. At least not in city centres. You don't have to worry about your kids coming across needles when they step out of the front door or go to the park. There's a real difference – it seems to be everywhere.'

'Organised crime's one of our top industries,' said Dolores, as if she was talking about financial services. 'The narcotics trade runs through our ports, our banks, our businesses. It pumps its cash through our society like a syringe. Of course there are more drugs here, Dan. It's like with Fiat – it's the home market.'

'They're turning their own children into drug addicts.'

'*Dai*, come on. You think the mafia is *The Godfather*? Marlon Brando and Al Pacino?' She laughed. 'And I used to say you were cynical!'

We were back in Piazza Verdi. 'All right,' I said. 'I'll speak to Vesuvio – he went to the conservatory. I'll ask him about this "entrance exam".' I looked towards the *Teatro Comunale*. 'It's sad,' I said.

The doors were open, well-heeled opera-goers beginning to gather in the foyer while the derelicts continued to sup their cans and play with their dogs on the porch.

'It's Italy,' said Dolores.

Chapter 7

The coroner had agreed to meet me the following morning. That spring we had finally installed air-conditioning into our apartment, so as usual it came as a shock to be hit by the heat when I opened the front door. It might seem churlish for a Briton to moan about an unrelenting procession of 'beautiful days', but I was looking forward to getting back into the cool again, even if it was over a dead body.

I descended the narrow stone steps into the courtyard where I came across Alba, who lived in an apartment on the ground floor. Her cotton nightgown was wrapped around her and she was next to a big fellow in jeans and a lilac polo shirt, one arm draped over her shoulders, the other pointing up beyond the two floors of the Faidate Residence's frescoed 'Romeo and Juliet' balconies.

'Dan.' Looking embarrassed, Alba wriggled out from under his arm. 'This is—'

'I know. Hi, Claudio.' Claudio was our go-to guy for electronics – be it fixing the TV or installing a tracking device. It appeared he had also become Alba's go-to guy. 'Problem?'

'Oh, hey, Dan. It's the roof.'

'He was just leaving,' said Alba.

'But we've just had it re-tiled.'

'When I was fixing the satellite dish I checked out the work,' said Claudio. 'They did a good job – should be fine. It's not *that* I'm worried about.'

'What then?'

'I'd need to go down.' He nodded at the steps leading to the *cantina*, or basement. 'Check the foundations.'

A door on the first floor, or *piano nobile*, opened. It had to be the Comandante. I caught Alba's panicked expression – her intimate goodbye was fast transforming into a family reunion.

'I'll leave you to it.'

I had last met the coroner, Doctor Mattani, over the mouldering corpse of Dolores' squatter friend, Paolo Solitudine, although it was better that the veteran anarchist's bloated body had not been her final memory of him. The old brick morgue where I had viewed Paolo had cast the scene in an even more baleful light, like something out of the hunt for Jack the Ripper.

This meeting, however, would take place at the more clinical setting of the university hospital of Sant'Orsola-Malphigi, the very place Professor Bellario had been conveyed and officially pronounced dead. The hospital was reputedly the largest in Italy – a sprawling mishmash of buildings dating from its foundation in the sixteenth century to the 1980s.

I passed beneath the nineteenth-century arch onto the hospital campus and followed the map I'd downloaded from the doctor onto my phone as best as I could, keeping an eye out for a sign pointing to *Autopsie Giudiziarie*, although I didn't hold out much hope – if Italian hospital signage was anything like the road markings, I'd end up in Maternity.

I followed a tree-lined thoroughfare, passing functional red and white tower blocks, their generators straining to maintain the requirements of air-conditioning, and earlier brick buildings which brought to mind the crude surgical interventions of yesteryear. Italian hospitals, though: I knew them well enough, from birth to death and points in-between. Notwithstanding the budgetary constraints common to any public health system, there was an air of calm and common sense I'd rarely encountered in the UK. Perhaps in this respect at least, the country's infamous resistance to reform helped: budgets might get cut, but at least everyone seemed to know what they were doing.

And there it was, along a slip road, at the base of one of those tower blocks – the autopsy *sala*. I hesitated – a pale blue Polizia di Stato *volante* was parked outside.

I walked back up the slope to the main road where I went a little further along and found a bench in the shade. I twisted around – I could monitor the *sala* entrance from here.

Ten minutes after my scheduled meeting with Doctor Mattani, the doors slid open and out stepped Commissario Rita Miranda, looking as pissed-off as ever. The uniformed officer she was with went around to the driver's side while she got in the back, her ear already pressed to her mobile phone. I turned away, shielding my face as the squad car went up the ramp and headed in the opposite direction.

'Sorry I'm late.' I ducked my head into the main autopsy room where the receptionist had told me the doctor would be waiting.

Doctor Mattani, dressed in hospital blues, was snapping off his gloves. 'You just missed the commissario,' he said. 'I'm sure she would have been delighted to see you.'

'Did you know she was coming?'

The doctor laughed. 'Hardly – otherwise I wouldn't have asked you to turn up now.'

'What did she want?'

'Like you – an update on our professor here.' He indicated the outline beneath a pink paper sheet. 'Quite the celebrity, at least now he's dead. What do you think?'

'About what?'

'Our new facility!' He gestured around the strip-lit, pale-blue-and-white-tiled room, which looked rather like an operating theatre only with fewer machines and a quartet of man-size steel tables. 'Quite a contrast to the old place, no?'

'I suppose so, yes.'

'You don't look very impressed.'

'It's . . . very nice.' He continued to look at me expectantly. 'A bit . . . sterile?'

'Well,' the doctor said defensively, 'it's supposed to be. It's a hospital, for heaven's sake!' he huffed. 'At least the bloody coffee machine works. Anyway.' He unceremoniously swept back the sheet to reveal the chalk-white body of Professor Ilario Bellario.

A broad crimson autopsy incision ran vertically down the professor's chest, another horizontally above his belly. Both were neatly stitched together with black mortuary twine, although his torso was still swashed with traces of dried blood where the excess had been sponged off.

At first I thought we had the wrong man, then I recognised

him, only he was perfectly bald. 'Looking for this?' Doctor Mattani produced the black wig like a rabbit from a hat. 'There are no secrets here!' He frowned. 'Well, perhaps that's not the whole truth.'

'Oh?'

'I've asked for further tests. I'll tell you: the commissario was not well pleased.'

'Why? Wasn't it a heart attack, then? A stroke?'

'Oh, it was a cardiac arrest, all right, which, for the lay person, we shall call a "heart attack". At least, his heart stopped, which is all that counts. Ventricular fibrillation – mechanical. Basically, the pump came to a halt, an "emergency stop", if you like. But coronary atherosclerosis – that's heart disease – well, it's entirely absent. There were no obvious defects. His other principal organs appear disease free. Despite his lack up top, your professor was fighting fit – look at him, not bad for a fifty-eight-year-old. I wish I looked so good.' I glanced at the man stretched out beneath us, naked down to his knees, then up at the doctor. Like most of the Comandante's contacts, he was of indeterminate old age, so probably older than the sixty-five he appeared. In fact, he was one of the group the Comandante had invested in the Cesenatico place with.

'So what caused it?' I asked.

Doctor Mattani shrugged.

'That's not much of a diagnosis, Doc.'

'Well, no, obviously, although sudden cardiac arrest has been known to happen out of the blue – there are a few hundred cases of sudden arrhythmic death syndrome annually – but obviously it's rare, which is why I have requested further tests – toxicology, stomach content analysis, etcetera. Until I get those results back I won't be able to confirm a cause. Hence the commissario was unhappy – she wanted to move ahead. Always in a hurry, that lady.'

'Will you get the results this side of the August break?'

'Let's hope so, eh?'

'So what else could have caused it? You mentioned "toxicology". Do you mean poison?'

The doctor laughed. 'Let's not get ahead of ourselves, Daniel. To be frank, that hadn't even occurred to me. Actually I was thinking – opiates, amphetamines. Marijuana, alcohol, barbiturates, or some other drug. Possibly something cut into the cocaine. Or it could be a legitimate medication. Anti-depressants?' He smiled. 'Viagra? He had a young wife, I understand. It could happen – the combination of a pair of medicines, the "two-plus-two equals five effect" we call it. It could have all sorts of nasty side-effects, especially if it's a mix of three or four, say Viagra, alcohol, cocaine, even aspirin, or a joint – they'd been heading home for the evening, maybe he was getting ready for some action.' He looked suddenly wistful. 'Or it could even have been an allergy. Who knows, but that's the kind of thing it'll cover.'

'So he couldn't have just had a heart attack?'

'As I said, there were no signs of obvious defects. If he had had a weak heart and simply dropped dead due to the sheer stress of the confrontation, I would have expected it to have occurred before now. What I mean is, I doubt he could have got to his age without a bit of stress in his life, which leads me to suspect instead he may have imbibed Colombia's leading export, possibly as part of a fatal cocktail along with

other stimulants. Anyway, the test will tell.' We both looked
back down at the professor. 'The Comandante was talking
about checking on the beach house. He's worried about these
tremors.'

'They haven't reached as far as Cesenatico, have they?'

'Not as far as I'm aware.' He smiled. 'It wouldn't surprise
me if he stayed down there – you know, just to keep an eye
on the place.'

'I've rarely seen him so enthusiastic,' I said. 'It's actually
quite disconcerting.'

'Well,' said the doctor, 'there's nothing to keep him here,
Despite this . . . *punto interrogativo* over the professor. I'm
sure the COD will turn out to be quite straightforward.
What is it? You don't look convinced!'

'*Dottore,*' I said, 'I've got a mugging that apparently wasn't
a mugging, and you've just given me a heart attack that had
nothing to do with the heart. To be honest, I'm becoming less
convinced by the minute.'

As chance would have it, Sant'Orsola's great sprawl began on
the other side of the Viale – the ring-road that traced the
course of the old walls – from Via Fondazza where Stella
would have her exhibition; where, in fact, she might currently
be setting up. I considered giving her a call but hesitated,
continuing along the portico as self-conscious as a schoolboy.
Christ, if ours really was like an Interrail relationship, why
did I feel as if Stella had months to run on her travel pass
while my train was due home any day?

I arrived at the point where Fondazza intersected with Via
San Petronio Vecchio. On the corner of the small piazzetta

was a church, beside it the gates that led to a university campus. The piazzetta was crowded with people unpacking crates, putting together exhibition equipment, and unloading plastic seats.

'Hello, stranger.' Stella – standing there in an old black T-shirt, shorts and a pair of battered DM boots. Her hair was pulled up into a bun, her face shone with perspiration. She looked immensely sexy. 'I didn't expect to find you here.'

'I was on my way back from the hospital.'

'Anything wrong?'

'Work thing. So – you're setting up the exhibition. I wondered . . .'

'You've come to help?' We stepped aside to allow a group of Civil Defence people decked out in their luminous orange boilersuits to troop by and into the church. 'The tremors,' she said. 'They're checking it won't fall on top of the orchestra.'

'So,' I said. 'Where exactly are your Rooms?'

'We're dressing a few of the nuns' old cells. Come over here.' I followed her to a pile of plywood sheets. 'They're a bit awkward . . .'

I took the other side of a three-metre square sheet and began to carry it with her around the side of the church.

'Before it was part of the university,' I said, 'it was a convent?'

'Of Santa Cristina. But you know, don't you,' she said teasingly, 'it's not a coincidence the show is being held here?'

'Of course I know.'

She laughed. 'Go back a few centuries and all this was a women-only world. One of the richest convents in the whole of Italy, never mind Bologna. It was mainly for the women of the aristocracy their families couldn't, or didn't want to, marry off.' I noticed a faded crest of crossed carbines as we passed beneath an arch – at some point, presumably, the old convent had also been a Carabinieri barracks. 'That was the choice in those days – baby factory or nunnery. Loads of the girls from wealthy families ended up in places like this – there were only so many eligible bachelors to go around.'

We arrived in a porticoed cloister around a large cobbled courtyard. 'Up these stairs. Anyway, a lot of them were really well-educated and Santa Cristina was famous for its music – the convent orchestra was one of the best in the city, and visitors came from as far away as Rome to hear it perform.'

We carried the sheet along a corridor overlooking the quadrangle. 'Then there's Lucrezia.' We entered a small, bare room with a window at the far end and laid the sheet against the others.

'Who?'

'Donna Lucrezia Orsina Vizzana. She became this incredible composer, something almost unheard of at the time: *What? A woman writing music?* But no one could deny her talent. What the church *could* do was shut the nuns up – literally.

'In fact, they'd actually begun cracking down even before Lucrezia and Isabetta, that was her sister, arrived, turning them into a closed order – basically, creating a women's prison – but the clergy were still rankled by the idea of women making music. They banned performances to outsiders, forbade them to use wind instruments – all that blowing, you see, provocative. I'm not kidding!

'Meanwhile, the nuns were trying to get around the

restrictions, using all the influence, the contacts they could muster, just so they could keep singing, performing, creating their music . . . to honour God, *obviously*.'

'Obviously.'

'Finally the Archbishop of Bologna, one Ludovico Ludovisi, had had enough and laid siege to the place – literally. Surrounded it with soldiers and tried to starve the nuns out. It's quite a tale.' Stella looked around the bare, former cell. 'Poor Lucrezia.'

'What happened to her?'

Stella shrugged. 'Nothing good – the constant tension got to her and there's no trace of any of her music after the siege. She died exhausted, paranoid, some say totally mad, although perhaps she had the last laugh – her compositions were transcribed. They've been recorded. In fact, for the show, an all-female orchestra will perform some of them.'

'And how are your Rooms connected to all this?'

'Barely at all. It's about *five hundred* years of resistance, right? Not just *The Sound of Music*.'

Chapter 8

Vesuvio was waiting for me in the shade of the portico opposite the *Teatro Comunale* box office in a cream suit and spats,
a matching fedora with a black band, and amber, retro-style
Persol sunglasses. He was smoking a cheroot.

'You're fucking kidding me,' I said.

'What?'

'Are you taking the piss?'

'I don't know what you're talking about. You mean the
hat? The sunglasses? It's hot, and you know,' he leaned closer,
'I have to keep a low profile. We don't want to get bothered
by the fans.'

'Well, thanks anyway for pulling some strings with the
Teatro – they would have probably still had us on hold.'

As we stepped into the gloomy box office, Vesuvio
removed his hat and glasses and the typically granite-faced
staff behind the glass-fronted counters rose as if to give him
a standing ovation.

'Pietro!' one lady called. 'He's here! He's here!'

From a rear office emerged another *Teatro* troglodyte,
'Pietro', presumably, an archetypal Italian functionary in a

T-shirt, sweatpants and trainers, although judging by the size of his belly and those chipmunk cheeks, he probably didn't get much exercise. The door beside the counter buzzed and he burst out, clamping fat fists around Vesuvio's hand.

'Huge fan,' he said, with no apparent sense of irony. His eyes lingered upon Vesuvio as if there was simply so much he wanted to say, but then he remembered himself. 'Please, please . . .' We followed him through to his inner-sanctum, an office crowded with filing cabinets, stacks of leaflets, bursting folders, and a pair of dusty Yucca plants. Behind his messy desk was a row of three decrepit-looking TVs, which clearly constituted the *Teatro*'s CCTV.

'Coffee? Water?' We shook our heads. 'Tell me, Vesuvio,' he said. 'When can we expect another tour?'

'In Italy? I believe something's pencilled in for next spring. Although I might be trying out some new material beforehand.'

'One of your "secret gigs"?'

'Possibly, around December. I could get you on the list, if you could stand it. Some of the material might be pretty rough . . .'

'Stand it? I'd love it!'

'Fine. Just drop my publicist a line with your details.'

'I will do, Vesuvio. Thank you!' He gazed at him adoringly.

'Well . . .' Vesuvio cleared his throat.

'You mentioned we might be able to see the CCTV?' I said.

'Oh. Yeah, yeah, of course.' Pietro did not take his eyes off Vesuvio. 'What did you want?'

'Footage from the evening Professor Bellario was at the opera,' I said.

'The professor,' Pietro tutted. He opened a file on his computer. 'A tragedy.'

'You knew him?'

'Certainly. He taught the musicology module of my Masters. I mean, I didn't know him well. He was – ah, this must be it – what you might call "a hands-off prof". He didn't take much interest in us, I mean his students, although . . . Hold on. Yes. This must be the one. You said you wanted entrance, interval and exit, right?'

We couldn't make anything out from the lobby footage of the audience filing in for the opening night of *Rigoletto*. It was only when we viewed the interval footage that I first spotted them – actually, Melodia, who I recognised instantly from the photo I had taken from the Delfillos. A striking blonde with a Raphaelite, heart-shaped face.

'Her?' said Vesuvio. 'Wow, a classic Florentine beauty. I bet she has blue eyes, too. *And there he is.*'

I still had the image of the professor's bald body laid out on that gurney, so struggled to recognise the living man sporting the black mop Doctor Mattani had held up like a trophy. I experienced vague nausea watching him guide his young wife through the crowd to pick up their drinks at the bar, blissfully unaware of what was awaiting him.

A woman was standing there as they arrived, handing them glasses of wine, raising her own mineral water in a toast, although they obviously made a joke of not clinking because to do so with water in Italy is viewed as bad luck. The professor was clearly complimenting her.

'She must be in the orchestra,' I said. 'Her black dress . . .'

'There are a lot of black dresses,' said Vesuvio.

'Can you pause it?' I took out the school photo, searched the faces.

'Her?' I pointed to a girl with a black, Louise Brooks-style bob at the edge of the group. While the other kids appeared genuinely joyful, she looked strained, as if that smile was taking all her effort.

Vesuvio clearly sensed it too, because he said: 'She looks a bit more cheerful there though?'

The trio parted and the Bellarios disappeared into the throng.

We fast-forwarded to the final piece of footage – the couple leaving the performance. There didn't seem to be anything amiss with the professor, who dawdled in the foyer to say goodbye to some fellow opera-goers. He certainly didn't look like a man about to drop dead.

We watched the couple give a final wave before stepping onto the porch and moving arm-in-arm in the direction of Via del Guasto. We slowed the footage to check if Guido was among the down and outs sat along the edge of the portico as it filled with the well-to-do, but couldn't spot him.

The couple descended the steps into the darkness.

'You don't have anything else?' I asked.

'There's another CCTV as you come out of the Via del Guasto,' said Pietro. 'But that's the Comune's, we don't have control over that.'

'And have the police asked to see this one?'

'Why would they? It took place around the corner, didn't it?'

'For completeness. This woman,' I tapped on the photo. 'Do you recognise her? *Is* she in the orchestra?'

'Maybe. That's not my area . . . I can take you down if you like?'

***

Pietro led us out of the box office and into the auditorium, always impressive, perhaps all the more so empty – four tiers of balconies reaching around the stage in the theatre's unique 'bell' design, their arches reminiscent of the city's porticoes.

We walked down the crimson carpet through the stalls towards the pit, where we could hear strings tuning up.

'What do you think you'll get out of talking to this woman?' asked Vesuvio.

'She was one of the last people to see the professor alive apart from his wife, who might not currently welcome a visit.' I shrugged. 'I like to have a full picture. Which reminds me.' We were almost at the pit. I caught Pietro's arm. 'Why did you say "although"?'

'I'm sorry?'

'You said the professor didn't pay much attention to you when you were a student, "although". Although what?'

'Oh,' Pietro flapped his hands. 'Well, you shouldn't speak ill of the dead. And really, it was nothing. Just rumours.'

'About what?'

'Like I said – gossip.'

'Pietro, my friend,' said Vesuvio. 'You can tell us.'

'Well, if you promise this won't go any further . . .'

'Absolutely,' I said.

'I heard, although it never concerned me – I mean, I loved musicology and couldn't have afforded to in any case – but it was whispered that if you were really desperate, the professor could give you private tuition to help you get through your exam.'

'Ah,' said Vesuvio.

'I'm sorry,' I said. 'I don't get it – is that so bad?'

'This is an exam Bellario would be invigilating, right?' said Vesuvio. Pietro nodded. 'I think in this context, "private tuition" should be regarded as a euphemism.'

'For a *bustarella*?' I said. 'A bribe?' The pair nodded.

Chapter 9

We arrived at the pit, where a dozen musicians in T-shirts and shorts were sitting. Two of the younger women were actually wearing black bikini tops. Beyond them – the barren stage, devoid of scenery, was hung with ropes, cables and pulleys. Bangs, booms and shouts filled its emptiness as stagehands rolled great crates up a ramp from a lorry visible through the open rear doors. No wonder the musicians were dressed as if for the beach – it was steaming in the pit, which was gathering the afternoon heat flooding in through that opening.

The musicians, a mix of young and middle-aged, sat among the empty seats of the full orchestra, sweating over their violins and violas. They looked irritably up at us.

'Er, excuse me,' Pietro began, '*maestri* . . .'

'Marco?' It was one of the older men, his *Teatro Comunale 2008* T-shirt plastered to his body.

'Hey, Gio!' Vesuvio waved. 'How you doin'?'

'Not as well as you, you bastard. They've even had to turn the ventilation off while they've got the doors open.'

'Can't they give you guys a break?'

'*Magari.* I see you're on *X Factor* now. Nice work if you can get it!'

Vesuvio smiled humbly. 'I can't complain.'

'What are you doing here anyway? Not looking for a job, I take it!'

I handed down the photo.

'We'd like to speak to the girl with black hair at the corner of the photograph, if she's about – we think she may be a member of the orchestra.'

One of the women in a bikini top leaned over.

'That's Amanda,' she said. 'Amanda Grimaldi. And in the middle, that's Guido – there's Melodia . . . and that's me! What's this to do with? Something about the professor? We've all seen the news.'

'I'm a private investigator,' I said. 'We're looking into the background – we saw footage of this Amanda talking to Professor Bellario during the interval. We wondered if we might have a word.'

'Someone mentioned her. The bass section was supposed to be rehearsing yesterday – she's a cellist – but she didn't turn up. In the end it didn't matter as it was cancelled by the section lead because of the heat.' She glared at an older man in a sweat-sodden shirt who, I intuited, had similar powers over the treble section but had chosen not to use them. 'I think they rescheduled . . . '

'You know Guido, then?' I said. 'You went to the same school?'

'Yeah,' she sighed. 'It was a shame.' Now she gave Vesuvio a hard look. 'He was working with you, wasn't he? Before he lost it.' Vesuvio nodded. 'Maybe you should have taken more care of him.'

'Do you know what might have made Guido confront the professor?' I said. 'I mean – did they have history? Was there bad blood?'

'Honestly, I've no idea – I knew Guido from school, but he didn't get into the conservatory, which was where I studied under the prof.'

'And Melodia.' It suddenly occurred to me. 'You all went to school together. Was there a "story"' – Italian for romance – 'between her and Guido?' The woman became evasive.

'I can't say. Guido, Melodia, they were both very . . . popular.' A middle-aged female violinist snorted. 'You'd have to ask her. It's really none of my business.' She picked up her viola.

'Vesuvio says Guido was very talented. Forgive me, but I've no idea precisely how talented you have to be to get into the conservatory. Highly, I presume. You studied with Guido – did you expect him to get in?'

'Oh yeah,' she said, clearly feeling on safer ground. 'He was one of the "stars". We were all shocked when he failed.'

'And this exam.' I glanced at Pietro. 'Was Professor Bellario involved?'

'He probably would have been one of the *professori*,' she said. 'Why?'

I shook my head. 'No rea—'

'We're just trying to get as full a picture as possible,' said Vesuvio.

Before we left, we returned with Pietro to the office where

he gave us Amanda's address. 'Although of course, I really shouldn't.' He smiled obsequiously.

We stepped out into the sunshine. Vesuvio put on his hat and shades. I retreated back under the portico.

'Thanks,' I said. 'You were a great help.' I held my hand out but he didn't take it.

'What are you going to do now?' he asked.

'I thought I would pay a visit to Amanda Grimaldi.'

'I'll come with you.'

'Really,' I said. 'It's fine.'

'Really,' he said. 'I've got nothing better to do.'

The huge gates at the address we had for Amanda Grimaldi, off Via Saragozza over on the other side of the old city, were already open when we arrived. It was in an otherwise sparse, narrow street marked on one side by small houses, the other by a high red-brick wall that had presumably once, like so many others in Bologna, contained the grounds of church property. Now it had become a different kind of sanctuary – a haven for the rich.

We crunched along a neatly-maintained gravel entrance where a builder's truck was parked – there was scaffolding across one of the ancient buildings inside the entrance to the compound – beside a small, private park-cum-orchard loudly broadcasting cicadas, towards a more modern mansion building perhaps little more than a century old.

'Not bad for a musician,' I said. 'I mean in an orchestra. I thought they were paid pennies.'

'Oh,' said Vesuvio as we inspected the post boxes. 'They are. Which was why I went the other way. I didn't come from money or have the contacts, which adds up to much the same thing. Frankly, you'd have to be mad or loaded to choose a career as a classical musician.'

According to the post boxes, Amanda was in 'Scala D/2', which meant literally 'Stairway D, apartment 2'. The first mahogany-framed frosted-glass double door signalled 'A'. Amanda's 'scala' had to be at the far end. Only then did it occur to me that we probably should have rung her bell, one among perhaps twenty upon the shining brass plate by the outside gate. But in a city where you were confronted by so many barriers, both solid and imperceptible, I'd clearly picked up the Bolognese habit of grabbing your chances when you had them.

We arrived at 'D' and pushed through the double doors. Directly in front of us was a broad Art Deco staircase curving languorously around a glass elevator. We took the stairs.

Vesuvio went first, climbing the steps two at a time as if he was acting out some kind of private fantasy, possibly involving *Chinatown*'s Jake Gittes. By the time I had arrived, he had already pressed the buzzer.

'No answer,' he said. He tried again.

He was about to try a third time when I stopped him. 'Can you smell it?' I meant that sickly-sweet stink; that gag-inducing, unmistakable signature.

He tapped his nose. 'Doesn't work so well these days . . . but, hold on, actually . . . *Jesus*. What *is* that?'

I bent down, opening my pick roll. I began to work at the lock.

'You shouldn't be doing that,' said Vesuvio. 'I mean, hell, I've broken a few laws but that's—'

I pushed open the front door. The stink hit us and we fell instinctively back, clutching our hands over our mouths and noses. I stepped to the side of the open doorway and snapped on a pair of plastic gloves.

'You're not going in?' said Vesuvio.

'Stay here.' He didn't look like he needed much persuasion.

Chapter 10

It was precisely the kind of place wealthy parents would purchase for their gifted daughter. Bright, renovated, compact. There were concert posters on one side of the entrance, on the other a series of original, black-ink cartoons featuring scenes from an orchestra; facing me, a full-length mirror framed by gold-painted notes – quavers, semi-quavers, and treble clefs – the sort of thing you'd be more likely to find in a child's bedroom, I thought, but perhaps Amanda had simply been fond of it.

It was only three more steps into the *soggiorno*, an open-plan, contemporary 'kitchen-diner' arrangement that was already partly visible from the entrance, but not the part in question – where I found the body.

Amanda Grimaldi was hanging by her neck from a wooden rail running along the edge of a mezzanine. Her face was a swollen mask; at least her eyes were closed. A grey tongue protruded between rubbery lips. Her fists were clenched.

She was wearing what looked like the same plain black dress she had on the night she had met the professor, her bare feet dangling above a contemporary ethnic carpet now splattered with dark spots, which also marked her calves and ankles.

I strode across the room and opened both sets of windows. It was almost as hot inside as out, and I checked the radiator – no, it had not been turned on to hasten decomposition. The place had probably just captured the sun through those big windows, which would make air-conditioning indispensable, especially at such an up-market address. I went to the kitchen, pressed the panel and it bleeped on. Well, it was working. I turned it back off.

There were two bedrooms – one used for music practice. Her cello stood on a stand, a bow lying on the floor next to it. There was a signed black-and-white poster featuring Jacqueline du Pré on the wall, which must have cost a pretty penny.

The main bedroom was a bit of a mess, but within the 'spectrum' of youth. I had seen worse in Rose's. The wardrobe doors were open. Some sports stuff was laid in a heap on top of a pair of trainers. Partially buried beneath the duvet was a copy of yesterday's *Carlino*, the one with the news about the professor. Was there a note? I scanned the room, her cluttered dressing table. I couldn't see anything, but this wasn't the twentieth century – a kid her age would have just as likely sent an email, message, or posted on 'social'.

I checked the bathroom, medicine cabinet. Some vitamins, women's stuff. *Sertralina eurogenerica* – proprietary name Zoloft, an anti-depressant. I opened the box – it was half-full. Women tended to end their lives using pharmaceuticals, but it was debatable whether there had been enough here to do the job.

I re-entered the *soggiorno*, where the full force of the stink had begun to dissipate, or perhaps I had simply grown accustomed. I circled back to the body. The young musician was hanging by a luggage strap, the sort possibly used to secure her cello case when she was travelling. I leaned closer, winced. The flat, black nylon of the strap had cut deeply into her swollen neck. The area surrounding it was marked by scratches, which stood out like old scars now the blood had stopped pumping. She would have clawed as she suffocated, whether she had planned this or not. Doctor Mattani was sure to find skin beneath her fingernails. *Only hers?*

I looked around. There was no sign of a struggle. The sole piece of furniture upset – the trendy Scandinavian dining chair that appeared to have been kicked away as she dangled a foot above the rug. I lifted up her sleeves. There was no apparent bruising, nothing to suggest her wrists had been restrained, something those scratches also appeared to confirm. Could she have been strangled and hooked up here afterwards? The dark, dry patches of shit down the inside of her legs appeared be aligned with those on the floor.

I went halfway up the wooden mezzanine steps so I was at eye-level with the wooden rail. It was just managing to keep her suspended there – the screws holding it into the upper parquet floor almost lifted out. Another tug and she might fall – another kick might have saved her life. I turned on my phone light and scanned the upper room, apparently used for storage. I took a few snaps.

I got back down and went to the kitchen where a phone lay flat on the counter. It was not plugged in. There was fourteen per cent of energy left. It was top of the range, so could

conceivably last more than a day without charging. I carried
it over to the corpse, hesitated, although admittedly not for
long, and lifted up her right, bunched fist. Fortunately I did
not need to pull back the fingers, simply raising the thumb
was enough to . . .

'What are you doing?'

It was Vesuvio, fedora and sunglasses in one hand, the
other pinching his nose. *There.* I was lucky, it had worked
almost first time. Amanda's phone lit up – a photo of the
philharmonic as her wallpaper. I went back to the counter and
took out my own phone.

'Man, we should call the police . . .'

'Leave the police to me.' I began scrolling through
Amanda's recent activity, snapping photos as I went.

'What happened?' he said.

'What do you think?'

'But *Jesus* . . .'

'Really, you don't need to be here. Go back out.'

'What are you doing? Do you think this has anything to
do with us?'

I placed the phone back where I had found it. Forensics
might discover when it had last been accessed, but frankly, I
doubted it would go that far.

'All right,' I said. 'Now I'll call the police.'

There are two main police services in Italy – the Carabinieri
and Polizia di Stato. Given my brush with the Polizia a year
earlier, which had ended in my being strip-searched and
thrown into the cells, I wanted to make sure we dealt with
the Carabinieri. But it turned out it wasn't that simple.

'I'm not sure I understand,' said Ispettore Umberto Alessandro. 'It's an ordinary suicide, no?'

'Something's not right. I think there may be more to it than that.'

'Not right about the suicide?'

'I don't know. Maybe. Not specifically. But everything seems . . .'

I could hear the sound of machinery, metallic clanking. 'Sorry,' said Alessandro. 'Ski lift, although no skiing, obviously. But I'm on holiday, the mountains, Cortina. You should join us when you tire of Cesenatico – the air's so much fresher. We're visiting the site of the Austro-Italian front this morning. They dug a kilometre-long hill straight up the mountain to supply the troops. Can you believe it? We're going to ascend—'

'Look—'

'You know, Daniel,' a hard edge entered Alessandro's voice. Holiday or no, mountain ascent or not, the *ispettore* was always on the job. 'Sometimes a cigar is just a cigar. If it looks like a suicide, tragic though that may be, and I understand it can be upsetting to see a young woman like that, but it happens. More often than you might expect, especially among that age group. . .'

'*Ispettore* . . .'

'All right, if you're *really* concerned.' His signal cut off.

'*Mio Dio.* What happened?' An elderly man was stood facing the corpse, his hand to his mouth. A woman, presumably his wife, entered behind him and gasped. They were dressed for travel, although whether coming or going I couldn't say.

'We've just discovered her,' I said quickly.

'*Mio Dio*,' his wife was now repeating, fanning a hand in front of her face. '*Mio Dio*.' She headed back to the front door, pulling out her phone.

I was about to call the general Carabinieri line myself when Vesuvio laid a hand on mine.

'I'd . . . Look, would it be okay if I . . .' He glanced at the elderly man, who was also apparently in the process of calling for help. 'They don't seem to have recognised me, but the cops, you know, the media . . .'

'Sure,' I said. 'Go. I can handle it.'

He squeezed me on the shoulder as if we were parting after a night out, and left. Now I tried the Carabinieri, but as I was saying the address, I heard a car pull up on the gravel outside. I went to the window.

Just my luck – not the dark blue roof of a Carabinieri *gazzella*, but the pale blue of a Polizia di Stato *volante*.

Chapter 11

The cops let the elderly couple – who were neighbours, thank God, rather than Amanda's parents – leave after taking their details, but took more of an interest in me, which came as little surprise.

'I tell you, Mario, no way – Miranda will break our balls if we let him walk.'

'But she'll break our balls if we call her over a simple suicide.'

'It'll come up, on the system.'

'You worry too much.'

'Guys,' I said. We were outside the building. They had already taped the apartment off. Fair enough – no one wanted to hang around that stink any longer than they had to. 'I'm not so sure it's that simple.'

'You? *Ma che cazzo* . . .' This was Mario, although the pair were almost identical – both male, mid-thirties, cropped dark hair, and with that laid-back yet vaguely threatening air of the Polizia – the federal police – which seemed largely absent from the more formal, by-the-numbers Carabinieri, the senior branch of the Italian military.

'What do you mean,' said the other one, 'not so simple?'

'It's hard to explain,' I said. 'But I think it could be linked to another case – Professor Bellario, who died outside the *Teatro*.'

Mario glared at me. 'My friend, you should want us to let you go. You say you opened the door to investigate the odour, but maybe you were breaking in and came across the corpse. *You* didn't call the police – the neighbours did.'

'Believe me, Officer,' I said, 'I've no desire to cause you any problems, or disturb Commissario Miranda, but we are where we are.'

'*Che cazzo* . . .' I was beginning to think Mario had some issues with the commissario himself.

'I'll call it in,' said his colleague.

The commissario arrived forty minutes later. By now we also had an ambulance in the driveway and the Municipal Police parked outside the main gate, supposedly to keep curious onlookers away, which on a side street like this didn't seem likely to be an issue, but in Italy there never appeared to be a lack of uniforms keen to be seen to be doing their job.

Commissario Rita Miranda got out of the rear of the *volante*. She cast a stony look at the officer who had made the call. 'Mario', meanwhile, had retreated inside his car and was apparently occupied with paperwork.

'The English detective,' the officer said. 'We found him in there. He may have broken in. He claims maybe it wasn't suicide.'

'What does it look like to you?'

'Well,' the officer glanced towards his colleague still sheltering in the car. 'To us – yes, suicide.'

'And the opinion of a pair of expensively-trained, experienced Italian police officers is worth less than this British,' now she acknowledged me with the kind of smile a cat might give a canary, '*hack*? Officer Pelotti,' she barked. 'Come here.' Mario almost fell out of the car. 'Is this your opinion, too?'

'I'm sorry, Commissario, I didn't hear.' The commissario might have been smaller and slighter than the pair, but in late middle age had preserved a craggy southern beauty that spoke more of Ancient Greek than Italian ancestry, and managed to evoke the terrible authority of the old deities. Certainly, the two cops visibly shrank in her presence.

'You believe the Englishman, then? There's more to it?'

Mario shook his head. 'I wouldn't . . .' He glanced at his colleague. 'Didn't say that, Commissario.'

Miranda surveyed the three of us with, it appeared, equal disdain, before brushing past me and setting off down the path towards the front door. As she opened it, she stopped and turned to look at me.

'Coming, Sherlock?'

The commissario slipped on gloves and a facemask.

'Here.' She pulled out a spare set and handed them to me. 'Remind you of anything?'

'You mean the last time we met? I hope you're not going to try and pin a murder on me this time, too.'

'What would *you* have done? You were the last person seen leaving the scene. You had a well-publicised history of conflict with the victim. It would have been remiss of me not to pursue it.'

'Except I was innocent.'

'Did I ever say you were guilty?'

'Yes. Repeatedly.'

'But I didn't charge you. Think of it simply as motivation, *caro*.'

'What do you mean?'

'Well, we cracked the case in next to no time, didn't we.'

'*We?*' A smile crinkled around the corners of the commissario's mask. 'Anyway,' I said. 'This is different.'

'So you say.'

I followed the commissario into the *soggiorno*. '*Oh, pòvera, pòvera ragazza*.' The commissario's flinty voice had become that of a surrogate mother. '*Mamma mia*, what have you done? Why? Why would you do such a thing? *Pòvera ragazza . . .*'

'I'd like to show you something,' I said.

'What is it?'

I led her through to the bedroom. 'You see the newspaper?' I told her about Amanda's link to the professor and Guido. 'There's something about all of this that doesn't add up. Okay, the professor's dead. But why should that lead you to kill yourself? And it doesn't even mention Guido in the newspaper, so she may not have known he was connected.'

'Why should her death be connected at all, Signor Leicester?'

'The newspaper . . . the coincidence of finding her here, right after . . .'

'Perhaps that's all it is,' said the commissario. 'Coincidence. Perhaps she had a history of mental illness, depression . . .' I thought of Amanda's medicine cabinet. 'Maybe it *is* connected, but it's not suspicious as you suggest – perhaps the news just tipped her over the edge. Note?'

'No, but . . .'

'Yes, yes. Electronic things, I know. Phone?'

'Kitchen.' I followed her through. She went over to the counter and looked down at it. 'I suppose you've already checked?'

'I . . .' Her perfectly plucked eyebrows arched. 'Nothing leapt out. But there *was* one thing.' I led her back to the mezzanine and up the first three steps. I shone my light along the floor a couple of metres from where Amanda still hung.

'If you look here, you can see a pair of marks on the parquet, and also down here.' I tracked the light to the edge of the mezzanine, beneath the bar, where there were a series of shiny stripes over the edge. 'It's the same width as the strap,' I said. 'I was thinking the first two could be from the rubber of trainers or shoes, maybe he was on his knees, and this – the strap.' I made a pulling motion. 'Maybe she was only attached to the bar afterwards. It certainly doesn't seem stable.'

Commissario Miranda stepped up and took a look. She sighed. 'You've certainly got an active imagination. These could literally be anything.'

'You could maybe check for fibres?'

'Well, well – look who's been watching *CSI*. I'll tell you what I'm more interested in, Signor Leicester – that knot. It's a proper slipknot. I'll check if she was a girl scout.' She went back to the kitchen counter, took a snap of the phone's position, and placed it in an evidence bag. I followed her out.

The commissario snapped off her mask and gloves and began to make her way downstairs. '*Che caldo!* What heat! It was you who opened the windows? You did well. That's quite a stink.'

'Judging by the newspaper she had been—'

'Of course, the newspaper! It's all about clues with you, isn't it, Sherlock.'

'What else would it be about?'

'Facts, probabilities, resources, statistics, budgets. You've no idea! You spend your life snooping about after unfaithful spouses and exposing poor bastards who doctored their CVs, so when something vaguely interesting comes along you're suddenly, yes, Sherlock fucking Holmes.'

'You've lost none of your charm.'

'We've already had one murder and two rapes this week, not counting your poor, misunderstood junkie, who quite literally scared a professor to death. And now – what? You want us to treat this tragedy as a murder enquiry? Have you any idea how much that would cost? And what about the parents? Do you want to tell them they can't bury their daughter? No, of course not.' We were back outside. The cops straightened up beside their *volante*.

'This is goodbye, then,' I said. 'Always a pleasure.'

'Oh, I wouldn't be in such a hurry, Signor Leicester. You'll have the pleasure of my company for a little while longer. Arrest him.'

'*What for?*' The cops placed my hands behind my back and snapped on the cuffs.

'You told me yourself, lad – tampering with the evidence.'

Chapter 12

The commissario had misled me – I would not be enjoying the pleasure of her company, at least not in the short-term. She had delegated my interrogation to one of her subordinates, who looked as bemused to find himself questioning me as I was to be wasting my time at the Questura.

'You were found at the scene of the incident, signore. How did you get in?'

'Picks. As you know, I'm a licensed private investigator. And a qualified locksmith.' I permitted myself a small smile – it was one of the qualifications I was most proud of.

'How do we know that you weren't breaking in?'

'The smell was plain from outside. I know what corpses smell like.'

'If, as you say, you know what corpses smell like, why not call the Polizia, or,' he smirked, 'Carabinieri.'

'Put it down to instinct. I wanted to see if I could help.'

'A corpse?'

'Who knew – maybe there was someone else alive inside. I had no idea. Anyway, I did it.'

'You discovered the body of Signora Amanda Grimaldi.

Yet still, you didn't call the police.'

'I had to let some fresh air in. It's not every day you discover something like that.'

'You took time to check her phone, too, as you confessed to the commissario. Isn't that the truth?'

'I think it's time I spoke to my lawyer, Avvocato Filippo Servi.'

'You've something to hide?' I shook my head. 'Then why would you want to speak to your lawyer? Why not just provide a straight answer to a straight question?'

I checked my watch. 'Haven't we both got somewhere better to be?'

'I'm being paid to sit here with you, signore. It's baking outside. I'm quite happy to be chatting in the cool. You, on the other hand . . . Well, I guess this must be costing you money.'

'Not me.' I thought of Vesuvio sloping off.

'And your client is?'

'Confidential.'

'You're not making life easy for yourself, signore.'

'A bad habit of mine.'

We played this game until the detective went for a coffee. He didn't return. Instead, a pair of uniforms – Mario and 'the other one' – entered. The cuffs were slapped back on, and I was led out of the room and along the corridor. I passed the glass exit doors and was steered down some steps.

'Jesus, what now?' We descended into a broad hallway with barred holding cells – more like cages – lined on either side. '*Dai*. You're kidding me.' They un-cuffed me, slid open the cell door, and shoved me inside.

Benches lined the cage on three sides. There were six pens in all, with a dozen men scattered throughout, although not evenly. There were four in the one opposite, for example, and another three in the one next to that, while I was alone in mine.

Bugger. There was no point denying it – I'd fucked up. I'd been complacent, too Italian, even. Perhaps the Mediterranean sun had finally got to me. I'd soaked up the pervasive sense of permissiveness – that each of us was, in our small way, a heroic resister to the rules and the only thing that truly mattered was not getting caught.

Breaking into Amanda's flat – although it wasn't the breaking in, *per se*, rather the not getting caught, the failure to cover my back, as the Comandante surely would have done. He would have been on the blower to his Carabinieri contacts the moment he had come across the corpse.

The admission about meddling with the phone to the commissario. Rookie error. Only I wasn't supposed to be a rookie gumshoe any more.

But there was no getting away from the fact I was still a rookie Italian.

I straightened myself against the bars. Well, Commissario Rita Miranda had taught me a lesson if I was prepared to heed it. The trouble was, I could be held in custody for twenty-four hours before being given access to a prosecutor. The usual trick would be to lose me in the system – 'Sorry signore, there was a mis-communication'.

Judging by the look of this lot, I could find myself transferred to *La Dozza*, the city gaol, before the paperwork 'caught up' with me, which could take days. The Polizia would have a good laugh at that.

I looked around – there were two guys in the cell next to me. A pair of Romanian gypsies. I signalled them.

'*Ragazzi.* How long have you been here?'

They looked at each other. The older one said: 'Yesterday.'

'Has the bus been? For *La Dozza*?'

He shook his head. 'No bus today.'

Great, I thought. No bus today – which meant it was probably still to come. I would have to get a message out from the prison. Bloody hilarious.

I began to pace the cell. It was only then I noticed the small guy in the pen on the other side of the bars. Not that he was trying to attract my attention – he was curled up on the bench, using his arm as a pillow as if he was sleeping off a hangover.

Skeletal hips exposed above slack jeans, skin stretched taut across fine features, an overgrown beard. He might look like a three-minute sketch of the teenager in that group photo, but without a doubt it was Guido Delfillo.

Chapter 13

'Hey.' He didn't stir. *'Hey.'* I rapped on the bars. He half opened his eyes. *'Guido.'* He appeared to focus on me, then out again. His lids drooped. *'Guido Delfillo.* Wake the hell up.' He looked at me again as if in a dream, although it was probably a methadone funk.

'I'm here to help you.'

He smacked his lips, rubbed his face, finally swung his legs onto the floor and sat upright, albeit as crooked as a crone. He looked as if he had been dragged backwards through a bush, both physically and mentally.

'You're . . .'

'Come over here.'

He lifted himself to his feet and waddled over. It was only now that I realised he was barefoot.

'Where are your shoes?'

'No idea,' he said vaguely. His feet were swollen and filthy. 'You're . . . my lawyer?'

'Your lawyer is Filippo Servi,' I said. 'He's the one that got you the methadone, right?'

'Yeah, Servi. Avvocato Servi, that's it.' Guido was

holding onto both bars. His hollow-cheeked face almost fit in-between them. 'So you . . .'

'I'm Daniel Leicester, a private investigator. I've been hired to get you out of here.'

'You're going to break me out?'

'Guido. Get a grip. No – I'm looking for information to help your lawyer build a case so you can be set free.'

'A case . . . okay, I get it.'

I could see no evidence from his expression that he had got it at all but I pressed on: 'I was going to speak to you at *La Dozza*, but since we're here . . .'

'*We're* here?' He seemed to grasp for the first time that he was not speaking to me on the outside, but that I was incarcerated along with him. He jumped back from the bars and slid along the bench, out of my reach.

'*Motherfucker.*'

'Guido . . .'

'What are you? Some kind of snitch?'

'Not at all. Like I said, I've been hired to get you out of here.'

'*Dai.* Servi couldn't afford to do this, hire someone like you – the state would never cough up for a private eye. My folks damn well couldn't afford it. You're a fucking snitch. Where are you from? Poland, is it?'

'England. But look, it's the truth. I've already spoken to your mum and dad in San Vitale. You told the police you were homeless.'

He stared at me. 'That means nothing.'

'Look – Vesuvio hired me. He said he felt guilty about giving you the push.'

'Vesuvio?'

'He feels responsible for the situation you find yourself in – with the drugs, I mean – although I'm beginning to think it was never quite as simple as that.'

Guido was shaking his head. 'So what are you doing on the inside? You know you could just have made an appointment.' It took me by surprise – that flash of humour in eyes that had seemed as dead as moons. Despite his drug-starved appearance, perhaps all was not lost for Guido Delfillo after all.

'I fell foul of a commissario who's got it in for me.' Guido nodded as if this made perfect sense. 'So, can we talk now?' He shrugged, reached back up to the bars and shifted a little closer. 'Do you want to get out of here?' I asked him.

Guido seemed to seriously consider the question. Outside or in, I understood, this place paled in comparison to the prison of his own making.

'You don't want to be convicted as a murderer, do you?'

'More like manslaughter. That's what the avvocato says.'

'Still, is this really what you want, when you claim you did nothing wrong?'

'I . . .' He looked down. 'I had something, once.'

'You mean your talent. Melodia?'

'Melodia?'

'Were you two an item? Is that what this was about?'

'Melodia? Oh no. Is that what they're saying? That it's something to do with her?'

'But you had a story . . .'

'*Beh*. Nothing serious. Melodia, she liked the older man.'

'Her professors?'

'Older students, although it came as no surprise that she ended up with a prof.'

'She said you pulled a knife.'

'She did? I did?'

'You mean you don't remember? The police didn't find a knife, but perhaps you threw it away before you returned to the scene.'

'I don't know anything about a knife. I don't carry one, you'd be crazy to – it's just the excuse the cops need.'

'Anything metal she might have confused with a blade?'

'Keys . . . No.' He laughed. 'No keys. The only metal is my spoon.'

'For heating the smack,' I said. 'Turning it into a solution.'

'To shoot-up. Can you imagine, waving my spoon at them? This is a hold-up!' Then he looked troubled. *'Actually . . .'*

'But the avvocato told me you're claiming it wasn't a hold-up.'

'Yeah, that's right.'

'What, then?'

A bilious ripple swept his face and I braced to jump aside if he threw up. Instead, he spat out: '*This*. This is what you've done.'

'You mean you said that to Professor Bellario?' He nodded. 'How so?' Guido was quiet for a long time. 'I can't help you if you won't help yourself.'

'Who says I want to help myself? *Look at me* – it could be this is precisely where I belong.'

'From what I've been hearing, it sounds like you've been bottling it up – all your anger, your frustration – too long, and that's why you've ended up in here. Come on – spit it out.'

'How was I to know he was going to drop dead?'

'So – then tell me what really happened.' Guido's grip tightened on the bars, his knuckles flushing white. He let out a long, hissed breath as if he was beginning to deflate.

'I'd always thought it was my fault. That I failed. When I failed, I thought – what *did* I think? – that it confirmed something I'd known all along . . . that it was all a dream, and finally, I'd woken up. *What was I doing here, in Bologna? Who was I to think I was top of my class?* Okay, among a bunch of kids, maybe, but when it came to the big test . . .'

'The conservatory exams.'

'I wasn't up to it.'

'But many of these kids you were with passed.'

'Precisely.'

'People fail exams all the time – then they take them again, and pass. When I was your age, I had to take my driving test three times.'

'I'd never failed an exam.'

'Your parents said.'

'The thought of being a year behind the others . . . *la vergogna* – the shame – I felt so small. It was like a confirmation.'

'You said that before, what do you mean?'

'These other kids . . . they were all from good families. You'd visit their homes . . . you could just see. *We* spoke Pugliese at home. At their homes, *dialect?* You've got to be kidding! *And the conversations.* Ours were food, football, family. You'd go to Melodia's and it would be politics, philosophy, literature, all sorts. Not to mention her folks not only knew who Padre Martini was, they could actually trace their roots back to him! I came from a long line of peasants. Not farmers, like they have up here, but *peasants*, proper peasants – my *nonni* used to work the land of a duchess from Naples.

'You know, it's not until you're in it, in that world, *their world*, you realise how little you actually know, what you've been missing, how small you are. That all the time when you were king of the world back home, in fact you were just a little peasant boy with a paper crown.'

'So you saw your failure in the exam as a sort of confirmation that you weren't good enough.'

'That's it.'

'But you got back on your feet – you did okay with Vesuvio.'

'It was all I was good for – pop music. To be an "entertainer".'

'It was probably that attitude that led him to fire you.' This raised a smile.

'Probably.'

'Which led to the drugs.'

'A "slippery slope", no? But it felt right, sitting at the feet of the concert-goers, playing for pennies. It was where I belonged.'

'So tell me, what led you to confront Professor Bellario?' Another long silence. '*Guido.*'

'It's hazy. We were sat around the corner of the *Teatro*. I was half out of it, coming down. Against the wall, in the shadows where they've set up that fish restaurant for the summer. You'd think people would be bothered by us stretched out there, but they're not – I don't think they see us. We're just part of the furniture. They'd probably use us as chairs if we obliged and bent over . . . Anyway, like I said, I was half coming out of it, in a kind of daze, but at that chilled-out point when everything's fine, good with the world. In fact, better: your senses are super-acute, it's like you're an angel dipping in and out of the conversations around you. Anyway, I remember sort of tuning into this chat on a table nearby and hearing them talking about it – about him, the professor, Bellario, and how he'd take a *bustarella* to get students through their exams. I don't know what exams, just exams, and suddenly *I got it.* I understood *why* I hadn't got in – I hadn't paid the piper! Or maybe someone else had and I'd been squeezed out! It's not as if my folks were the types to make a fuss. They could barely speak Italian!

'But don't get me wrong, it didn't upset me. Actually, I didn't feel a thing, which is what it's like, you know, but hell, I did need to piss. My God, how I needed to piss! So I got myself up and went around the back where they've put those urinals.

'In fact, I remember chuckling to myself about it, and trying to remember, or at least to remember to remember, because it did seem kind of important, what I'd heard. It was only as I was coming out and saw him, and her – you know, the perfect, gilded couple . . .'

Guido's expression hardened, and I glimpsed how he might have appeared the night he emerged from the shadows. 'Suddenly, it didn't seem so funny. I can't remember, not properly, but I stood in their path. They tried to get around me, but I went the same way. Excuse me, he said. I said – do you remember me? He looked – it was obvious he had no idea. No? You don't remember? Really?

'*Is it Guido?* That was Melodia. *Guido, what are you doing? Are you drunk?* I wanted to explain to them – what I was, what I'd become. I don't know – that may have been where the spoon came in. It was dark, the metal . . .

'They fell back, the look on their faces – and now I was shouting. I can't remember precisely what. They just stood there. In the end, I don't know . . . I suppose I had run out of words. I walked away.'

'Then you heard a scream and returned.'

'I did. To be honest, I hadn't gone twenty paces before I'd forgotten what I'd been so angry about.

'When I heard it, I didn't even connect the two, I mean, about me confronting them. I was just drawn back out of curiosity. And that was when I found her on her knees beside him.' Guido looked surprised. 'Yes, that's what happened.'

'Why didn't you tell Avvocato Servi all this?'

'It wasn't clear like now. I had flashes, but . . . I just felt all this anger, all this shame. I'd forgotten about the conversation. Instead, I thought I'd just confronted this professor, made some accusations, but they had no basis. It was only now I remembered the talk at the table. When I spoke to the avvocato, I thought it was just more of me being a loser.'

'Amanda Grimaldi. Name ring a bell?'

This evoked a smile. 'Amanda. I remember her – quiet, studious. I used to help her with her composition. Anyway, what about her?'

Chapter 14

I was being lined up by the Polizia Penitenziaria for the bus to *La Dozza* along with the others when Mario came down and pulled me out.

I gave Guido's arm a squeeze – *'Coraggio'* – before allowing myself to be led back up the steps and towards the exit. Mario pushed open the doors, closing them behind me without a word. I looked up at the clock in the entrance hall. I'd lost the afternoon.

I checked my phone. If I had been expecting a rash of missed calls from worried colleagues or loved ones, I would have been disappointed. Just a WhatsApp from Rose asking what was for dinner. I felt way too weary to attempt to make anything myself, so replied: *crescentine*, which I knew would make her day. 'And order me a beer, too.'

We didn't live far from the Questura, but I took my time walking home. I needed to process, let the imprint of Amanda Grimaldi's grotesque death mask fade; breaking the news to the kid – Guido.

'But why?'

'I've no idea.'

'But she had everything . . .'

'Sometimes it's not enough.'

Despite the indomitable blue sky, I felt clouded by suicide, police cells and bad news; sweat-heavy, grime-sheened. In fact – I stank. Of course – death sticks. I'd spent too much time with the girl and the stink had combined with my perspiration, so no matter how sweetly deodorised I might have been when I'd set out that morning, I gave off the vague odour of garbage.

A day of dead bodies, sob stories. And all too plausible explanations – I particularly liked Guido's for the knife, which seemed to embody the kind of absurdity that so often characterised real-life crime and that prosecutors couldn't wait to ridicule. A spoon-wielding mugger? The kid would be laughed out of court, or rather straight back to *La Dozza*.

And the professor himself? Was Doctor Mattani correct in guessing the professor's heart attack was linked to some deadly cocktail of illicit, but routine, substances?

And could Bellario's death, whether Amanda was aware of Guido's involvement or not, have pushed her over the edge to commit suicide, as the commissario suggested? There were the pills in her medicine cabinet. Those marks upon the mezzanine I noticed could have been just that – from shifting boxes. Perhaps Commissario Rita Miranda was correct and I should amend the old adage to: '*clues* do not equal causation'. And yet . . .

I crouched down to tie my shoes. I had reached the portico of Via Solferino, just around the corner from home. Through the crook of my arm, I couldn't see anyone behind me apart from an old lady wheeling her shopping trolley some distance away. But I still wasn't happy. Straightening up, I turned fully around, surveying the doorways sunk in the shadows. I gazed across the street in case there should be someone lurking behind a column. I waited for signs of movement.

Nothing.

Just my imagination? I continued to wait, and nothing continued to happen, except that old lady drew slowly closer.

True, I was tired, stressed-out. It could simply be paranoia. But I had learned to respect these feelings – these echoes, perhaps, of some long-dormant mammalian sense that warned me I was being watched.

And I duly noted it.

The JUST EAT kid was waiting at the opening gates when I arrived at the Faidate Residence. I took the order and handed him a tip. Across the courtyard, I noticed Stella emerge from the steps leading down to the *cantina*.

'Hey,' I called, ducking my head back out through the gates for a final look before they closed behind me – nothing. 'If I'd known . . .'

I held up the bag of warm *crescentine* – a cousin of the *piadina*, they're basically fried dough closed like a pancake and containing a choice of savoury fillings. 'I'd have asked Rose to—'

'I added some to the order,' Rose called down from the balcony.

Stella had paused at the top of the steps. 'I've something to show you,' she said.

'What?'

'In the *cantina*.'

'Claudio thought something might have happened.' I waited for Rose to come for the *crescentine*. 'That maybe the tremors had affected the foundations.'

Rose slapped down the stone stairs barefoot and snatched up the piping hot bundle. I followed Stella down into the gloomy, brick-arched basement.

The *cantina* of the Faidate Residence was said to date back half a millennia, although when we had had the archaeological team from the Superintendent of Fine Arts down for an inspection, one of the experts had tapped a lower section of red-bricked wall and said: 'You know what that is, don't you? Roman.' So it was anybody's guess how far back the building truly went.

I followed Stella around one corner, then another. It was a labyrinth down here. The family had used it to shelter during the bombing raids of the Second World War, and Nonno Faidate – that would be the Comandante's father, Rose's great-grandfather – had constructed false walls to shelter partisans, an especially shrewd move on his part considering he was also deputy chief of police throughout the fascist administration, something the family history tended to gloss over. But it was those fake walls that had attracted Stella in the first place – she had wanted to recreate one of the 'hidden spaces' for her show.

'Over there.' She nodded at a narrow stretch of corridor supported by a pair of steel braces. 'I bumped into Claudio with the Comandante and a builder. They were talking about having to pour some more concrete in to underpin it or something. Apparently they're sinking . . .'

'Jesus. How much will it cost?'

'Never mind – I might have a solution for that.'

'Solution?'

'So, I was taking some photos . . .' We appeared to be facing a solid wall of old, flat medieval bricks. Stella took one step forward and another sideways, vanishing behind the false wall Nonno had created during the war. I followed her. She switched on a bright-white photographer's lamp set high upon a tripod, stripping bare the cell-like space that might have concealed half-a-dozen partisans in its time. 'Over there.' She pointed to a small pile of bricks in the far corner, a dark patch above them. There was some kind of hole. 'I'm sure it wasn't here when I was down the last time. I was thinking it might also be connected to the tremors.' She handed me a torch. 'It's another room.'

'Christ, I hope Nonno didn't wall up any Nazis inside here, too.' I held up the torch and peered through. She was right about a room, although it was much smaller than the one we were standing in – the size of a deep cupboard or closet. I tilted the torch downward. Beneath a layer of dirt I thought I could make out a large box.

'That's . . . interesting.'

'I was wondering – some kind of illicit loot?'

'The thing is,' I said, 'if Nonno put it there, and never came to retrieve it, do we really want to know what's inside?'

'You can't be thinking of leaving it!'

'I'm not saying that, but who knows what he got up to – the family legend was he was playing a double game. Maybe it was a triple one.'

'He was a collaborator, you mean?'

'That was what the Germans thought – that he was on their side – and perhaps they were right.'

'That's what fascinates me about these hidden spaces,' said Stella. 'That one of Chiara's? A strongroom – the family used to literally sleep on top of the family silver, only now it's used to store the loot *her* father got hold of during the war. There are paintings down there he bought cheap from Jewish families, or said he would look after – Chiara's a little vague on that – but in any case, they were never returned and she's always been afraid to show them. Or at least *she was* – I've persuaded her to let me "discover them" for the exhibition. It should create quite a stir.'

'What about your own stuff?'

'There'll be plenty of that too, but these old paintings, they've been waiting for such a long time to see the light of day, poor loves. Anyway,' she began working at one of the bricks by the hole as if it was a loose tooth.

'Hang on,' I said, but I was too late – she had wrenched it out and half the wall along with it. We retreated back into the corridor as the dust billowed after us.

'*Cazzo*,' she said, coughing. 'The whole thing must have been held together by sand.'

'Or mud. You know – I'm beginning to wonder if that wall isn't such a recent addition.'

'What do you mean?'

'Nonno's cement's still holding up – this new space may have been part of the original building. Perhaps even Nonno didn't realise it was here.'

We ventured back inside. The dust hung like a rusty mist in the lamplight. Most of the wall had now collapsed into a ragged pile of bricks. Beyond it – the bulk of a chest strapped by black iron and secured by hefty locks with crude keyholes.

Stella and I looked at each other with childlike wonder. 'Doesn't seem modern,' she said. Then: 'Hold on.' She crouched down by the light and opened her camera case.

Stella began photographing the discovery from every conceivable angle while I looked on, my natural curiosity tempered by what little I knew about the family history.

The Residence had been in the family for hundreds of years. The Faidate had been traders of the higher caste but I suspected that, situated as they were between the aristocratic *palazzi* of Via Solferino and the wealthy monasteries in the hills, yet midway along a street once famed for its brothels, the ancestors had had a sizeable moral hinterland.

So what was in the chest? Bologna had endured frequent sieges, occupations, as well as violent feuds within the walls, hence the still-formidable fortifications that shielded *La Residenza* from the street. But if the chest had contained 'the family silver', why would it still be here? There had been plenty of lean times over the centuries, and I doubted the Faidate could have afforded, like Chiara's family, to have simply sat tight upon their wealth. Could it have been forgotten? That was perhaps a possibility – the person or persons who had hidden it had been struck down, even the entire family, by disease, conflict . . .

Or – it simply contained something they had not wanted to be found.

Stella was tugging at the locks when Rose appeared.

'Nonno says to get a move on before the *crescentine* get— What's that?'

Stella's grin reflected brilliant white in the light.

'Okay,' I said. 'Let's take a break. We'll leave it, for now.'

'*What?*' said Stella.

'Get something to eat. I'm starving, and it's been quite a day – did I tell you I had a sidekick? Your pal Vesuvio . . .'

'We can't just leave it!'

'The chest will still be here after dinner.'

'Is it treasure?' asked Rose.

'It's locked,' I said.

'Oh,' said Stella. 'We could easily knock these off – see how they've rusted? It probably wouldn't take—'

'*Let's just* . . . slow down for a moment,' I said. 'We can talk to Giovanni upstairs. Perhaps he might have some idea about what it contains.'

'Don't you want to know?'

'Of course I do – and that's precisely why I think we should talk to the Comandante. But, you know, this isn't *The Mummy* . . .'

'Hope not,' said Rose. 'He came to life.'

'What I mean is – we *really* don't know what's inside. It could actually be something dangerous, like gunpowder.'

'*Beneath the house?*' said Stella.

'They'd have had to put it somewhere. Come on.'

I ushered the ladies out, feeling like a proper killjoy.

I cast a wary glance back at the chest and reached up to switch off the light. Killjoy, perhaps, but something told me it contained nothing good.

Chapter 15

'You did well to wait,' said the Comandante, as happy to dig into a *crescetina* stuffed with prosciutto and creamy stracciatella cheese, washed down with a bottle of Menabrea beer, as he might a veal fillet topped by shavings of white truffle accompanied by a glass of Sangiovese Superiore. 'I suspect if it had been filled with golden sovereigns, priceless artworks and diamond necklaces, we would have known about it by now. You're sure it's . . . ancient?' Giovanni Faidate clearly harboured similar fears about his father's wartime record.

'Take a look yourself.' I pulled my *crescentina* out of the oven. 'I'd say it's a couple of hundred years old at the very least, judging by the lock.'

'The most likely outcome,' said the Comandante, 'if it contains organic material like clothes or cloth, is there will be nothing left.' He looked oddly hopeful.

'Although it seemed pretty dry in there.'

'We should keep this between ourselves for the moment,' he said. 'We certainly don't want the authorities to hear about it. Or the media.' He was looking at Rose.

'What?'

'He means don't tell your schoolmates,' I said. 'Including Stefania. She'll blab to her mum and we'll have crowds of freaks outside thinking it's the Arc of the Covenant or something.'

Rose rolled her eyes. 'I'm not a kid any more, Dad. I know how to be discreet. I don't tell anyone anything, do I?' I considered this. It was more or less the truth – at least, these days. 'But I can tell Uncle Jac? Dolores?' I nodded.

'I'll ask one of our friends to take a look before we open it,' said the Comandante.

'Massima?' I asked.

'I think she should have the requisite equipment.' His steel-grey eyes softened as he turned to Stella. 'I suppose you consider us very stuffy.'

'It seems a bit over-the-top, Giovanni. Dan was actually talking about gunpowder . . .'

'Oh, yes,' the Comandante gave me an approving nod. 'Quite possibly. Or a bastard child.' Rose gasped. 'Or a servant's,' he added as if that would make it any better. 'Even a legitimate offspring. It could have occurred during an outbreak of the plague and rather than consigning the body to a mass grave, as would have been required by the authorities, they may have preferred to lay it within the grounds.' He shrugged. 'And if that's the case, then the bacillus could still be active. Only the other day I was reading how health officials in Padua had been obliged to don protective clothing when they were clearing a church crypt precisely for this reason.'

Stella looked at the pair of us. '*Gunpowder. A bastard child. Plague.* They hadn't even occurred to me. What kind of people even *think* like that?'

'Oh,' said Rose between mouthfuls of *crescentina*, 'that's easy – detectives.'

Stella announced she had better be going – another reminder, if any were needed, that we had yet to achieve the easy familiarity of staying over.

As she rose to leave, sadness swept the Comandante's face. Did Stella's presence, however obliquely, recreate the little family he remembered, that had departed forever with his late daughter? I didn't want to dwell on that. I walked Stella to the door.

'You won't forget to let me know about the "grand opening"?' she said.

'I'm sorry. I'm sure your other boyfriends would have simply got a hammer and knocked the locks off.'

'For sure,' she smiled. 'And in the process they might have blown us to kingdom come.'

'Well, at least you'd have gone out with a bang.'

She laughed. 'I'd prefer my Wiki entry not to end – *She was blown up trying to break open an ancient chest filled with gunpowder.*'

'I don't know – there are worse ways to go. *Stay.*' I pulled her towards me.

'It's not that I don't want to. It's just—' My daughter emerged from the kitchen.

'Are we okay for tomorrow?' Rose called as if there was nothing unusual about finding her art tutor in a clinch with her dad.

'Sure,' Stella said. '*A domani.*'

'*A domani,*' said Rose, continuing along the hall to her bedroom.

'*A domani.*' Stella gave me a peck on the nose. She backed out.

I followed her onto the landing and waited for her to step from the stairs into the courtyard, watched her make her way across the grass. She disappeared beneath the silver elm before emerging again by the gate, pressing the glowing green button and waiting for the doors to open. She looked back. Part of me wanted to duck out of sight, but it was too late – she had caught me. I waved. She blew me a kiss before slipping through the opening doors and into the night.

I returned to the kitchen to find the Comandante filling the dishwasher. We tidied in silence then stepped onto the balcony where he could smoke, and I could watch him smoking.

With the chime of the nine o'clock bell from San Procolo came *il vento della sera*, the breeze that blew east across the city each evening like a relieved sigh for having made it through another day. We watched a solitary yellow balloon float across the sun-baked roofs, bob upon the flesh-dark tiles.

'You've had a busy day, my contacts tell me,' said the Comandante.

'You spoke to Alessandro,' I said. 'Did he make it up the mountain?'

'Also our contact in the Questura. You were arrested!'

'It was silly,' I said. 'A complete waste of time. Vindictive. But I did get to speak to our boy, Guido Delfillo. According to him, the whole thing was a misunderstanding. He had a go at the prof, yes, but over his exam result. There was no attempted hold-up.'

'What about the girl, Signora Amanda Grimaldi?'

'Precisely. I don't like it. Commissario Miranda gave short shrift to any connection between Amanda's death and Professor Bellario . . . I mean any sinister connection, and I could see her point, but . . .'

'It does seem quite a coincidence.'

'We should look at the footage from the opera house again, but this time focus on the girl. I sent pics of her phone's contents to Jacopo.'

'You haven't seen his email?'

'It's been a long day, Giovanni.'

The Comandante put on his reading glasses and opened his phone.

'It says here there didn't seem to be anything out of the ordinary on the photos you took of the telephone, however, in the final shot he remarks,' he cleared his throat, '"It looks like the SpeakSafe app was uninstalled on the Monday morning at ten-o-twelve." Obviously we will have to wait for a professional's opinion, but how long would you say the unfortunate girl had been hanging there?'

'Long enough for significant decomposition to take place: she was bloated, stank like hell. The windows were closed, and although the heating hadn't been turned on, well, it would hardly have been necessary, providing the air-conditioning was turned off – which it was. It was baking in there.'

'*Necessary*, by which you mean – if the purpose had been to speed up decomposition with the intention of obscuring any possible evidence.'

'Quite,' I said. 'There's just one thing – why would she have been wearing her dress? The others were dressed light, casual, for the rehearsal.'

'What does that tell us?'

'Bellario died after the Saturday-night performance. Amanda didn't show for the Monday rehearsal and there wasn't another performance scheduled until the Tuesday evening. We found her the Tuesday afternoon. Yet – the *Carlino* dates her death after the Monday morning, so that means she died between the Monday and Tuesday when we discovered her. In short, I can see no reason for her to be wearing the dress.'

'Unless she wanted to look her best,' said the Comandante. 'It can be a statement, even if they don't leave a physical note – their final word to the universe. I wrote my thesis on the suicide epidemic among the bourgeoisie of *fin de siècle* Vienna. What?'

'I'm sorry, I didn't know you had a degree. I thought as a *carabiniere* . . .'

'I was a simple plod?' The Comandante looked amused. 'Actually, that was for my Masters – applied psychology. My first degree is in criminology. Anyway, there are categories of suicide, and that's one of them.'

'If it was all about looking one's best, it's a shame she didn't consider she'd shit herself, or be puffed up like a balloon.'

'*If* that was her intention. Alternatively, someone could have simply set the scene – you know, it's the little details that can swing an investigation one way or another. An informed murderer might know that. This mobile telephone application "SpeakSafe". It sounds like some kind of secure messaging service, is that right?'

'It is.'

'How easy would it be, for someone to gain access to her phone post-mortem?'

'Well, I did.'

'Not that difficult, then.' The Comandante permitted himself a smile. 'Or she did it herself. It could merely be a coincidence. The challenge is to discern coincidences from clues.'

'The commissario wouldn't like to hear you say that. According to her, it's not a question of clues, but budgets, resources . . .'

'Which is why the difficult crimes so often go unsolved, and the rich escape unpunished. Fortunately, at least for now, we have money on our side. What do you propose, Daniel?'

'Until Doctor Mattani gets back to us with the toxicology test on the prof we'll be a bit in the dark. In the meantime, I would like to square off Guido's "alibi", such as it is – establish there's some truth to his allegation.'

'And of course, there's the wife – Melodia,' said the Comandante. 'Of the trio who met for a drink at the interval of *Rigoletto* – the Professor, Signora Grimaldi, Melodia – she is the only one who remains alive.'

Chapter 16

The courtyard of the conservatory echoed with instruments – from one room a piano, from another a pair of violins, and from yet another, brass, practising diverse pieces to generate a cacophonous, though not discordant, sound akin to one of those abstract works only classical aficionados can really appreciate.

But sitting here in one of the city's most evocative enclosed spaces – beneath a portico that had once cloistered yet another closed order of nuns, surrounding a quad that was almost English-green with its grass and tall trees – the sound had its own peculiar appeal. Perhaps it was precisely this kind of experience that had inspired experimentation, although there was a time and place for everything.

I continued to scroll through the document on my phone.

The report had come through a few minutes earlier – Alba's profile on Melodia di Battista.

Age 27. Spouse of Professor Ilario Bellario. The professor's third wife (previous spouses Maria Fannelli and Felicita Davide). Four children from two prior marriages, two apiece. With Fannelli, two school-age girls. With Davide a boy, Giovanni, 22 and girl, Eva, 26.

Melodia is the daughter of composer and former Professor of Composition at Conservatorio Giovanni Battista Martini – Marco di Battista – and wife, pianist Eroica Fulmine. She graduated (viola) from the *conservatorio* among the top third percentile. She belongs to a quartet which appears to specialise in the baroque. I couldn't get into her Facebook page. I think I found her Instagram but there's not much – just ads for their concerts and a few pics of string instruments. She's got quite a low profile but maybe she's just the serious type – after all, she got married young to an old man. It's true she *is* related to Father Martini, which I got not from her but from the Wiki on her dad, who seems to have leant a lot upon the family connection throughout his career, although he's dead now – he was 65 when he met Melodia's mum (who was 30) so, yes, considering Melodia also married a man thirty years her senior that does seem a bit creepy . . .

'Anything interesting?' It was Vesuvio. 'Well – don't look so surprised to see me! We had an appointment.' True, although I had been hoping he might have felt like giving it a miss considering the circumstances in which we had parted. Still, at least he had reverted to standard rocker jeans, T-shirt and sunglasses for the conservatory, where apparently he wasn't too worried about being recognised.

'This place is called Giovanni Battista Martini,' I said. 'That's after "Father Martini", right? So he's clearly pretty famous, but before I began to work on this case I'd never heard of him.'

'He was, basically, the musical godfather of Bologna,' said Vesuvio.

'Composer?'

'Theorist, mentor, teacher, an expert of counterpoint, and he collected thousands, maybe tens of thousands of musical texts. At the time, it was probably the world's leading library of music. And because Bologna was the centre for church music – I mean, it had all these churches, right? – as well as having the oldest university, all the great musicians of the time came to study here. But hey,' he looked up, 'the maestro can explain better.'

The 'maestro' looked like a character out of Dickens – physically shaped by his environment. A tall, spindly man with snow-white hair swept back to his collar, long and bony *Nosferatu* fingers – albeit without the talon-like nails – a hollow chest and a stoop, he seemed incomplete without being wrapped around a cello or harp. Yet he had a keen smile; the jeans, sandals and T-shirt reading YOU CAN'T BEAT HOVEN beneath a picture of the composer with a purple Mohican, transformed Ebenezer Scrooge into one of the Fabulous Furry Freak Brothers.

'Marco.' He and Vesuvio embraced.

'Daniel,' said Vesuvio. 'Let me introduce the Dean.' We shook hands. 'Maestro, Daniel would like to ask some questions about the admissions process, and Professor Bellario.'

'Ah, Ilario, poor man. Uh-huh. Okay!'

We followed him along the portico, up a sweeping staircase and along a shabby, strip-lit corridor. The *palazzo* had been battered by centuries of public use. Peeling paint, chipped plaster ... we passed arbitrarily bricked-up doorways and windows, vast spaces divided by flimsy partitions. Contemporary Italians occupy old buildings in much the same way medieval Romans once did the ancient Forum – like squatters. But it would be unfair to say the buildings are unloved; on the contrary – the kids sat smoking upon the stone bench where parents once lingered with novice daughters; the frescoed private chapel now a practice room – give life to buildings that elsewhere might have become perfectly preserved mausoleums.

Having said that, there were few signs of dilapidation in the dean's suite of offices. The principal was the size of a salon and facing away from the courtyard, instead over-looking Piazza Rossini. There was not a crack in the bright Renaissance frescoes, and the black-and-white marble floor, worn dull with age, was scattered with fine Persian carpets. The dean's huge antique desk had its back to the windows and a pair of flags – the Italian tri-colour and the European Union – stood boldly behind it. He directed us to an ageing tan leather sofa I recognised as a classic design from the 1970s, while taking a similarly upholstered chair. I didn't know about the maestro, but previous deans had certainly enjoyed the fruits of office. Vesuvio appeared to confirm this: 'The old place hasn't changed,' he said. 'Except the occupant.'

'No regrets, I presume?' said the dean.

'No point,' said Vesuvio. 'As I was saying, Daniel, I decided to seek my fortune elsewhere. The maestro here, and the then dean, tried to persuade me otherwise.'

'One of our finest,' the dean said sadly. 'But . . . I *did* understand. Ours can be a capricious business, as Marco memorably pointed out at the time. Especially in Italy.'

'Especially in Italy,' Vesusvio incanted. He turned to me. 'Signor Olivietto was my composition tutor.'

'Tell me, Signor Leicester.' Despite his hippie attire, Vesuvio's 'maestro' had the eyes of a hawk. 'What is it that you want, precisely? Ilario Bellario, you say? A tragedy. But what has that got to do with us? He moved on some time ago.'

'We are trying to verify a story that his alleged assailant, Guido Delfillo,' I paused, but the dean hadn't appeared to recognise the name, 'provided. He says he confronted the professor with the claim that he was somehow cheated out of his place at the conservatory.'

The dean smoothed back his hair. 'And this caused Ilario to drop dead?'

'Apparently.'

'Well, I must say, I never realised he was such a sensitive soul.'

'He may have misinterpreted the situation. Certainly his wife . . .'

'Felicita?'

'No, Melodia.'

'Oh, he's got a new one, has he? I see.'

'Claims to have seen a knife, although she may have been mistaken.'

'So what is this lad saying, precisely? He was "cheated" out of his place? Sounds like sour grapes. I mean, he wouldn't be the first candidate to fail an exam.'

'He claims the professor was corrupt, that he took bribes.'

'Well, he can claim what he likes.'

'It's true, though, Maestro,' said Vesuvio, 'that numbers are limited every year, so if you are lower down the list, you have less chance of getting in.'

'I remember you came in quite high, and it was downhill from there!'

'So, say a prof took a *bustarella* to up the marks of one candidate,' Vesuvio continued, 'another would have to lose out. And I mean,' he indicated a pair of yellowed pages of musical notation framed on the wall beside the dean's desk, 'it's not as if it's unheard of.'

'Really, Marco, this again? As the dean told you at the time: it was 1770. And that was Mozart.' He said to me: 'The poor man almost had a coronary when he began waving it about.'

'I'm sorry,' I said. 'I'm not following you.'

'You mentioned Father Martini, Daniel,' said Vesuvio. 'If you look – the bottom sheet is a real mess, full of errors. It was Mozart's exam – an antiphon he was asked to compose to get into the *Accademia*. The one above is the version that was actually submitted in his name after it had been "corrected" by Father Martini.'

'He was thirteen, Marco,' said the dean. 'And – *he was Mozart.*'

'Could the same sort of thing happen today?' I asked. The dean was shaking his head.

'There are checks, balances. There's a board.'

'But was the professor on the board?'

'Illario was involved in the process, yes.'

'Is there *anything* about the professor you could tell us,' I said. 'Strictly off-the-record, that might help? Why he moved on, for example . . .'

The dean looked at me. 'There's really *nothing* I can tell you.' He then looked at Vesuvio. 'I'm sorry.' He held his hands together in a gesture that implied they were tied by invisible strings.

'Nothing you *can* tell us, Dean,' I said. 'But could you do us a favour?'

'It depends what that favour is.'

I nodded at his computer. 'Could we see the records of the two students?'

'Oh, they would be confidential.'

'Their results? For their entrance exams?'

'Ah.' His eyes darted between the pair of us.

'They were public, weren't they?' said Vesuvio. 'I remember having to come here. They were posted up in the hallway.'

'They were,' the dean said finally. He got up and went over to the desk. 'Names?'

'Guido Delfillo and Amanda Grimaldi.' Again – not a twitch of recognition from the dean.

After a bit of fannying around trying to get the printer in the outer office to work, the dean returned with a pair of print-outs. I took a look and passed them to Vesuvio. 'You can probably make better sense of these.'

Vesuvio skipped through Amanda's, his finger following the grades. He then turned to Guido's. He paused mid-way down.

'What?'

'It doesn't make sense. The kid did brilliantly in his practical exercises, his audition, if you will, but flunked composition, which surprises me, as he was often helping us out with recording arrangements – orchestral scores and so on.'

'Perhaps he had picked it up by then,' said the dean.

'And Amanda?'

Vesuvio shook his head. 'Nothing special. Well – performance-wise she was weak. Scored high on composition, though, which would have lifted her into the middle-percentile.'

'Whereas Guido . . .'

'Lower percentile. Waiting list.'

'Only he didn't get in. Odd, especially considering he was giving Amanda extra help with composition.'

'He could always have re-applied,' said the dean.

'So – Professor Bellario moved on,' I said. 'Was he in any way pushed, Signor Olivietto?'

'The reputation of the conservatory is second to none,' said the dean. 'And it is my duty to ensure it remains that way.'

'I'm not sure that's exactly an answer.'

The dean checked his watch, rose to his feet. 'That's all I can tell you, Signor Leicester. I'm sorry I can't be of any more assistance.'

As the dean accompanied us back along the dingy corridor, he said to Vesuvio: 'I hear you've a new album in the works. Paolo Bersani at your label was telling me. He said it would have quite a significant live orchestral component. I was thinking – perhaps you might consider hiring some of our final year students.'

'Sure, Maestro, when it comes to that . . .'

Ahead, a door was flung open and the upright neck of a wooden instrument emerged followed by an elongated, triangular body mounted upon a wheeled trolley. It was followed by two more of these monsters, navigated by a woman on either side. They proceeded towards us. As they passed, the lead woman, bespectacled with a tied-back bun of grey hair, nodded to the dean. They trundled past.

We reached the top of the stairs. The dean turned to watch the final unwieldy string instrument round the corner. '"Tromba Marina" or "Sea Trumpets". You saw the first lady? That's Professor Gloria Penna, Ilario's number two. She's now the acting head of the musicology department at the university. Probably the future one, too, knowing how these things work. I guess she came out on top in the end.'

'How so?'

'She was the original shoo-in for departmental head when the post came up, until the debate at the festival of music. After that – well, she was out, and Ilario was in.'

'What happened at this festival?' I asked.

'Oh,' the dean surprised me with his subsequent choice of words. 'He crushed her.'

We walked back down Via Zamboni beneath the tall portico that runs alongside the church of San Giacomo until we arrived at Piazza Verdi.

'Well,' I said to Vesuvio. 'Thanks again.'

'At least no dead girls this time.'

'No,' I said. 'Are you all right?'

'About what?'

'It must have been a shock, to see Amanda hanging like that.'

'At least it'll give me something to talk to the shrink about after the holidays – Elvira had it written into the pre-nup. Why do you think she did it, the girl?'

'Hard to say. Could be any number of reasons . . .'

'Like what?'

'That's precisely what's bothering me,' I said. 'I have to admit, I'm discovering the world of classical music is unexpectedly murky.'

Vesuvio slapped me on the back. 'They're the worst – us rockers, we're in bed by nine with our teddy bears and warm milk.'

We found ourselves setting off in the same direction – towards Via delle Belle Arti. It turned out Vesuvio lived in the grey stone bulk of Palazzo Bentivoglio, a huge palace erected by a minor branch of the family a couple of centuries after their original palace had been demolished.

'So what are you doing in my neck of the woods?' he asked.

'My daughter,' I said. 'I'm meeting her for lunch at Comix.'

We stood outside the open doors of Palazzo Bentivoglio, its massive courtyard visible through the baroque iron lattice-work of the inner gates. 'Say hi to Eros and Marco for me,' said Vesuvio. He winked. 'And give Stella a kiss, too.'

Chapter 17

Comix Café took its name from its theme: the world of *fumetti*, or the graphic novel.

Fumetti hold a particular fascination for Italians – youth and adults alike – and it is common to find pre-teens perusing the racks of comic books beside elderly *professori*, the selection ranging from Mickey Mouse *Topolino* paperbacks to bulky hardbacks on weighty themes like the Yugoslavian civil war or the philosophy of Nietzsche, painstakingly drawn across page after page of carefully researched detail. Perhaps it is because the Italian is such an obsessively visual culture – one in which the Old Masters, recounting biblical scenes across walls and ceilings for a largely illiterate public, could be said to have been the original graphic storytellers.

I wondered how Vesuvio knew that Stella would also be here. Well – it was his local bar, perhaps he had even spotted them on occasion: Rose had her weekly lesson, which had continued after Stella and I had become an item – indeed, it was Rose's sole condition when I had revealed, or rather, she had deduced, I was dating her tutor – and I was happy for them to meet at Comix, notwithstanding its proximity to

Piazza Verdi, because I knew the guys behind the bar would keep an eye on my girl. It was also air-conditioned, which was a joy in this weather. I let out a relieved sigh as I stepped in.

'Tough morning?' asked Eros.

'I've actually had worse.'

A pair of what looked like highwaymen entered behind me. Despite the heat, they were draped in capes bedecked with gold and silver filigree, tri-corn hats and Venetian-style half-masks, except there was little *Carnevale* sparkle about them; on the contrary, the masks were grotesquely comic – sprouting huge papier-mâché noses flushed red by booze, and bushy eyebrows and moustaches like a medieval Groucho Marx.

A group of kids, sat at the far end beneath shelves packed with comic books, let out a cheer. The pair bowed, and began to de-robe.

'Theatre students,' Eros said. He nodded at the masks. 'Balanzone.'

'What?'

'*Il dottore* . . . one of the characters from *La Commedia dell'arte*. You know, the old theatre. Balanzone's from Bologna, obviously, a professor. Figure of fun because he knows everything about nothing. *Niente cambia!*'

'It's connected to this event? The five-hundred years thing?'

'Although I'm not sure what the *Commedia* has to do with "resistance".'

'Ah!' Angelo, one of the cartoonists who frequented Comix, placed his finished coffee on the counter. 'Surely *commedia*, or satire, is the first and finest line of resistance: to mock the learned and powerful. And you see – the performers are actually both women.

'Because the actors of the *Commedia* sported masks, Italian theatre could employ both sexes. So while Shakespeare was using boys for female parts, here they had the real thing.' A chuckle emerged from the depths of his bountiful, bushy grey beard that expanded like a bib across his barrel chest. He may have been a cartoonist but he had the wild vigour of a thriving castaway. 'In Stratford, his Romeo and Juliet would have actually been Romeo and *Julian*. So that's the idea – they're going to have females playing the male roles and men the female.' Now he tugged at his 'mouth mane' as Stella called it. 'Or something like that. A "gender fluid" production, that's what they're saying.'

'What would Duke Magnesio think?' I was referring to his comic strip.

'Oh,' Angelo's quick blue eyes twinkled. 'The Duke would take it in his stride – fashions come, fashions go, but there's one thing that never changes.'

'Which is?'

'Revenge! Sicily's the home of the vendetta, after all.' This was the setting for his bitingly sardonic super-hero. Angelo glanced around the crowded bar. 'The young, the blessed young, see life as a procession, but that's just on the surface – the foundations never change, the old stories: love, pride, greed, envy, betrayal . . . and the longing for a hero to impose justice upon an unjust world.'

'That's what I love about Italy,' I said. 'You wouldn't expect a conversation like this in your pub back home. It would all be about the football.'

'Oh, you don't want to talk about that here,' said Eros. 'Have you seen how Bologna are doing?'

'More to the point,' Angelo winked, 'how is your invest-igation moving along? The dead professor, the young girl? Nasty, that. Very nasty.'

'How on earth did you hear about it?'

'We were just talking about it, weren't we, Roberto?' He nodded to a gent with crazy white Einstein hair sat at a table cleaning his pipe upon a copy of *La Repubblica*. In his khaki shirt and shorts, he could have been perched at a riverbank contemplating a fishing float.

'We were, Angelo.' Roberto didn't look up from threading through the green and red pipe cleaner. 'Indeed we were.'

'So it's hardly a secret.'

'You heard about it here? Or the Osteria della Luna?'

'Personally,' said Angelo, 'I think Vesuvio has more money than sense, but that's hardly a controversial opinion.'

'Unless he's buying,' muttered Roberto.

'Well, yes. It's true – then I keep my opinions to myself. But it seems he got more than his money's worth when you two stumbled in on that girl. He rolled into the *osteria* as white as a sheet!'

'Maybe he'll write a song about it,' said Eros.

'Good material,' agreed Roberto. 'Oh yes, indeed.'

I looked at Eros.

'Rose?'

'Around the corner.'

Rose was sat with Stella, a series of Polaroids spread across the table like playing cards. I pulled up a seat.

'*Allora*,' I said – an almost untranslatable Italian word that stood for everything and nothing.

'Hey!' said Rose. 'Guess what!'

'What?'

'Stella said I could include some of my own work in her show!'

'Really?' I looked at Stella, elegant in the white summer dress she had probably worn for her lecturing gig at the art school further up the road. She turned her huge brown eyes towards me.

'Well, why not?'

I might have replied – because you're a moderately famous local artist and my daughter is a fifteen-year-old schoolgirl, and I'm not sure how that will go down with the exhibition's curator – Alberto Fini, head of the art school and public intellectual – but I could see Stella's pitch already, about giving voice to youth, and so on. She might not compromise on her art, but she knew how to work an angle.

'Congratulations,' I said to my beaming daughter. 'Your mum would be proud.'

It just slipped out, though neither Rose nor Stella seemed to notice, continuing to natter about the exhibition, but it left me with a lump in my throat.

So I thought of something else: the Delfillos, perched on the edge of their sofa in that dark little apartment. How happy they must have once felt, to have this prodigy as their son.

I took out the photo – *The Laughing Cavalier* – all the potential in Guido's fresh young face, all those young faces, even Amanda's. I remembered Guido's heroin-hollowed cheeks, Amanda's rubbery leer. I closed my eyes. Opened them: rattling from the bar area, the tinkle of glass. Our table trembling.

It was over.

A whoop, a smattering of applause. Rose laughing along with the rest of them. The kids were all right – at Comix Café we were among the immortals. Stella caught my eye. She gave me a look as arch as an Italian Marlene Dietrich, then broke into a smile that transformed her otherwise austere beauty.

I looked down – my phone was continuing to vibrate upon the table, but that was as it should be – Doctor Mattani. I went back through the bar and out onto the portico.

'*Dottore.*'

'Daniel.' The coroner sighed.

'Is everything okay, *dottore?*'

'It looks like I may have to delay my own trip to Cesenatico. The toxicology came back negative – no cocaine, Viagra, not even paracetamol. So it looks as if you'll be having your test for poison, after all.'

'Are you saying . . .'

'I've re-examined my initial findings.' Another sigh. 'Bellario *was* exceptionally fit for his age. I can't find any under-lying factor or indication of an inherited condition that might have caused his death without the intervention of . . . some kind of agent. Or at least this seems more probable than . . . *divine* intervention.'

'Thank you for letting me know.'

'No problem. To be frank, I've been putting off the call to the Polizia. The commissario is really going to break my balls.'

Chapter 18

'I thought they were going to be in the church.'

'Apparently it's been declared unsafe,' said Dolores. 'Although, to be honest it makes more sense to hold the performance out here – can you imagine how hot everyone would get?'

It was early evening and I was, unexpectedly, back at Santa Cristina, standing in the shadows of the porticoed cloister while a dozen musicians practised on their strange-shaped string instruments in the cobbled courtyard. This was the all-female orchestra that would be recreating the sounds of the sisters of the former convent.

I had asked Dolores to keep an eye on Melodia – 'follow' would be too strong a word – although as it turned out that is precisely what she had done when the young widow had left her local bar and come here, where she was now propping up a cello at the rear of the horseshoe of musicians – a mix of young and middle-aged, with the older women playing the more eccentric-looking instruments – around the musical director, who I immediately recognised as Professor Gloria Penna.

'How does she seem to you – Melodia?' I asked Dolores. 'Her husband dropped dead in front of her a couple of days ago, and yet here she is carrying on her life.'

'She didn't look happy in the bar,' said Dolores. 'I mean, she wasn't joking and laughing. Pale face, puffy eyes, kept to herself. But maybe, you know, this was something she wanted to continue.'

'She claimed Guido had a knife, that he held them up. He had an entirely different version.'

'It was dark,' said Dolores. 'She was traumatised. In any case, it's his word against hers.'

'Whose side are you on?'

Dolores tilted her sunglasses down to the bridge of her nose. 'I didn't realise it was about sides, Dan.'

'Then you're in the wrong business – we're on the side that's paying us. Her mother also married an older man. Her father was sixty-five when she was born. The Bellarios live in Via Galliera, an impressive address.'

'Legally, Melodia will only get half of whatever he left, if that's what you're getting at. The rest will go to the kids.'

I admit I was a little surprised by Dolores' grasp of inheritance law. 'Maybe it's a big half. Why shake your head?'

'You're being ageist.'

'Am I? Is that oldist or youngist? I confess, I struggle to keep up.'

'What I mean is – she did seem pretty upset to me, if you're implying she only married him for his money or whatever. It's not always like that. Maybe she just loved him. Not everything's a "motive".'

'He was probably poisoned, you know – Professor Bellario.'

Now I had her attention. 'At least that's what the coroner seems to believe; he's got to do some more tests.'

Dolores frowned at Melodia. 'Then do you think it *could be* an act?'

'Most people are murdered by someone they know,' I said. 'The reasons don't change – greed,' I thought about what Angelo had said, 'revenge, jealousy . . . She was his third wife, perhaps she was worried about a fourth.' I watched Melodia's translucent face turn intently towards the *professoressa*. 'Amanda Grimaldi,' I added. 'Was she a part of this group?'

'No idea – I'll find out. Do you think Bellario could have been after her?'

'He may have been,' I said. 'Or Melodia may have thought he was. Personally, I find it hard to believe, looking at her, but as you say, perhaps I'm being ageist – after all, he'd bagged one young woman. What *is* that sound?'

'That's them!' Dolores nodded to the triangular instruments. 'That's what the nuns used – they had them made to recreate the sound of the horn section when they were banned from using brass.'

The erstwhile sounds of the sisters of Santa Cristina filled the cloisters, possibly for the first time in half a millennium.

Proud, pithy notes generated by the strange instruments bounced off the columns, the high convent walls that had enclosed the women. Despite being dressed principally in T-shirts and shorts – even the older women – it wasn't so hard to imagine the sisters sat here all those centuries ago, hidden from the lecherous or reproachful eyes of their male custodians, practising their music in the shade.

I was about to leave Dolores to it when a guy turned up

with a trio of large cardboard boxes balanced on a trolley, wheeling it around the orchestra to stand beside the professor, his fingers drumming impatiently on top of them as if she wasn't in the middle of conducting a complex early-Baroque composition.

At first Professor Penna tried to ignore the man, but even I could tell his presence was throwing the musicians off. She finally stopped and, with an exasperated sigh, signed for the delivery.

The women gathered excitedly around. Through the crowd we saw a ribbon of bright red, another, as the musicians withdrew outfits from the boxes. Of course, red – the colour of protest and, post *The Handmaid's Tale*, especially female protest, although as a violinist with a mauve mop of hair, having thrown me a recalcitrant glance, stripped down to her bra and panties to try one on, I realised these outfits were anything but the 'modest' robes of the 'handmaids', instead light cotton dresses buttoning from the front, with plunging necklines and ending above the knees. They were outfits that *celebrated* the women's sexuality, even if I was a little surprised that the older musicians were also up for wearing them. But that, I supposed, was precisely the point.

'Wow,' said Dolores. 'They're pretty revealing.'

'I'm glad you said that. Hello,' I added. '*Carpe diem.*'

'What?'

'Seize the day?'

'*I know what it means.* I don't know what *you* mean.' I nodded at Melodia coming towards us, a red dress draped over one bare arm. In her white vest, cut-off denim shorts and flip flops, Signora Bellario definitely looked more like a student stepping away from a beach volleyball session than the widow of a fifty-something professor.

'You speak to her,' I said. Dolores shot me an alarmed look, but I was already sitting down on the low wall separating the portico from the courtyard and pulling out my phone. In the old days, I would have fished out my cigarettes.

I heard Dolores say: 'Hi, excuse me. Um, Melodia?'

'Er . . . yeah?'

'I thought it was. I'm Dolores . . . Pugliese. I was really sorry to hear about the professor. I mean your husband, Professor Bellario.' I glanced up from my pretend activity. Melodia's rather sublime features were swept by a sorrow that wouldn't have looked out of place in a gallery or church wall.

'Were you in Ilario's class?' she asked.

'Not exactly, well, I . . .' Dolores glanced down at me and Melodia followed her lead. Smiling sympathetically, I got to my feet and held out my hand. Melodia's was damp.

'I'm sorry,' she said. 'The heat . . .'

'Don't worry. We apologise for troubling you, signora, but we've been asked by the lawyer to look into the circumstances surrounding your husband's passing. You were with him at the end, I understand.'

'Yes.' She held the dress up to her chest.

'And of course, Guido.' She looked at me as if I had spoken Chinese. 'Guido Delfillo.'

'Oh. Yes, yes of course.'

'You said he had a knife.' Melodia nodded listlessly. 'Are you sure about that?'

She blinked, and a pair of tears rolled down her cheeks. 'I'm sorry?'

'He's claiming it was simply a spoon.' Melodia didn't look surprised. 'Signora . . .'

'I can only say what I saw.'

'Guido apparently made some kind of accusations about the professor—'

'He came out of the shadows. Shouting . . . raving about money but nothing made sense, it was just stuff, incoherent stuff. The knife . . . The face. His face like a phantom, or a horrible tramp. *Guido? Is that you?* He ran away. I turned to Ilario and he had just . . . gone. I looked around – he wasn't there. Then I looked down . . . and there he was.' She held the dress up to her face.

'I saw you.' Professor Gloria Penna had materialised beside us, holding a litre bottle of water like a club. 'Earlier, at the conservatory. Melodia,' she put a protective arm around her, 'it's all right, dear.' She looked at us. 'And you are?'

'Professor Penna,' I said. 'Let me explain—'

'I said – who are you and what are you doing here? Are you journalists?'

'They've been asked to investigate the circumstances,' said Melodia.

'Who by?'

'They said something about a lawyer.'

The *professoressa* scowled at me. 'What lawyer?'

'As I explained to the signora, we've been asked to look into the circumstances surrounding the death of Professor Bellario, who I believe also used to be the head of your department at the university? I was just wondering, *professoressa*, was Amanda Grimaldi also a member of your troupe?'

'And *I* asked who you are if you're not journalists.'

'We're private investigators.'

She grimaced as if she had bitten into a clove of garlic. 'Then you can fuck off.'

'That's not polite,' said Dolores, probably as surprised as me to be insulted by this otherwise respectable-looking professor, notwithstanding her UniBo T-shirt, baggy shorts and the faded green tattoo of a cartoon gecko on her ankle. 'We are entitled to ask questions.'

'Not here, you're not – now, bugger off.'

'We're not going anywhere – this is a public space.'

The professor shook her head. 'There you're wrong, signora. The complex is owned by the university, a foundation, and the women's library, of which I am a trustee. So it is private property and I repeat – fuck off, before I call the police.'

'Oh! Now wait a minute . . .'

I took Dolores' bony arm, nodded to the professor. 'Congratulations on the promotion, by the way,' I said. 'I hear it was a long time coming.'

Professor Penna, her arm still protectively around Melodia, watched as we walked away.

We emerged onto the little piazetta. 'Coffee?'

'I could do with a beer,' said Dolores.

'Fair enough.' It was *apero* hour, after all. We went to the little bar on the corner and took a table outside.

'So what do you think?' I asked.

'About Melodia? I get what you say, but she didn't *seem* like she was lying, she appeared to believe what she was saying. She seemed . . . I don't know.' She searched for the word. 'Really *soft*.'

I had to smile. If there was one thing Dolores was not it was soft.

'That can be an act, obviously,' I said. 'Simply a way to get what one wants. People tend to chart the most direct course through life, fill the role they've been assigned in life, as often as they make the part their own – maybe Melodia's role is "little girl lost".'

'Hence marrying the old man, father figure.'

'Now let's not be ageist, signora.'

'But she stuck to the knife story. Who do you believe?'

'Guido,' I said. 'It's too ridiculous to not be true.'

'Then she's lying.'

'I don't know. You're right, she also seemed convincing. Apart from the implement, the scenario both she and Guido described seems to match up – it would be perfectly reasonable for her to mistake that flash of metal for a knife. To be frank, in Guido's smack-raddled mind, it's equally possible that although he *believes* he pulled an innocuous piece of cutlery, somehow he had got hold of a blade. But the police didn't find a knife and I swung by the Guasto on the way over and couldn't see any sign of a spoon, either.

'Neither could be lying, both could be mistaken, but let's be clear about this – there's only one of them a court will believe.'

'And *if* Melodia was involved in her husband's death,' said Dolores, 'which is now being put down to an attempted robbery, she has every reason to stick to her story. It's like Guido simply fell into her lap. So, what's next?'

I thought of Professor Penna with her protective arm around Melodia.

'If foul play *was* involved – I mean, other than this alleged attempted robbery – then the wind's currently blowing in just one direction: towards the pair most likely to have benefited from Bellario's early demise.'

'Some wind. Now that would be nice, no?'

'For that, Dolores Pugliese, we will have to wait until sunset.'

Chapter 19

Incrocio Montegrappa was a traditional restaurant, run by a pair of identical twin sisters, which Claudio particularly esteemed for its tiramisù, an indication, if any were needed, that he intended to get through the full four courses this lunchtime, plus a bottle of wine, at my expense. Unlike our trainee investigator, neither he nor Jacopo, who had joined us, appeared to harbour any qualms about fine dining.

'Tell me, *signori*,' I said, 'what magic you've got to help crack the case.'

He and Jacopo exchanged a glance. 'You know,' said Claudio, rubbing his big hands, possibly in anticipation of his invoice, 'there's a lot we can do. We can bug this Melodia, for example. We could enter her home when she's away, set up some audio, cameras even, although you want to be careful with that – *la privacy*.'

I had to laugh – it was no coincidence that the Italian lexicon did not contain a word for 'privacy'.

'Isn't *all* of it illegal?'

'But cameras – it's like voyeurism, isn't it? Especially a woman. Won't be looked on kindly by the courts, unless of course they've requested it. Audio, however, well, it's easier to get away with. Considered somehow "cleaner".'

'And we can probably gain access to her telephone messages,' said Jacopo. 'Even listen to her calls with a little help.'

'How about gaining access to a SpeakSafe account, if she has one?'

Jacopo shook his head. 'End-to-end encryption,' said Claudio. 'Even more secure than WhatsApp.'

'There is a back door,' said Jacopo. Claudio looked surprised. 'Yeah – well, sort of. If you register a new device with them, SpeakSafe will send you a code. So, technically, if you can clone the number . . .'

'Then you will be sent the code to access the account,' said Claudio. 'I'm thinking the SIM – right?'

'That's it,' said Jacopo. 'If we could get hold of the SIM card from her phone and clone it, I could speak to our contact in SOG about getting the operator's key. We should then be able to receive the pass-code from SpeakSafe to access her device.'

'The Special Operations Group?' said Claudio. 'Of course,' he added appreciatively. 'The Comandante.'

'I thought that was why you were dating my cousin,' said Jacopo. 'So you could gain access to our contacts in the Carabinieri.'

'Ha. Got me.'

'And of course there's her cooking,' I said.

'Oh, there's that, too.'

'So what I'm hearing,' I said, 'is we'd have to get hold of her phone, copy the SIM and, presumably, so she doesn't get wind and delete the lot, replace the phone before she realises anything is amiss?'

'That's about it,' said Jacopo.

'All right,' I said. 'And there's someone else's SIM I'd like to clone, too. A *professoressa* . . .'

'I'm sorry,' said Jacopo. 'Maybe I made it sound too simple – getting hold of one phone will be a big enough ask, but two . . .'

Claudio reached over and re-filled my wine glass, or at least as far as they fill them in Italy.

'Don't worry about that,' I said. 'Focus on what you'll need to hack this app.'

Never mind that bottle of Sangiovese, followed by the complimentary limoncello, simply sitting inside the air-conditioned comfort of Incrocio felt intoxicating in this heat, and I was in no hurry to venture outside again, even if it was only a twenty-minute walk back to the office. But I finally left the guys to finish off the lemon liquor and stepped out, sunglasses on, head down. I suddenly envied Vesuvio his ridiculous hat. Instead I ducked under a portico and plotted my path back to Marconi involving as little exposure to the sun as possible.

It definitely felt hazy outside – the scorching, irradiated air, stone-dead silence. There were no trees here in the city centre, no cicada saw.

I didn't make it far along the portico before I stopped, removed my sunglasses and wiped them with the corner of my shirt, battling a wave of weariness, no doubt abetted by the booze.

A pair of footsteps came to a halt behind me.

A young woman stood checking her mobile phone. I replaced my sunglasses and continued to a bar, where I ordered a *caffè lungo* and a large glass of water. Downed the coffee, absent-mindedly tugging at my middle, certainly none the slimmer following that meal. Even though I had managed to skip the *secondo*, I had been unable to resist the bloody tiramisù.

I glanced out of the window. The woman from the portico was staring straight at me. All right – she still had her phone pressed against her ear. She could have been listening – she certainly wasn't talking – but it seemed like a pose. Indeed, the moment I looked at her, she looked away and *began* to talk, turning and heading off along the portico.

I dug into my pocket, slapped some change on the counter. I was about to charge after her, but hesitated. There was respecting your suspicions, and acting upon them. Had she been a guy, then fine, I might have got away with waylaying him and asking some pointed questions – but a lone young woman? With the taint of liquor on my breath?

I straightened myself up, made my way calmly to the exit. I looked in the direction she had gone – the portico was empty. The other way, then, as if she could have somehow sneaked past the bar without my noticing.

Nothing. I walked along the portico the way she had gone. It was a lengthy stretch, and she would have had to have moved exceptionally quickly to make it to the end before I emerged from the bar. Could she have entered a store along the way? We were at the dog-end of lunchtime, coming on for three in the afternoon, and all the shops – from hardware to women's fashion – were closed, although I paused outside the dress store and discreetly tried the door. Locked.

The portico was raised about three feet off the main, cobbled road. Usually the street would be packed with parked cars but, this being a lunchtime in July, most of the slots were empty – people had gone home, or to the beach. From the portico, those cars that did remain appeared unoccupied, as did the cab of a refrigerated van, probably associated with Gelateria Gianni across the road. The only other place I could see where she could have gone was the church, Santi Gregorio e Siro, along the same side as Gianni.

I took the four steps down onto the cobbles and into sunlight that sliced across the street to the façade of the church. I strode across, up the metal ramp and through the sun-bleached green doors.

Icing-white walls and columns belied the church's plain red-brick exterior, like a wedding cake turned inside out. That vaulted ceiling, marble floor, achieved a contemplative cool despite the sunlight pouring in from high windows; a sense of peace, despite the Catholic pomp. The church appeared empty – I couldn't see a soul among the polished oak pews, not even a tourist taking a breather or an old lady reciting the rosary.

Still, I walked down the centre aisle, checking as I went.

As I neared the Baroque altar with its surprisingly modest, time-creased painting of a rather wan-looking Jesus, my eye was drawn to a side alcove, a painting.

It was the conventional Christian trope of John baptising Jesus, yet it drew you in: the sashes of crimson clothing draped around the Baptist and Messiah, the Eternal Father and his trumpeting angels, the panoply of exquisitely executed supporting characters drawing your gaze inwards.

I'd always teased Rose you didn't need to be an expert in art because a genuine masterpiece would declare itself.

On closer inspection, I discovered the painting was a Carracci. I backed respectfully away and lowered myself onto the end of the pew, gazing upward.

A wooden clap as the church door closed. I twisted around. No one. But had there been *someone*? Had they seen me and ducked out? I made to stand up but the blood rushed to my head, so I sat back down, drew in a few breaths, tugged guiltily again at my midriff and looked up at the masterpiece as if to ask for guidance, but John was busy pouring Jordan water over the Lord's head from a dainty little jug. Jesus had his head bowed, eyes cast downward. He looked very young, not dissimilar to a Bolognese student; not that different to my photo of Guido Delfillo.

I lay back, keeping my feet flat upon the floor. Above – the frescoed ceiling. Those oval-framed paintings were no masterpieces, I decided. But they had a chocolate box simplicity, schoolbook innocence. Perhaps, in fact, they had been designed with bored schoolchildren in mind – casting their own, restless gaze upwards during some interminable mass.

Icing sugar sprinkled upon my face. I licked my lips. It tasted dry, chalky.

I woke with a gasp. The dust, or perhaps it was plaster, still hung in the air: there had been another tremor.

My phone began to ring. I looked around and found it face-down upon the floor. I rolled onto my side and almost fell off the pew.

'Alba,' I croaked.

'Where have you been? Didn't you see my message? Claudio and Jacopo rolled in drunk – I told them to get out before the Comandante caught them – and they said you had left earlier. Is everything okay?'

'Yeah . . . fine. I just . . .' I sat up. I was still alone in the church. I checked my watch. I must have been out for half-an-hour. I then checked my back pocket – my wallet was still there. 'I got waylaid. Was following up something. Or rather,' I began to remember what had led me here, 'I was following someone. Or being followed. Anyway, I'm fine.'

'Are you sure you're not drunk?'

'I'm sure.'

'Good to hear it, because the Comandante wants to see you.'

'When?'

'Now.'

Chapter 20

Sitting on the Comandante's Chesterfield sofa: a couple. The Grimaldis, Amanda's parents. Despite their fine clothes and vigorous physical appearances – Signor Grimaldi, the prosperous businessman, his wife a similarly successful professional, a lawyer perhaps, or medic – they were cowed like the Delfillos, worse: any trace of hope had been extinguished by a single brutal act. These people weren't just beaten, they were broken for good.

'*Do you want to tell them they can't bury their daughter?*' Commissario Rita Miranda had asked.

Not without a damn good reason, I thought.

'Our visitors,' the Comandante explained, 'heard you were the person who discovered their daughter, that this was part of an investigation being conducted by our agency, and wanted to know more.'

'We want to know everything,' said Signor Grimaldi. 'Everything you know.'

'The first thing,' I said – this was no time for condolences – 'is that it was not an investigation into your daughter, but the circumstances around a crime that we thought your daughter might be able to shed some light upon.'

'Your boss said something about a mugging, a photo . . . but what had this to do with Amanda?'

'The accused was one of her former classmates. We simply wanted to ask her for some background. Then we arrived, and . . .'

'You spoke to the police,' said Signora Grimaldi. 'They say it was a suicide. Did it look like a suicide to you?'

'Well,' I said. 'She was . . . hanging. I could see no obvious signs of forced entry. The apartment appeared undisturbed. I couldn't find a note. Did she—?'

They shook their heads. 'Nothing,' said the father.

'No messages at all?'

'Not as far as we know. We've asked all her friends, had people check every account.'

'Among yourselves – your family – what messaging app did you communicate with?'

'WhatsApp.'

'Not SpeakSafe?'

'What's that?'

'Just another app. But . . . so, this came as a surprise to you. She had never tried anything like this before?' They shook their heads again. 'She didn't suffer from depression?'

'She's anxious, an anxious girl,' said the signora. 'Would get quite worried before performances, playing new pieces, but she always pulled it off. Always! She's a hard worker.'

'So she never mentioned troubles to you – with any romantic partners, work, anything like that?'

'Nothing out of the ordinary. I mean, she was fine, as far as we knew – we'd spoken on the Sunday. In a fortnight she was going to Florida with a group of friends. Once the opera was over. It was all she talked about. She was really looking forward to it. She was happy. The happiest she'd been in a long time.'

'Despite her anxiety.'

'Like I said – before she began a season. But once she got going . . . she had already got through half-a-dozen performances, was beginning to relax . . .'

'She called me once,' said the father. 'A couple of weeks ago, when I was at the office. It was a bit odd.'

'Why?'

'Well, it was during the day, a work day. She usually only calls during the weekend.'

'Did she want money?' said his wife. She looked at me. 'He's the soft touch. Maybe she called you when she knew I wouldn't be about.'

He shook his head. 'She sounded, I don't know, a little upset.'

'You didn't tell me.'

'It wasn't anything . . . I mean, now, of course, you think about it, but then, really, it wasn't anything I would have . . . I mean, I would never have thought . . .'

'What did she say?' I asked.

'That was the thing. I was with a client, I told her. I said – is everything all right, darling? She said, yes, yes, everything's fine. Okay, to be honest, I thought she was going to ask me for money, but she didn't. She just said it was nothing. She said she had a free moment and just wanted to say hello.'

'And did she do that often?'

'To be honest, no, not during the day.'

'*Why didn't you tell me?*' said his wife.

'I . . .' He closed his eyes. His thin lips quivered. I wanted to help him.

'It was probably nothing.' I turned to the wife. 'Can I ask you – did Amanda find it difficult to gain admission to the conservatory?'

'What's that got to do with it?'

'So, you're saying that she did?'

'On the contrary – she worked really hard, as usual. She was worried, yes. But as it turned out, she had nothing to be worried about, like I told her. She passed the exams with flying colours.'

'And you didn't provide her with any additional . . . assistance?'

'Yes,' she said. 'Actually, we did. She had a number of tutors.'

'Was Professor Ilario Bellario among them?'

'I don't know.' She looked at her husband.

'That name doesn't ring a bell,' he said. But the emotion had drained from his voice. He looked not so much like a grieving father as a poker player.

'You said she would often come to you for money, Signor Grimaldi,' I said. 'Around the time of her entrance exam, did she come to you for any sums that were, shall we say, out of the ordinary?'

The signora was shaking her head. 'Not at all, I would—'

'Twenty thousand euros,' said her husband. 'Cash.'

We walked the Grimaldis to the door.

Signor Grimaldi spoke. 'If you discover anything . . .'

'By the way,' I said. 'Amanda. Was she keen on camping? Ever a girl scout, sail, anything like that?'

'No,' said Signor Grimaldi. 'Her whole life had been her music ever since she was little. The Polizia asked us the same thing. Why?'

'Standard question.' The wife seemed to buy it, the husband, not. He gave me a grave nod, and opened the door for the signora, who passed through it without acknowledging him.

The Comandante and I waited at the top of the stairs as their footsteps descended the four storeys. The street door closed.

'Coffee?' he said.

If the Comandante was going to talk shop out of the office, he preferred to do it away from Via Marconi at Caffè del Poggiale, a small bar on Via Nazario Sauro where the proprietor, Max, had gone to school with Lucia. As usual, one way or another, Giovanni liked to keep any discussions, even those in danger of being overheard, somehow within the family.

We went inside and ordered *caffè shakerato* – cold coffee served with crushed ice in cocktail glasses – at the bar.

'Well, my boy,' the Comandante clinked his glass with mine, 'it seems we may be dealing not only with one, but potentially two murders.' Max, cleaning the glasses on the other side of the bar, looked suitably impressed.

'And just before the holidays, Comandante.' He chuckled.

Giovanni gave him a wry nod. 'I had so been looking forward to getting away.'

'Cesenatico, right? We'll be going down ourselves. Hope to see you there!'

'Hope so, Max.' The Comandante turned to me.

'So,' I said, 'I take it you believe Amanda was murdered, too?'

'Quite possibly – her lack of expertise in tying knots . . .'

'She could have got it off YouTube. That's what everyone does these days.'

'This deleted messaging application,' said the Comandante. 'Her apparently up-beat mood before her "suicide".'

'Despite possessing anti-depressants.'

'I had Alba look into that,' said the Comandante. 'The brand is also prescribed for anxiety. The marks you noticed on the mezzanine. And, of course, there's the bribe she paid to the professor to have her accepted at the conservatory, presumably at the cost of Guido Delfillo.'

'I was struck by Signor Grimaldi's apparent lack of curiosity about the purpose of the twenty thousand,' I added.

'Clearly he understood why Amanda required the money. But chose not to enquire further.'

'She could have decided to kill herself out of guilt – she discovered Guido had been arrested and was so upset by the sorry turn of events she decided to end it all.'

The Comandante moved his head from side to side as if weighing this possibility. 'But Amanda Grimaldi poisoned Ilario Bellario,' he said.

I looked at him. 'What? Why? How?'

'The final question is easier to answer than the others.' The Comandante opened his briefcase and produced an iPad. Frankly, I wasn't sure what was more shocking – the revelation about Amanda or that he knew how to use the device we had bought him three Christmases ago. But he certainly seemed to know what he was doing, and soon brought up a video file. 'This was sent over by the gentleman at the *Teatro* after Alba asked the client to place a request.'

'Vesuvio? Perhaps we should be paying him.'

'Now, let's see . . .' He traced his forefinger along the bottom of the screen. 'Coming to the scene in question . . .' I immediately recognised it as the interval at the opera, but a little while before the section of the video we had viewed in the back office.

The catering staff were finishing setting up, placing drinks orders along the bar before the audience members began to arrive. Through the curtained entrance being used by staff, Amanda emerged, unmistakable with her black bob and long dress. She joined the early birds, checking the drinks receipts until she stopped by a pair of glasses of white wine. She picked them up, turning to face the entrance, before returning them to the bar, presumably having realised there were no other free surfaces available. Amanda's back was to the camera, shielding the drinks, but she appeared to ask the bartender for something. He went to the far end and bent to open a fridge.

The Comandante paused the film. He ran his finger back so it rewound to Amanda entering through the curtains. 'You see here,' he said. 'Her right hand is closed. She appears to be holding something tightly. She doesn't let it go.' He then swiped forward as her hands disappeared onto the counter while the bartender's back was turned. By the time he had returned with a bottle of water and glass, her hands were by her sides. Giovanni enlarged the view as her right hand apparently slipped something into the band around her waist before dropping to her side again and hanging open.

The bar began to fill. Amanda picked up the drinks – balancing her own water between the two glasses – and weaved her way to the far end of the bar, where she set them down again.

'Now look,' said the Comandante.

He paused the film again to point at a bin by the corner. Amanda's right hand fingered whatever was snuck under the band and dropped it in. She then picked up the glasses and turned to face the entrance to the bar, and the camera. With that dark bob and pale face she looked like a silent film actress performing a scene of high tension in which only her expression could convey the emotion of the moment, until it suddenly vanished – replaced by a broad smile as she raised the glasses.

The Bellarios were arriving. She handed them their drinks, taking her own and they joked about toasting with a glass of water. But now I watched as Amanda's eyes never left the professor's glass as he sipped his drink.

'Damn it,' I said. 'I suppose it would be too late to get hold of the contents of that bin.'

'I have already asked,' said the Comandante. 'They are emptied at the end of every day. I suppose it may be possible to have some kind of analysis done – if we could find the bin in question – but as for the actual item . . .'

'But if Amanda *is* the murderer, why would she then end up being murdered? And by whom?'

The film was frozen on that moment, the three of them pinned like social butterflies in black and white.

'Or you might ask me why I don't believe it is suicide,' said the Comandante. 'Certainly in my long career, I have come across murderers who took their own lives, but these have been men – and exclusively men – who acted after killing loved ones. I have never come across a premeditated murder outside the family where the perpetrator ended their life. And poison is most certainly a weapon of pre-meditation. So if Amanda actually did kill herself, I very much doubt it was out of remorse. It seems more likely her death was either instigated, or executed, by at least one other.'

'But why would Amanda poison the professor?'

'Well, that *bustarella* appears to cement their clandestine relationship. Might she have sought his death because of this? Was he holding her past over her? It seems unlikely, given he would be condemning himself along with her. On the other hand, as an "anxious" person, she might have feared one day the truth would come out. According to Guido Delfillo, people were apparently talking openly about it.'

'The dean made it pretty clear that this was the reason he moved Bellario on, "To protect the reputation of the conservatory."'

'So she may have worried that her career was at stake. Certainly, anxiety should not be mistaken for cowardice. To overcome one's anxiety, as the anxious person must – as Amanda did before her performances – means manifesting a great deal of courage. The frightened person who overcomes their fear is likely braver than the ordinary, unencumbered soul, even if that fear may distort their perspective and lead them to act recklessly.

'What we may have, therefore, is a person with a heightened sense of danger, and perhaps a greater readiness to do something about it. Do you mind, Max?' Only then did I notice Max leaning on his elbows across the bar – he must have listened to the whole thing.

'Go ahead, Comandante.' Giovanni took a bowl of olives and placed it on the bar before us.

'This I see as option one – that Amanda killed Bellario to protect her reputation. Yet, experience tells me that had she done so for this reason, she would have been highly unlikely to have then ended her own life.'

'What if they were having an affair,' I said, 'but he wouldn't leave his wife? A case of if "I can't have him, then nobody can".'

'Not unless he had provided her with a refund for that *bustarella*,' said the Comandante. 'Who could be attracted to a man like that?'

'Melodia.'

'I'm sorry, Daniel,' he shook his head. 'I don't see it. And in any case, then why not kill the love rival? No, I think a more plausible option,' he moved the napkin holder beside the olives, 'is that a person, or persons unknown, somehow manipulated Amanda into committing the murder, possibly via this deleted application, then compelled her to kill herself. Or, more likely, staged her killing to look like a suicide.' Now he plucked a napkin from the holder and wiped his mouth. 'Hence my suspicion that not one, but two murders may have taken place.'

'Heh.' Max, straightened up. 'Bravo, Comandante.'

'But if that's the case,' I said, 'there's still the "why". If Amanda *wasn't* the driving force, why would they want the professor dead? And why kill Amanda?'

'Amanda – because she knew too much. It tied up a loose

end. Professor Bellario . . . well, the man was corrupt. He may have simply crossed the wrong person. However, this connection to Amanda does appear to narrow the field somewhat. Dolores has confirmed that although she was not a part of this women's orchestra, Amanda Grimaldi had recorded with them.'

'I've already a plan in train,' I said. 'To clone the SIMs of Melodia and the *professoressa*.'

'Good,' said the Comandante. 'But tell me – what is a "SIM"?'

We were settling up when I said: 'You know, Comandante, we really should inform the commissario about this tape. It would certainly help Guido's case.'

'And what do you think would happen if we did?'

'She might ignore it. Or she might run with it – put the cat among the pigeons.'

'And what do pigeons do when pounced upon by a cat?'

'The lucky ones fly away.'

'Precisely, which would be a shame for Amanda, and her parents. Better to let them peck away until we are in a stronger position to pounce. It would help everyone – young Guido and, I dare say, even your friend Commissario Miranda, if we are able to provide a full rather than partial picture. But I do think we should get a move on.'

'Before this cop gets to the film, too, you mean?' said Max.

'Quite, Max,' said the Comandante. 'As soon as the coroner has confirmed poison as the COD, the commissario will be obliged to bring considerably greater resources to bear, and then . . . ' His phone buzzed.

'Paff,' said Max. 'The birds will have flown.'

'It's from Massima,' said the Comandante. 'She's ready to open that box.'

Chapter 21

There was a little crowd gathered in the courtyard when we arrived. Alba, Claudio and Rose were chatting to Massima, who was wearing, perhaps out of habit, the white plastic overalls she donned during her day job for the Forensic Police Service, although the hood was pulled down around her thick neck.

'No Stella?' I asked Rose. I had messaged her on the way, and tried to call but it had gone through to her answer phone.

'I think she's teaching,' she said.

Dolores and Jacopo arrived, Jac carrying a pair of bolt cutters.

'Batman and Robin,' said Massima. 'Dig the shades, girl – had a pair like that myself back in the eighties. Shoulder pads, too.'

'Says the woman dressed like a polar bear,' said Dolores.

'Look,' I said. 'I don't suppose we could delay this? I promised Stella we would wait for her.' They all looked at me – even the Comandante, despite his initial reservations – as if this was an absurd suggestion.

'Massima has confirmed there are no explosive substances,'

he said. 'And neither do there appear to be any organic ones.'

'I drilled in,' said Massima. 'Took a sample. Whatever's in there, it's inert.'

'Treasure,' Rose said with confidence.

'All right,' I said. 'But you're supposed to be her collaborator, right? Make sure you take a video of the opening.'

'Will do!'

We trooped down into the *cantina*. Rose turned on Stella's lamp, and there was the chest – brushed clean of grime and with a peppering of sawdust where Massima had drilled through the top. We gathered around it.

'My goodness, Claudio,' said the Comandante. 'If the partisans had all been as big as you they would never have managed to fit in!'

Jacopo knelt down and placed the bolt cutters around the lock.

'Hold on,' called Rose. She leant over his shoulder with her phone. 'Okay – action!'

Jacopo squeezed and the lock gave a satisfying crack. He turned to Rose.

'Okay?'

'Okay.'

He began to lift up the lid. I suspect I was not alone in experiencing a shiver of anticipation – it was a scene as old as stories. But even as Jacopo raised, with some difficulty, the iron-strapped top, I was asking myself – what if this story was not *Treasure Island*, but *Pandora's Box*?

Something snapped and the lid flew back, clattering onto the ground behind. A dusty funk filled the small space while Jacopo sat back, covering his mouth and nose. We all did

– but it was not the noxious stink of yesterday, just the sigh of very, very old air.

'Oh.' Rose perhaps spoke for us all. 'Books! It's just books!'

They were stacked one atop the other – great volumes bound in hide, their leather tough and irregular with thick un-embossed spines.

The Comandante stepped forward. 'Hold on,' said Massima. She handed him a pair of gloves. 'You never know.'

'You think this could be like *The Name of the Rose*?' I asked.

'Hardly. But books that age – fingertip grease could leave an alkaline residue, ruin them. And hey.' She winked at Rose. 'Maybe they are valuable, after all. Precious manuscripts. Who knows?'

'Heretical volumes?' I wondered. That would make sense – squirrelled away down here by a family of secret Protestants. The Comandante gave me an admonitory glance as if to defend the reputation of his ancient forebears.

He lifted up the cover of the first book, turned one tan page. Another.

'Well?'

'As far as I can tell. I don't know . . . my Latin is not what it was but . . .' The pages crackled. 'What it looks like to me is that they're some kind of ledgers.'

'Ledgers?' asked Rose. 'What are ledgers?'

'Accounts,' I said.

'Yes,' continued the Comandante. 'There appear to be columns of . . .'

'Accounts?' Rose said.

'You know – company accounts. Like accountancy.'

'*Accountancy?*' She lowered the phone. 'Oh. My. God. I don't believe it!'

'I'm sure there's a reason they were placed there,' I said.

'Unbelievable! This family is so boring, even its secrets are boring!' She pocketed the phone and pushed past me.

'Hold on,' I said. 'Where are you going?'

'To walk the dog.'

'Generation Instagram,' said Jacopo. 'Honestly.' He glanced at his father. 'I don't know why she would be so surprised.'

'Can I take a look?' Dolores stepped through the gap left by Rose and crouched beside the Comandante. She took one of his gloves and began leafing through the pages. 'Yeah, that's what they look like – well, actually, this is some kind of directory of suppliers.' It was easy to forget that our trainee investigator, despite her thrift shop clothing, was an archaeology graduate and fluent in Latin. She flicked back to the first page. 'That's what it says here – Preferential Arrangements, Faidate Brothers, 1632.' She lifted out another book. 'Ah, yes, now this one appears to be actual accounts – profit, loss. Same year.' Then another. Although this was bound like the other books, it appeared packed with loose sheets of varying quality. Some literally floated in fragments onto the floor. '*Woo.* Now this is in Old Italian. Receipts, invoices . . . Jesus, to think they had the same old crap back then. *Niente cambia.*'

'Any dates?' I asked.

'Yeah – all the same, 1632.'

'Does that year mean anything to you, Giovanni?' He shook his head.

'Dolores?'

'Not my era, I'm afraid. I mean – it was the counter-

Reformation. Middle of the Thirty Years' War. What you were saying about heresy wasn't far off, Dan. There was a lot of suspicion, crackdowns. Cultural as well as religious – conservative backlash, hence "counter". Things must have been pretty intense, for traders especially, given they would rely on business across borders, maybe even stuff that was no longer strictly legal. '

'There's profit to be made in war,' said the Comandante. 'As well as loss. And no shortage of risk. Perhaps they placed these documents here because they had undertaken questionable transactions. It would make sense, instead of destroying the records to conceal them in case they required them for future reference.'

'Then the danger passed,' I said, 'and they were simply forgotten.'

The Comandante nodded.

This rational explanation appeared to dispel what tension remained in the chamber. I found myself sympathising with Rose. Although I was relieved the contents of the chest hadn't been dangerous or distressing, there was no doubting the discovery was a little bit of a letdown. *Bloody Faidate* – my girl knew her family all too well.

Claudio mentioned something about 'lasagne in the oven' and he and Alba went back up.

'So what shall we do?' I asked.

'We should move them, now it's open,' said Massima. 'The humidity will get in otherwise.'

'I'd be happy to take a closer look,' said Dolores. 'What?' She was responding to Jacopo's sceptical look. 'I'm interested – it's history. We find out more about how the ancients lived from their rubbish tips than their tombs. This is the real thing.'

'I could do with a beer,' said Massima.

'Of course, my dear,' said the Comandante. 'You certainly deserve one. How about we go across to Bruno's while the young people tidy up. Shall we leave you with the books then, Dolores?' Dolores gave him the thumbs-up. 'Naturally, you'll let us know if you do come across a treasure map or some other document that might be of relevance to the "boring" family history.'

'On it, chief.'

Dusk had descended when we finally emerged up the canteen steps carrying the books.

My phone, tucked in my back pocket, rang. By the time I had laid the ledger upon the flagstones and taken it out, Rose had rung off. I was about to call her back when she called again.

'Rose,' I said. 'What's up?'

'Dad!' Her voice was shrill, panicked. She was out of breath. 'He took him!'

'What? Are you all right?'

'He took him, Dad!'

'Rose, listen to me – *are you all right?*'

'Yes, yes, but he took him, he took Rufus!'

'What?'

'*A man.* Took *Rufus.*'

'What man?'

'I don't know!'

'Okay. I'm coming – where are you now?'

'The park. San Michele in Bosco.'

'Rose! I told you to steer clear of there!'

'I forgot!'

'*Forgot*, how could you? Never mind. I'm coming. *Now.*'

'Hurry up, Dad!'

'You just stay there – right where you are!'

'I'm in the road now. But . . . Dad!'

'What?' Her phone went dead.

Chapter 22

I was out through the gates and half-up Via Paglietta when Rufus came the other way, barrelling into me and almost knocking me backwards – he was a medium-sized dog but bulky with it, so it was like being hit by a furry cannonball.

'What happened?' I asked him uselessly. He still had his lead, so I grabbed that and kept going in the direction he had come – towards the Viale.

There was some kind of traffic jam on the main road itself, cars blocked from turning up Via San Mamolo, and two of the three lanes were stuck, horns blaring, while the traffic on the third, outer lane, sped past. We waited for a break then went for it, weaving between the stationary vehicles, over the cycling lane that ran down the middle of the Viale, and across the empty eastbound highway.

I ran along Via San Mamolo, a narrow road sandwiched between the church of Santa Annunziata and a string of shops and bars.

Up ahead, a crowd had gathered in the middle of the street. I was on my phone again.

Now my daughter's phone was ringing but there was no answer, so I began to shout: 'Rose!'

It wasn't until I had almost reached the crowd, still calling her name, that a young woman emerged from the throng.

A young woman, I realised jarringly, who was my daughter.

'Rufus!' Rose cried. The dog broke from my grasp and ran to her. 'I thought I'd lost you, Oh God, I thought . . .' She buried her face in his fur. I crouched beside them, took the pair in my arms.

'What the hell happened?' I said. '*I thought something had happened.*' I repeated hopelessly: 'What the hell happened?'

'I was mugged.' Her face, her bare arms, slick with perspiration – we both were, sat in the middle of the road on this dirty, muggy night. Car horns sounding, sirens distant, but approaching.

'Were you hurt?'

'Oh no. He,' she gestured towards the crowd, 'the mugger said, "Did you say Rufus? Is this your father's dog?" I said, "What do you mean?" He said, "Never mind" and just grabbed the lead from me. Rufus tried not to let him and pulled the other way, but the man just picked him up and began to run. I was going after him but then . . . Oh Dad, it was awful. I was chasing him. Shouting – "Stop, thief!" I was calling for help, the police, but there wasn't anyone. He dropped Rufus and was dragging him along the street. I mean, he had him by the lead.

'I remember him looking back at me shouting at him as he began to cross the zebra, and . . . I don't know. There was this *boof*, and a big SUV hit him. I don't know where it came from. What I mean is, it must have been on the road, but I didn't notice it pass, maybe it was parked. Then *splat* he went right over the top – I thought, Rufus! That he might have gone under, and I was running down when I realised the car I thought had stopped in front of the restaurant was moving – backwards. It ran him over again! Then it went forward and he'd vanished.' Rose gulped as tears finally glazed her eyes. 'It must have dragged him underneath . . .'

'It's all right,' I said. 'You don't have to . . .'

'Then there was this sort of *bumpety-bump*, and it sped off.' She nodded upwards, towards the hills. 'I went over . . . and there he was. Blood was smeared behind him on the road like . . .' she shuddered. 'Like strawberry jam.'

Dolores and Jacopo appeared. 'Let's get you out of the street,' said Dolores. We walked her to the pavement, sat her on the church wall.

Rufus placed his head in her lap.

I went to see who was behind this.

I pushed through the sweat-sticky crowd. The man was laid flat on his back like a busted toy, his legs swept unnaturally sideways and unmoving. His chest rose and fell in short, panicky breaths. His mouth was bloodied, eyes swivelling with shock. I knelt beside him. Beyond the belt of the crowd, I heard a vehicle pull up, sirens stop.

'Pasquale Grande,' I said. *'What the hell were you thinking?'* His eyes fixed on me. He tried to say something but only blood bubbled from his mouth. *'Is this your father's dog?'* He must have remembered me calling Rufus when I encountered him and his mistress in that clinch on the hill beneath San Michele. Our client, Signora Grande, must have revealed the film, with God knew what consequences. And this? Some kind of ill-begotten revenge? Presumably, he had been waiting for me, rather than the dog, but in my absence, the dog must have done.

There was commotion from behind. The bright red uniform of a paramedic bent beside me, another. 'Please, give us space.'

I got up, stepped back into the crowd as another pair of medics arrived laden with equipment, followed by a group of *poliziotti*, who began to create a corridor through the crowd.

The Comandante came to stand beside me.

'Our dognapper?'

'Apparently.'

'He's that fellow,' said the Comandante. 'From your film.'

'That's right.'

'The adulterer, Grande. You would usually take the dog for his walk at this time of the evening, wouldn't you, Daniel?'

'But he found Rose, instead.'

More cops arrived, widening the cordon. Municipal Police began to close off the road and re-route the traffic. The flame-red outfits around Pasquale swelled until we watched him being lifted onto a trolley. They wheeled him in a huddle to the ambulance.

We went back to Rose, still sat on the wall with the others.

'Is he dead?' she asked. I shook my head. 'There's no way,' she said, 'he could survive that. No way.'

'How are *you*?'

'Me?' She looked at me with her mother's shining eyes. '*I'm* all right.'

'Are you sure?'

'Bloody right. Worse for him, though. And we've got Rufus back, and that's the most important thing, isn't it, Rufus?' The dog looked up appreciatively from her lap. Certainly Rose seemed to have recovered from her initial shock – they were a hardy lot, the Faidate. Especially my girl, I thought. But then, she had been through infinitely worse.

'Okay,' I said. 'Let's get you home.' I looked at the Comandante. 'Can you inform the police, presuming they need to interview witnesses?' He nodded.

'I'm sorry,' Rose said as we set off.

'What on earth are you sorry for?'

'I didn't get it.'

'Get what?'

'The registration number of the car. I only thought about it once it had gone.'

'Don't worry about that, love.'

'I should have, though,' she said. 'We are detectives, after all.'

Alba and Claudio were waiting for us in the courtyard when we returned.

'Come here.' Alba clasped Rose to her ample bosom, although, I noted for the second time that evening, how much my daughter had grown, that she was almost equal, at least height-wise, to the adults surrounding her. 'It must have been a shock. You're sure you're okay?'

'Fine,' said Rose. She breathed in the aroma of lasagne from the foil-covered tray held by Claudio. 'Hungry . . .'

'Go on then.' He handed the tray to me.

'Hold on, Rose,' I said. 'But what are you two going to have?'

'Oh, we'll eat out,' said Claudio. Alba nodded, as if they were a well-established couple, whereas I had surprised them here in the courtyard just a few days earlier. Things were clearly heading in the right direction.

Because Alba and Claudio were a couple with, let's say, a healthy appetite, there was plenty of lasagne not only for Rose and me, but also the Comandante.

'I'll miss this,' he said. My daughter and I looked at him, but we didn't need to ask what he meant.

'I'm happy for her,' I said. 'They seem a good match.'

'That's not fair,' said Rose.

'What do you mean?'

'Well, I like Claudio and everything but . . .'

'But what?'

'Well, he's not exactly . . . *stylish*, is he. And Alba's always liked a well-dressed man.'

'Maybe that was the trouble.'

'What's *that* supposed to mean?'

'Um . . . that she's tended to go for style over substance. Looks over personality.' Rose considered this.

'Maybe you're right,' she said. 'They love her and leave her. They can't handle a big woman.'

'Rose?'

'That's what she always says – they can't handle a big woman. They only want skinny little girls. Men – they're just like children.'

'Alba tells you that?'

She looked at the two of us. 'Well, present company excepted, obviously. You've fallen on your feet with Stella.'

'Thank you very much,' I said. 'Does Alba say that, too?'
Rose laughed.

'*I* do. Alba can't stand her! She's jealous.'

'Because of Vesuvio.'

'Alba says you ought to be careful, she's out of your league.'

'Duly noted,' I said. 'And what do you think?'

Now she looked me straight in the eye, with those, her mother's eyes, and said: 'I think you deserve to be happy, Dad.'

The two 'excepted' men were left to do the tidying up while Rose went into the *soggiorno* to Skype – or whatever they called it these days – with Stefi about the evening's events. Afterwards, I offered the Comandante an *amaro*.

I opened the doors to the balcony, closing the ones through to the living room, ostensibly to keep out the mosquitoes, actually so Rose wouldn't overhear. The Comandante took out his cigarettes, looking longingly at them before glancing towards the balcony.

'Okay,' I said. 'As long as Rose doesn't catch you.' He got up and brought the ashtray in from outside. He lit his cigarette and surveyed me through the blue smoke.

'You know,' said the Comandante, 'he resembled you.'

'Who?'

'Signor Grande.'

'He must be ten years older.' In all the time I had been on his trail, it had never occurred to me.

'Same height, build, hair. In the dusk it can be harder to distinguish details than in the dark.'

'You're not suggesting . . .'

'But it would usually be you with the dog.'

'Yes, I suppose that was why Pasquale was waiting.'

'Perhaps not only him? Could someone else have wanted to "confront" you?'

'Who?'

'That's what I would like to know,' said the Comandante. 'Who might want to hit *you* with an SUV then reverse back over to make sure?'

We surveyed each other through the smoke as if it might offer up some kind of clue.

'No, I don't see it, Giovanni. Really I don't.'

'What?'

'All right. I *have* had a sense of being followed recently. I mean, I haven't spotted anyone, at least not anything I could confirm, but . . .'

'Do you think this Pasquale fellow might have hired a detective agency himself?'

'Perhaps,' I said. 'Although if that was the case, it would be by-the-by now.'

'You mentioned Vesuvio had been talking about the Bellario investigation at La Luna.' The Comandante let out a weary sigh. 'He may as well have published the news in the *Carlino*. And, of course, there was your encounter with the *professoressa* yesterday . . .'

'You don't think it might have something to do with that?'

'We have two deaths and one apparently in the works, my boy.'

The Comandante rested his cigarette upon the rim of the ashtray and reached down. He lifted his briefcase onto the table, rolled the combinations and snapped back the catches.

There appeared to be little inside except for a few documents and a folded-up copy of *Il Corriere* until he fiddled with a catch and lifted them out. They sat on a tray, beneath which was another compartment containing a small torch, a pack of disposable gloves, a first aid kit, some sort of aerosol, a Leatherman-like tool, and a Beretta handgun.

The Comandante took out the pistol and placed it on the table between us.

'I think it's fair to say you may be over-reacting, Giovanni,' I said.

'Humour me.'

'You know if I got caught with that . . .'

'You won't get caught. In any case, I'm sure it wouldn't be a problem.'

'Only if I'm stopped by the Carabinieri, who tend to be spread lighter in the city than the Polizia. And in any case, what am I supposed to do? Shoot a speeding SUV? I'm not sure this would have much impact.'

'As I said, Daniel, humour me.' Through the smoke the Comandante looked as serious as a prophet. 'We have passed the point where it would be wise to put this . . . *confection* of incidents down to coincidence. For safety's sake, we should presume a person or persons is behind them – all of them – at least until we establish otherwise. And if that's the case, then I'd say being prepared is the least one should do, particularly as you are the ultimate guardian of my granddaughter.'

That was what had spooked him – how close all this had come to Rose.

'If you carry a gun, Comandante,' I said, 'you should be prepared to use it.'

'You've carried a gun before.'

'I didn't use it.'

'Well, my boy.' The Comandante got to his feet and closed the briefcase. 'True, you didn't actually pull the trigger. But only because you had another weapon at your disposal. Not dissimilar to the one employed this evening, in fact.'

'I'm not sure if my poor old Punto was in quite the same dangerous weapons category, Comandante.'

'It did the job, however.' He took the ashtray and his glass to the sink before bidding me goodnight. The gun remained conspicuously where he had left it. After he closed the front door behind him, I pulled a chair out from beneath the table and set the Beretta on the top of a kitchen cupboard, out of sight.

Chapter 23

'Will you stop it, you're putting me off.'

'Stop what?'

'Walking up and down behind me,' said Rose. 'I can't concentrate.'

'You're playing a game on your phone.'

'I'm watching *Chi l'ha visto*.' Partly true – the missing persons show was on the TV. 'For work – maybe there'll be a local person. You can bet all the other detective agencies are watching.'

'The only work you have to worry about, darling, is *homework*.' She looked up from the sofa.

'Go out,' she said. 'Go and see Stella.'

'What about you?' I said.

'What about me?'

'Well,' I said. 'After this evening . . .'

'Oh, *that*. Don't worry about that, Dad. We'll be fine.' She dug her bare feet into the flank of Rufus, sprawled at the other end of the sofa. He looked around at me as if to say – *you're still here?*

'Fine,' I said. 'But, you know, if you . . .'

'Sure,' she said, looking back down at her phone. 'I'll call you.'

The Bolognese turned nocturnal for the summer months. Having sheltered, and frequently slept, throughout the day, *il vento della sera* drew them outside to reacquaint with family, friends and neighbours along porticoes bathed night-red.

In contrast to the tranquillity to be found behind the battlements of the Faidate Residence, it felt like the rest of the city was at *festa*. Young people were gathered smoking and drinking outside bars and restaurants, older folk and families leant against columns or sat upon chairs inside their stretch of portico.

It was simpler to take the roads squeezed between the medieval buildings, tarmac still sticky beneath the soles of my shoes, until I reached the cobbles and flagstones of the city centre, where the young almost entirely held sway.

I finally arrived at the Osteria della Luna. It was one of the few places you would still find a healthy demographic mix – students, grizzled politicos and writers, assorted other reprobates and recidivists. I had messaged my old pal Luca, who used to host a discussion group in the *osteria*, but without much hope – as I expected, he replied with a photo of his squidgy-faced new-born. His days of Sangiovese-fuelled activism were over, at least for now. Still, I would claim to be looking for him when I waltzed in – since I'd begun dating Stella Amore, I'd tended to avoid La Luna. I didn't want her to think I was keeping an eye on her, or bothering her, or that she had to pay more attention to me; ultimately, I just didn't want to appear too clingy.

I slipped through the crowd in the lane and entered the *osteria* which, in contrast to outside, was unexpectedly quiet – between the bar, where Stella was slouched against a fridge talking to another woman – and the interior courtyard used by smokers, also standing room only, there was a wilderness of empty tables dotted with a handful of quiet-talking couples.

There was nowhere to run, nowhere to hide. Stella looked at me without shifting from the fridge. Seeing her, in her tight black T-shirt and jeans, unmade-up face – her natural, striking beauty – Rose's words pinged into my mind like a smartphone notification: *'You ought to be careful, she's out of your league.'*

'Talk of the Devil,' she said. The other woman, a similarly tall art school beauty, perhaps a decade younger than Stella, looked surprised.

'That's him?' she said.

Stella straightened and came over, lifted up the counter. 'This is the one.'

'Ah,' I said. 'I thought Luca would be here.'

'Come on you,' she said. 'I need a smoke.' I followed her outside to the fringes of the crowd. Watched her open a tobacco pouch and produce a pre-rolled joint. She lit up and took a deep drag.

'All right,' I said. 'I admit it – I wasn't really looking for Luca.'

'You knew,' she said, 'I was supposed to be there for the Grand Opening of the chest in the *cantina*. Didn't we have a deal?'

'I did. I called, messaged . . .'

'I was working. I never look at my phone when I'm working.'

'So, what was I supposed to do?'

'Hang on?'

'I was . . . everyone was . . . look, I asked Rose to film it for you.'

Stella's huge eyelids closed like a camera shutter on a painfully slow setting, then opened again. 'Never mind,' she said. 'I've thought of something else.'

'What do you mean? Was there a problem?'

'I had a concept, for the filming. Rose did a good job but . . . Well, it doesn't matter – I've decided we'll take the box in its entirety, for use in the exhibition. Would that be all right?'

'I'm sure it would. But you might need some help.'

'I will certainly need *your* help.'

'Not a problem.'

She took a final drag and handed the joint to me.

'Look, I'm sorry.' Now she pressed a finger to my lips.

'Some of the best art is by accident, apparently. Anyway, I should go back inside. Will you wait for me?'

'Of course.'

She laughed. 'Well, you said that last time!' A brilliant smile, a blown kiss. I watched her ascend the steps and disappear inside.

A voice in my ear. 'Are you going to hog that?' Vesuvio plucked the joint from my fingers.

'Fancy bumping into you here.'

'Sheer coincidence,' he added in English. '*Mite.*'

'Sheer coincidence you're here every night?'

'Is that how you speak to all your clients?'

'*You* asked for *me*, remember,' I said. 'Consider it a favour.'

'Does that mean it's on the house?'

'It means,' I took the joint back, 'I don't need your money.'

'Now, now.' This wasn't Vesuvio, but Angelo with Roberto standing beside him, pipe smoke trailing in his wake like an olden day locomotive. He looked at me as if I was some kind of zoological specimen. 'Vesuvio just happened to be with us when you came out.'

'And he does own the place,' observed Roberto. 'Indeed he does.'

'Well, part,' said Vesuvio. 'It's the only thing that stops the old dump being converted into another bloody tourist spot.'

'Then it was you who was behind putting Stella on the night shift?'

A smile played at the corner of his lips. 'I don't manage La Luna, Daniel, and frankly, I could do without her being here every night – I bet half the crowd think I'm still mooning after her, not only you. My bet is she took the job because it pays more. I mean, nothing personal, but that was always her priority – not the money, obviously, but the time for her real work. And if she can earn a little more to support it, then . . . anyway, in a sense we're in the same boat.'

'How so?'

He glanced towards the door, then back at me. He seemed about to say something, then changed direction. I could almost hear the sound of screeching brakes. 'We're both, um, satellites, right? Around the planet that is Stella Amore. Ha! "Star", right? Yeah,' his gaze drifted back to the doorway. 'Stella's the real star.'

'How's your wife doing in the Caribbean?'

'She's happy, thank you for asking, and so are the kids. Stella never wanted kids. Does that bother you?'

'Not at all.'

'Well, I guess you've already been there. But seriously,' he nodded thoughtfully. 'I'm not being doe-eyed – she deserves all the praise she gets.'

'So are you going to stick around, Englishman?' said Angelo. 'Roberto's going to the bar.'

'Thanks,' I said. 'A Menabrea.' Roberto looked at me expectantly.

'He's going to the bar, *mite*,' said Vesuvio. 'Remember we don't do rounds here.'

I dug into my pocket. Vesuvio laughed.

'Just put it on my tab,' he told Roberto. 'So, how's the investigation?'

I told him about Pasquale Grande.

'That's three dodgy deaths in as many days.'

'Well, we don't know if Pasquale is actually dead,' I said. 'As yet.'

'Still – the poisoning, Amanda, and now this. Leads?'

I glanced at Angelo, his wine-dark tongue poking out to seal the edge of a roll-up cigarette. I suppose it hardly mattered – Vesuvio was providing the entire *osteria* with a running commentary.

'We're looking at the wife,' I said, 'and Bellario's deputy, that *professoressa* the dean pointed out. Basically – the two people with the most to gain from Ilario Bellario's death.'

'*Cherchez la femme*,' said Angelo. 'I used the title in a Duke. Ah . . .' He took the glass of wine Roberto had brought over on a tray.

'She said when you bring the tray back, she'll be ready to go.' He looked at me curiously.

'What?' I said.

'What?' he said.

I turned to Angelo. 'Your friend here always looks at me as if I'm a rat in a laboratory maze.'

Angelo burst out laughing although Roberto continued to stare, apparently unperturbed.

'That's scientists for you! The animal kingdom is a mystery to him – men and women in particular!'

'You never mentioned that Vesuvio actually owned La Luna,' I said to Stella as we walked along the portico of Via San Felice.

'It was going out of business and he stepped in,' said Stella.

'Why?'

'Oh, I don't know.'

Stella pressed herself against me. 'That ice-water English blood of yours beginning to simmer with a little Latin jealousy, after all?'

'Maybe the heat's beginning to get to me.'

'It gets to us all in the end, that's why . . .'

I kissed her, I pulled away – looked down at that lovely face, those huge eyes. Maybe Vesuvio was right – we were all just satellites in Stella's orbit. Perhaps when he was a footnote in musical history and I was just a story someone was telling in La Luna about the Englishman who became a detective in Bologna, her work would feature in grand exhibitions. Future generations would be moved by her interpretation of the world and her work would command exorbitant prices on the international market. But no one could hold her as I could now.

'Are you all right?' she said. 'That weed's pretty strong, you know.' I looked at her, blissfully befuddled.

A cough. Through the tangle of Stella's hair, I thought I saw someone, or their shadow, stood behind a column in the portico on the opposite side of the road.

'What is it?'

'Nothing, I . . .' Another cough, then a woman stepped out, followed by a shadow, a man – a couple had paused to light their cigarettes. They continued on their way without a glance in our direction. 'I might be becoming a little paranoid,' I admitted. 'I keep having this sense of being followed.'

'Who by?'

'I'd wondered if it had to do with the guy who snatched the dog. Now . . . I don't know.'

'You're tired.'

'I am. In fact, Stella Amore, I'd come to La Luna looking for somewhere to rest my weary head.'

'Then,' she drew my face back towards hers, 'you came to the right place.'

Chapter 24

We were in the boardroom in the Marconi office, for once that long polished dark-wood table was getting some use. Present: the team, minus Dolores, who was over at the university checking out the background of Professor Bellario, plus Claudio and Vesuvio. It wasn't entirely unheard of for a client to come in for an update – after all, they were paying – but more often than not they preferred us to simply get on with it and present them with the end results – the photos, videos or other evidence of miscreance, the missing person or item in question. But I had let slip I was having a catch-up the previous evening, and now here was Vesuvio, in his designer T-shirt, artfully ripped jeans, and the sunglasses he did not remove throughout the meeting – both a very rock star and very Italian look, although my guess was this was actually down to his drinking long into the night with his cronies after I had left.

'You've contracted us to get Guido Delfillo off the hook,' I said to him. 'Let's try not to forget that. I've spoken to Avvocato Servi and he has already filed for bail based on the suspicions of the coroner, but the commissario is having none of it.'

'Anyone might think she had it in for you,' said Vesuvio. 'I heard the rumours.'

'Small town,' I said. 'But I genuinely don't think our shared history has anything to do with the reaction of Commissario Miranda. She simply plays the numbers game, and isn't interested in going down rabbit holes, which may be why she has one of the highest clean-up rates in the city.

'When the coroner comes back with something more solid about any poisoning, well, she may let Guido off the main charge. In fact, on that note, I have a duty to advise you we could simply wait to hear from Doctor Mattani before pursuing the investigation any further. We could suspend our activity and save you money.'

Vesuvio dismissed this. 'The girl, Amanda.' He visibly shuddered. 'What about her?'

'It looks as if she paid Bellario a bribe to get into the conservatory. Arguably, Guido was the fall-guy.'

'But she didn't just top herself!' He shook his head. 'The sheer *coincidence*, man.'

I looked around the table. There was no point in pretending we didn't feel the same way.

'You're right,' I said. 'It does seem suspicious, presuming there may be some connection between the two deaths.

'Okay, let's begin with Professor Bellario. At the moment, one of my colleagues is looking into his affairs to see if we can come up with something. Then, as I mentioned yesterday evening, we're also looking at Melodia, his wife – whether the crime could have been motivated by greed or passion. What would she inherit? Did he have insurance? Did she have a lover? Her presence at the scene, along with her contact with

Amanda, also places her in the frame.

'Then there's Professor Gloria Penna, who you will remember also had much to gain from Bellario's death. It turns out she also worked with Amanda, and as the dean mentioned, there could even have been an additional motive.'

'That debate,' said Vesuvio. 'Where he "crushed her".'

'Of course, these ladies may be entirely innocent . . .' I saw Jacopo about to butt in and shot him a warning look. 'But given what we currently know, they represent our strongest leads.'

'What are you going to do?'

'We have already begun to watch Melodia – which actually led to a link with the *professoressa*. We now want to . . . well, in short, gain access to their phones to see if we can establish if one or both of them are involved in some kind of conspiracy – if they have been communicating with each other in one form or another, or were in contact with Amanda.'

'How are you going to do that?'

Now I nodded to Jacopo. 'During their performance at Santa Cristina tomorrow evening,' he said. 'They've reserved a room to change in, store their stuff. We should be able to do it there.'

'Won't they have their phones with them?'

'They're forbidden,' I said. 'The *professoressa* apparently scolded one of the orchestra when their phone went off during rehearsal and reminded them to leave it "upstairs" during the performance.'

'I was asked to watch them during the dress rehearsal,' said Alba, who usually tried to avoid 'the sneaky stuff' as she put it, although she seemed happy enough to report to

Vesuvio. 'Their skimpy little dresses didn't even have any pockets. Probably on purpose.'

'Yeah,' Vesuvio chuckled. 'That sounds like a maestro. Every conductor is a tin-pot dictator. Hell, me too, in my own humble way.' He smiled warmly at Alba who looked like she could melt. Claudio looked icily on.

'They'll probably feel safe enough,' said Jacopo. 'They're locked in an office in the women's library, which will also be locked.'

Vesuvio looked at me. 'You'll be able to pick those locks, too?'

'They're too complex, I won't have the time. We need to bring some specialist equipment into play.' I nodded at Claudio, who gave me a thumbs-up.

With not a little trepidation, I hopped onto the back of Jacopo's Vespa for the trip back across the city to the scene of the Pasquale Grande hit-and-run. The stretch of Via San Mamolo where the incident had taken place was a narrow but busy artery so there had been no question of closing it for more than a few hours.

We took off our helmets.

The only evidence that remained was some detritus along the gutter – shards of headlamp glass, scraps of fluorescent tape, plastic wrappers and mangy paper towels.

'Why didn't you tell Vesuvio about Amanda acting suspiciously during the interval?' Jacopo asked.

'That's proper evidence,' I said. 'I didn't want Vesuvio broadcasting it to La Luna and from there getting back to the cops, and Lord knows who else. And neither did I want

Amanda's parents to know, at least until we have the full picture. They're suffering enough. Speaking of which, what's the news on Signor Grande?'

'Intensive care,' said Jacopo. 'Serious but stable. Our contact said he had damage to the internal organs, including a ruptured spleen and liver, along with a smashed hip and two broken legs, one of which was an open fracture. They think he'll pull through, although there may be some permanent damage.'

'Is he talking? Have the police questioned him?'

'She thinks not.'

'All right. The Comandante wants us to check this out, but it's off the Vesuvio account, so don't spend too much time on it.'

'Won't the cops cover this, Dan?'

'In their own time, Jac, in their own time. So, I want you to ask the people in the restaurant, passers-by – dog walkers especially, because they'd be regulars. Say we've been hired by the insurance company.' I looked around. 'I can't see any CCTV, but the SUV came down from San Michele, then after the incident headed up San Mamolo towards the hills, so I suggest you do the same. Tell the owners of any likely cameras the same thing, and that they'll get a slice of the payoff – say seven per cent – if they provide us with something that leads to a settlement. That should motivate them.'

I handed him back his spare helmet. 'Where are you going?' he asked.

'The university.'

Chapter 25

Bologna, *La Rossa* – The Red, for its brick, its politics. *La Grassa* – The Fat, for its food. *La Dotta* – The Learned, in some senses, this most of all.

Certainly, just as there was an Oxford before its university, there was a Bologna – it had been the Manhattan of the early medieval era, its dozens of family and guild towers sprouting out of the sump of the Dark Ages as the city-state established itself as the mercantile hub of north Italy; before then, *Bononia*, a thriving Roman city, but Bologna, *La Dotta*, was the city's abiding source of fame and fortune. A font of learning dating back to 1088, rivalled for centuries only by Paris, its alumni included Dante, Erasmus, Petrarch, Copernicus and Cervantes.

Yet despite this ancient pedigree, you would search in vain for any dedicated faculty building older than the Archiginnasio, constructed in the sixteenth century. The mystery of that missing university is like the secret of the city itself – its source of power is no single location, but its entirety. Bologna would not be the city of porticoes if for centuries students hadn't flooded to Europe's premier seat of learning and required accommodation – the Bolognese built outwards to add additional rooms, and curtained off the sheltered pavement below to accommodate the poorer scholars, hence the private ownership of each stretch of pavement that remains to this day. And as the leading families fell and the university's wealth exponentially grew, it had little need to construct premises when so many grand buildings became empty. So between palaces and porticoes, it would be fair to say much of Bologna *is* the university, setting aside churches, and 'UniBo' owns a fair number of those, too.

Hence I would find Dolores in Palazzo Poggi, one of the great palaces that lined sweeping Via Zamboni, now almost exclusively seats of learning.

Our trainee investigator was sitting, illuminated by a desk lamp, at an oak table, one of a dozen that ran down either side of the library, walled and terraced by ancient books with the busts of great thinkers scowling down from the balcony. It was coming on for lunchtime and there were only a handful of students, although there was another kid on a computer at the far end of Dolores' table. She, meanwhile, had one of those old books we had found in the *cantina* open in front of her.

'Research,' she whispered.

'Is that really necessary?'

'Honestly,' she said. 'It's fascinating.' She ran her finger down the precise, amber-aged script. 'By seeing what the Faidate were purchasing for their clients, it's like a record of how people used to live. And how the Faidate did, too. It looks like they were the middlemen for a lot of the Hundred.'

'The what?'

'It says here,' she tapped another old book, 'the hundred families of Bologna – they were the people who ran the city, had a place on the legislature and so on. But the Hundred wouldn't dirty their hands with business. In this one,' she meant yet another weighty volume, 'it reveals the head of the Faidate household at the time, one "Dante Hercules" was made a *cavaliere*, a knight, which was apparently the only way he could deal with Bologna's aristocrats – it meant he could mix in their social circle. It was all a question of rank.

'Judging by the ledgers it looks like books and manuscripts were actually their main business. These were like the prestige products of their time. Especially in Bologna, I suppose. But there are also records of tapestries and even silks, which cost a bomb as they were imported from China, or "Cathay", as they put it. Speaking of which, they also dealt in exotic herbs and medicines – and look at this.' She produced a slip of yellowed paper. 'I found it among those loose leaves. It's an order from the Botanical Gardens for – get this – the infirmary at the convent of Santa Cristina della Fondazza.' Her face lit up like Indiana Jones. 'It's like touching the past!'

I leaned closer, saw only a long Latin list.

'Returning to the present, Signora Pugliese . . .' I sat back, acknowledging the lad at the other end of the table who had stopped work on his computer.

'Oh, this is Mirko,' said Dolores. 'He's a PhD student, working on his thesis – Professor Bellario was his supervisor.'

'So you knew the prof well,' I said. 'I'm sorry.' Mirko shrugged. He didn't seem too upset.

'Mirko has some footage of the famous debate between

the professors,' said Dolores. 'Where *Professoressa* Penna was supposedly "crushed". In fact, he was the one invigilating.'

'Really?' As if on cue, Mirko slid across next to me, along with his laptop. He looked questioningly at Dolores.

'Go on, then.' He brought up the Vimeo website.

'It was part of the festival of music,' he explained. 'I didn't want to do it, but the professor insisted.'

'Professor Bellario, you mean.'

'He had me set the whole thing up, invite the *professoressa*, and so on. It wasn't even related to my thesis.'

'Which is?'

'Colouration, Sesquialtera and Hemiolia in the fifteenth century.' Dolores and I exchanged a blank look.

'Okay, go on.'

'Well,' he passed me his headphones. 'You can see for yourself.'

The title of the Vimeo was *Does Music Have a Herstory?*

The pair were sat in chairs flanking Mirko. The camera was positioned behind an audience of around thirty – a mix of students and academics judging by their age and appearance. Bellario looked much as I remembered seeing him as he ushered his wife through the opera house – confident and vigorous. He was sat back with his legs crossed widely, manfully, contemptuously even. Professor Penna, on the other hand, looked frankly nervous, closed – her long-skirted legs were pressed together, her hands cupped upon her lap. The professor was all smiles, bestowing welcoming signals to the audience. The *professoressa* looked jittery, friendless.

Mirko the invigilator coughed, glanced nervously at Bellario, requested the *professoressa* speak first. She went to stand rigid behind the lectern. She shuffled her papers, fiddled with the computer projecting onto a screen behind her. Eventually she got the slide up – a painting of nuns posing with musical instruments in the background, which may or may not have depicted the sisters of Santa Cristina. Certainly that was her theme: how, although it was male composers who had been remembered, and their works transcribed, women had always played a central role in the evolution of music, whether it was the creation of traditional folk, sung while gathering or planting, or the daughters of the wealthier classes schooled in the arts of entertainment, not least music, so they could play for family and guests, essentially, as the *professoressa* put it, to 'advertise their wares – themselves – to prospective suitors.' The culmination of these traditions could be seen in the music of the convents where, behind closed doors, the daughters who had been raised to become 'ornamental breeding machines' were able to give full expression to their potential in a world without men.

The *professoressa's* presentation was received with polite applause. I found her argument persuasive, but her manner – she came across as both defensive and hectoring – was not one calculated to endear her to the audience. Or perhaps she had simply misjudged them, treating them as if she was delivering a lecture to a hall of uninterested undergraduates rather than her peers. In any case, as Professor Bellario unfolded from his seat with a cheery smile, one could almost sense the relief. He grasped the lectern with both hands as if it were the hips of a lover.

'Of course there's a herstory.' He sat down again. Cue nervous laughter and calls for him to return, which he did with a show of reluctance. 'Oh? You want more? Are you sure? Because, well, it would be heresy for me to suggest anything else, wouldn't it? And those of you who know me, know I am never, ever, a controversialist!' There was more laughter from the audience. 'Okay? Really? You really want to hear what I think?'

'Tell us!' came a cry.

'Okay, well, basically, I sympathise with everything my esteemed colleague said.' He looked fondly at the *professoressa* who smiled uneasily back. 'And yet, sadly, happen to know she is almost entirely in error.' More laughter. The *professoressa*'s face fell. 'Sadly, because I wish her central thesis was true. But what is truth? It can only be arbitrated by facts – and yes, the fact is that some truly *wonderful,* although let's be honest, minor, compositions came out of the convents, which rightfully have a place in the *his*tory of music. But as academics, it is bad practice to promote theory that lacks an evidential basis, as I am sorry to say the *professoressa*'s does. Yes, she notes the folk influences in the compositions of Mozart, Beethoven, and especially Liszt and Bela Bartok, all this is indisputable and the reason why so much of what we might consider relatively contemporary music, albeit from the eighteenth or nineteenth centuries, has roots that stretch back centuries, "into the mists of time". And thank goodness, it's a wonderful thing.' And now he paused, apparently moved. 'It is a wonderful thing to think that these songs from the souls of our ancestors continue to speak to us through the DNA of classical compositions. However, as for claiming that this soul is *female,* well . . .' The professor went on to ruthlessly deconstruct the *professoressa*'s thesis, beginning with the heroic male poets, passing through the production of American Spirituals and Sicilian *lamentazioni* and concluding with: 'In almost any early society you would care to name, men were the instrumentalists, and thus, arguably, but almost certainly, *the chief producers of melody.*'

There was a firm round of applause. Some of the audience rose while others let out whoops and whistles. The thought struck me that Bellario had not only outshone Penna, but also packed the audience. This was a man looking for a new roost, and he had his eyes on the *professoressa*'s nest.

I paused the video.

'Well, you can see why she might be upset.' I took off the headphones.

'There's another hour where they wrangle over chromatics and hermetics and conclaves or something,' said Dolores. Mirko winced. 'It gets pretty technical.'

'But Bellario hobbled her out of the starting gate,' I said. 'A pretty bold move. It goes with the profile – a risk taker. And I suppose he had to take his chance if he wanted the job – nothing to lose in a sense, go for the big win. "Crush her".'

'And there's more,' said Dolores.

Mirko looked hesitantly at Dolores. She nodded encouragingly. 'I know where the key for his office is,' he said.

Mirko led us past the reception at Palazzo Gotti, a little further down Via Zamboni, then up a stone staircase to the second floor, instructing us to wait while he went to the lecturers' common room. According to Mirko, the professor routinely kept his key inside an envelope in his pigeonhole. Apparently, he often had his PhD students stand in for him during lectures, so they needed access to the filing cabinets in his office.

'Helpful chap,' I said. 'Well done.'

'All part of the service,' said Dolores. We watched Mirko lollop back down the hall with the key. I'd half expected him to say it had mysteriously disappeared, but no. We followed him to the end of the corridor, where he unlocked the heavy oak door. He was about to step through when I stopped him.

I stood in the threshold. The office was tidy and apparently undisturbed. It wasn't quite as spacious as the dean's back at the conservatory, but certainly a cut above some of the habitats of other university academics I'd seen, with their workspaces crudely sectioned off by flimsy partitions beneath flaking frescoes. For starters, the professor had an entire room to himself, complete with a window looking out onto the street, and a stone fireplace, albeit now stacked with student papers. His large, glass-topped industrial-style desk faced the door, and the rest of the furniture was contemporary, too, perhaps a statement, along with his young wife, that he was still a forward thinker. Pricey, too – I was pretty confident that was an original Eames chair by the window.

'I can't see anything out of the ordinary,' I said.

'Except *that*.' Dolores stepped past me. On a stand between the Eames and a book cabinet was some kind of instrument that looked, especially silhouetted by the light, like an upright, uncoiling boa constrictor.

'Oh, that,' said Mirko. 'That's one of the professor's collection of serpents. They're wood-brass, ancestors of the tuba. He always said that they not only sounded, but looked beautiful.'

'Cost a pretty penny, too, I imagine.'

'That one? Yeah, I believe it's from the eighteenth century.'

'Along with all this,' I meant the furniture. 'Hard to imagine being able to pay for all this on a professor's salary.'

'I . . . I never thought about it,' said Mirko. Dolores switched on the computer.

'Any idea of his password?' she asked sweetly.

'I . . . Actually, I'm not sure you should be doing that.' The kid was getting cold feet. It may have been a mistake to mention money – whatever spell Dolores had cast seemed to be wearing off.

'Come over here *un attimo*,' she said. He did as he was told. I decided to step back and examine the bookshelves while Dolores jokingly quizzed Mirko about possible passwords. The guy – a shy, cloistered academic, after all – was soon trying to guess along with her.

Of course, I'd always recognised Dolores Pugliese was charming, and knew Jacopo harboured a heavy crush on her, to which she had always appeared oblivious, but listening to her play this kid, I realised there was very, very little oblivious about Dolores Pugliese, and probably never had been.

Men, I thought. Such dunderheads.

'We're in!' she exclaimed.

'You are?' *That*, I hadn't been expecting.

'It was the name of his latest serpent, the one he was planning to buy,' said Mirko excitedly.

'They have names?'

'This did – I remembered him telling me. *Sextus*. And that was his password!'

'Well done.' I thought it might be my turn to distract

Mirko while Dolores did some digging. 'You were saying you used to get notes out of his filing cabinets?' I gave the drawer a tug. 'Locked.'

'Oh,' he plucked the keys out of a coin-filled ashtray, and brought them over. 'But you won't take anything?'

'Of course not! Just a quick look, honestly.' I noticed Dolores slip a memory stick into the side of Bellario's computer. I needed to keep Mirko talking. 'So, how did you find the professor? As a tutor, I mean. You didn't seem very keen about hosting that discussion for him.'

He shook his head. 'It was shortly after Professor Lepori's death . . .'

'Sorry, Lepori?'

'He was the departmental head. Very sad, he drowned.'

'Really? You mean in the sea? On holiday?'

'In his bathtub. But he was an old man – slipped getting in, banged his head. It was actually him that accepted me onto the doctorate.

'Anyway, I was involved in the festival and Professor Bellario, who at the time was at the conservatory, suggested it. I wasn't very keen, but he said he had developed an interest in the subject and thought it would make for an engaging discussion. On the other hand, the *professoressa* . . .'

'Penna.'

'Who was filling in for Professor Lepori, wasn't very enthusiastic, but, well, Professor Bellario had somehow got the rector . . .'

'Of the university?'

'That's right, involved – I think they were friends,' he sighed. 'And so she changed her mind.'

'I get the impression you weren't too keen on the late Professor Bellario, either.'

'I . . .' Mirko hesitated. 'He just didn't seem to have much time. For us, I mean – the students who had been selected by Professor Lepori. He only truly seemed interested in his own people.'

'The ones he had chosen?' Mirko nodded. Over his shoulder I could see Dolores was still busy moving the mouse about, frowning with concentration.

'So I unlock it here, do I?' I asked.

'Yes, that's it.' I pulled out the top drawer.

'How does it work, then? The filing system.'

'Oh, it's quite straightforward.' As Mirko explained, I watched Dolores swiping the mouse across as if she was loading stuff onto the stick.

I made a show of going through the files, which seemed to be exclusively music-related, until I arrived at the bottom cabinet, which appeared full of meticulously filed receipts and invoices concerned with the professor's serpent collection. Then I came to a final green file containing a batch of estate agents' literature relating to a development of a *palazzo* in Via delle Belle Arti under the auspices of a developer, EdificioBo, along with various floor plans.

'Mean anything to you?' I asked. Mirko shook his head.

'Maybe he's collecting property, as well.' It was a remark so dry I couldn't tell whether he was joking or not.

'What do you think you're doing?'

Professor Penna was standing in the doorway. She was wearing a colourful dress, her grey hair down and face made-up, despite the heat. She looked as if she was about to attend a wedding reception – I guessed she was going to sit on a jury at a *Laurea* ceremony.

'We were just leaving.' I straightened up. Dolores rose from behind the desk, snatching the memory stick out of the computer, which let out an offended bleep. The professor pointed at Mirko.

'*You* let them in?'

'On the contrary,' I said. 'He just discovered us here and was asking us to leave.'

'You broke in?'

'The door was open,' I said. 'Wandered in, to be more accurate.'

The *professoressa* pulled out her phone. 'I'm calling the police.'

'Go ahead.' I moved towards her and she fell back into the corridor. 'It's Faidate Investigations,' I said. 'They know where we are, if you really want to waste their time.'

Dolores and I made our way briskly back along the corridor and down the stairs. For all my swagger, I didn't really want to deal with cops, be they Polizia or Carabinieri.

We reached the bottom of the stairs, where we were blocked by a large group of students filing into the reception. Mirko caught up with us.

'She said to make sure I saw you leave.'

'She hasn't called the cops?' asked Dolores.

'No.' He looked at her like a dog that had just returned a stick.

I nodded to a dark-wood panel set high upon the entrance wall listing names and dates stretching back to the seventeenth century. At the far end, the workman was finishing stencilling: *Prof. Dott. Alfonso Lepori.*

'That's your late professor, isn't it? The one before Bellario.'
The gold gleamed fresh, along with six other names above.
'Recent additions?'

'It's not been a good year for the academic staff,' said
Mirko. 'But then, it's a big university, and they tend to be
getting on. Professor Lepori was eighty-two.'

'They don't retire then?'

'Not unless they want to.' He sighed. 'It doesn't leave much
space for my generation. But isn't that the problem with Italy?'

'They hand the jobs out to their pals,' said Dolores. 'Or
it's dead man's shoes.' The Thwarted Youth of Italy shared a
moment.

'We had better get going,' I said.

We said our goodbyes, Mirko stuttering his, at least to
Dolores. I knew he would love to ask for her phone number,
or whatever it was they did these days, and also that he
wouldn't dare. I felt for him, but only a bit – if he wanted to
play the cloistered academic, then that was the price. When
I'd met Dolores, she'd been dating another student – only he
hadn't been the cloistered type, but the radical. What 'type'
she went for now was anyone's guess and, I decided, none of
my business.

We began to cross Piazza Verdi, passing Via del Guasto
and the front of the *Teatro* with the usual menagerie camped
out beneath the portico.

'So what did you find on the computer?' I asked her. 'You
seemed very busy copying things over.'

'It was mainly from his personal email – there was stuff
about some property he was planning to buy, in cash.'

'EdificioBo? I saw that.'

'Thought it could be interesting.'

'Where do you put all that money from kickbacks you don't want to declare to the taxman?'

'Precisely.'

'Or your wife? We might want to check to see if she knew about it. There were no recent insurance policies, anything of that sort?'

'Nothing sprang out. There were a few emails between the pair of them, but they seemed routine. You know, house, holiday stuff.'

'Threatening messages?'

'Yeah, I probably would have mentioned if I had seen any, Dan. But anyway, I did a big data dump, so we can have a proper trawl later.'

'That kid, Mirko.'

'What about him?'

'Oh, nothing.' Mirko was on his own with that, I decided, as were we all.

Chapter 26

The most important thing to remember about the opening of *500 Years of Resistance* wasn't Stella's *vernissage* or breaking into the library to copy the SIMs, least of all celebrating Bologna's resistant spirit or memorialising the benighted nuns of Santa Cristina. No, today was all about Rose and the three charcoal and crayon sketches she had laboured over, quite literally late into the night, since Stella had invited her to participate in the exhibition. They were going to be placed in *The Room of Infinite Histories*, where Stella and I had actually moved the now empty, but still quite filthy, case from the *cantina*. It would be closed – a kind of 'Schrödinger's Chest', I supposed was the concept – although when Rose asked me what the hell I meant by that, I confess I got my science a little mixed-up.

'But how can the cat be dead and alive at the same time? *It doesn't make sense.*'

'Well, I suppose Stella's idea is that while the chest is closed, anything could be inside.'

'Yeah, I get *that*,' said Rose. '*That* was the whole point of my pictures. Hold this still, will you?' I kept the paper in place upon the mat board on the kitchen table while Rose pinned the sketch down. It was both poignant and sinister – an infant wrapped in swaddling, its eyes closed as if it was sleeping, but in fact it was dead, as my fifteen-year-old had made explicit in the label below – *Bastard Daughter Smothered at Birth*. The other two were: *A Pair of Dancing Shoes* and *Curse* – a raven with broken wings – all brilliantly executed and stylistically not unlike the canon of Stella Amore, although I supposed that was to be expected. I had a vision of Rose in twenty years' time glaring unapproachably at drinkers behind the bar at La Luna. I pushed the thought away – if worse came to worst she could always work for the family business. She might have the potential to be a fine artist, but I suspected she would also make a rather formidable gumshoe.

It was four in the afternoon. We were all set.

Fooled into a false sense of security once again by our glorious air-conditioning, I opened the door to an oven. The pair of us wavered at the threshold.

We took the plunge.

I followed Rose down the steps as she balanced the A3-size sketches upon wooden blocks placed one on top of the other. If you subtracted the cicadas' frantic saw from the foliage of our courtyard's solitary elm, the city was silent.

The Alfa, sharing the shade with the insects, chirped open and I switched on the air-con full blast. Another life-changing development – our new SUV. After our old Punto had rather spectacularly bitten the dust, I'd given in to my daughter's campaign to buy the same kind of car as the other families among her rather middle-class milieu, albeit insisting on a smoky grey, and Italian, model, rather than the usual white or black German brand. And as much as I did miss whizzing around town in the rattling Punto, I had come to appreciate the Stelvio's space, modernity, *air-con*; its raised eye-line and, given the ubiquity of SUVs in Bologna, relative anonymity. Most of all, it was a damn sight more comfortable to sit in over the endless hours of a stakeout than our rickety old Fiat.

Although it was a bit of a tank when it came to navigating the medieval streets, and I wasn't even going to try to park near Santa Cristina. Instead we took the Viale and I dropped Rose at Porta Maggiore, from where she just had to cut down a side street to get to the convent, while I went to find parking along a tree-lined avenue on the other side of the ring road.

In no hurry to expose myself to the heat, I sat in the parked car and read my emails, then called Jacopo to check everyone was ready for the job. 'Remind me – how long does it take to copy one of these SIMs?'

'I've just practised. Less than a minute.'

'So, providing we can get hold of the phones, then we should be in and out of the library pretty quickly.'

'That'll be the thing. Claudio says the locks are solid but standard – they're used to having the main gates of the complex locked outside office hours, so they're pretty secondary.'

'And the library will be closed – no one will be there?'

'Dolores called to check.'

'Okay, and Alba will arrive early to photo our targets' clothes and bags? I'm not going to have a chance – I'll be with Rose and Stella.'

'No problem – everything's cool.'

'Cool! Well, that's one thing we could do with some more of.' Something was glinting in my driver's side mirror. I toggled it to see a scooter halted a few parked cars behind my own. It pulled out and passed by, stopping at the junction by Ospedale Sant'Orsola. It, or rather, she, the rider, was wearing a blue T-shirt and denim shorts along with a white helmet, which matched her scooter.

She turned right, for the second time.

I expanded the view on my sat-nav to see where it might be possible to leave the main road and drive in a loop so you ended back where you began. I looked into my side mirror and waited.

It would have only taken around five minutes for the woman to come around again and I was about to put it down to my paranoia, get out and head over to Santa Cristina, when something glinted again in the wing mirror. I toggled it outward and there she was – back up the street, parked along the other side of the road in the shade of the trees, legs astride the Vespa. She had taken off her helmet and was holding a phone to her ear. She was quite a way off, but I had little doubt – it was the woman from before.

I got out. Any thought of a mad dash in her direction was forgotten as I slammed the Alfa's door closed. She had already put her helmet back on and was revving the machine. I habitually patted my pockets for my wallet, phone, and locked the door. Despite the heat, a chill ran through me – I suddenly wished I had that gun.

I manufactured a casual glance up and down the road. Traffic was running normally in both directions. She would need to be a pretty dab hand to navigate the traffic with one hand, and take aim with the other. Still, I made sure to keep to the pavement, ready to duck behind the parked vehicles should she make an attempt. If I reached the end of the street unscathed, then I wanted to get her off that scooter and even the odds a little.

I arrived at the junction with Via Mazzini.

I risked another look – there was no sign of her.

I hesitated, then, instead of turning towards the old city in the direction of Santa Cristina, I dashed across the road and through the entrance of Ospedale Sant'Orsola. I passed beneath the gatehouse and took a sharp turn right.

I stood flat against the wall to see who would come after me – would it be the woman, or were they working as part of a team? That in itself might tell me a lot about what was going on. Only it didn't take me long to realise this wouldn't work – the late afternoon sun was shining straight into my eyes and whoever came through the gatehouse was momentarily dazzled too, so keen to get out of the light as quickly as possible, making everyone appear to act suspiciously.

And of course I was suffering too – I made for the hospital campus and the shade of a chestnut tree where I could watch arrivals with my back to the sun.

'You didn't have to come in person, you know – I could have told you over the phone.' I looked around. Sitting on a bench was Doctor Mattani, a bottle of fizzy water in one hand and a cigarette in the other. His white coat was open and beneath it he was wearing a pink polo shirt, jeans, and loafers. He was sockless.

'You're dressed like you wish you were elsewhere,' I said. 'Do you mean the autopsy of Amanda Grimaldi?'

'Ah, that poor young lady! The Comandante told me you had some questions about her, and in fact I have just filed the PM. Death by hanging. She had an elevated furrow to the back of the head, whereas if she had been strangled then hooked up to make it look like suicide, there would have been damage to the back of the neck. Having said that, I have sent skin samples found beneath her fingernails away for analysis, but judging by the state of her neck, I wouldn't count on it coming up with anything. No – it seems you've struck out.'

'Struck out? What do you mean?'

The coroner took a deep drag on his cigarette. 'I couldn't find anything on your professor, either,' he said. 'Toxicology came to nothing.'

'Nothing? At all? Are you saying Bellario wasn't poisoned?'

'We tested for Antifreeze, Arsenic, Cyanide, Strychnine. There was no evidence whatsoever.'

'But, you said . . . Aren't there other poisons?'

'These are the poisons cited in the literature. I mean, Daniel,' he took another sharp stab at the cigarette, 'it's not as if poisonings happen every day in Italy, let alone Bologna. These days it's extremely difficult to get hold of these things – well, other than anti-freeze – precisely because there was such a . . . *boom* in the olden days, nineteenth, early twentieth century.' He smiled. 'Mainly women getting rid of their husbands with rat poison or other widely available household compounds, hence their popularity in the fiction of the time. But,' he waved his cigarette like a tiny wand, 'precisely because I knew I would be pressed on this, and not only by you, I sent samples to Milan for more sophisticated tests. They checked for sodium fluoroacetate, basically another form of rat poison only licensed pest controllers can get their hands on, thallium, aconite, antimony – you might like this, it was used by a British murderer christened "the Teacup Killer" – botox . . . no? It's only the most poisonous substance known to man – perhaps people should remember that when they get some hairdresser to inject it into their forehead. Batrachotoxin,' his voice dropped, 'extracted from the golden dart frog, no less. Hemlock, made famous by your Shakespeare. Ricin, and even polonium, the signature toxin of the KGB, although why the Russian secret service might wish to assassinate a musicology professor at the University of Bologna, I could not begin to tell you.

'I would like to claim credit for being so thorough, but these were actually suggested by the lab as sort of a bonus package. To be frank, I wouldn't have bothered with half of them, but we had some money left over in the budget, and whether it was you or the commissario, once you've got the bit between your teeth . . .'

'So none of these . . .'

'They were all negative. I admit, having spoken to the relatives, there does not appear to be evidence of hereditary disease that might have led to sudden arrhythmic death syndrome, but we have asked them to undergo tests and I am sure something will come up, so although it's not yet official I'm considering it natural causes.' He stubbed out his cigarette on the arm of the park bench and took a swig of water. He began to rise.

'But Doctor, we saw film of Amanda Grimaldi putting something . . .'

The *dottore* shook his head and began walking away. 'He wasn't poisoned, Daniel.' He raised a hand then brought it down like a lightning strike. 'Apparently it was an act of God, after all. Perhaps I had better go back to church.'

***

I stood beneath the chestnut tree, watching the coroner make his way across the grass towards the autopsy *sala*, hands stuffed deep in his white jacket pockets. He actually had a bit of a skip in his step – demob happy. No doubt the next time I saw him would be at the beach in Cesanatico, his deep-tanned, wrinkled body basted in sun cream with a copy of the latest Carlo Lucarelli thriller open across his sleeping face.

'*Balls*,' I said, which lacks the appropriate resonance in English. '*Palle*,' is what I actually said, as in '*che palle*' – what balls – an Italian expression commonly employed in response to the frustrations of everyday life, although discovering your poisoned murder victim was not, apparently, poisoned, or indeed, therefore, likely to have been murdered, probably went beyond the everyday Italian experience, at least for most people. I added a string of expletives in English that didn't require any explanation.

So what the hell now? I began to walk down the road that ran through the campus in the direction of the Viale.

Bellario wasn't poisoned – I kept repeating this as I headed towards the exit, oblivious now to the likelihood of being followed – and if Bellario hadn't been murdered, *then the whole thing had just been a dreadful accident*, a synchronous series of events that had turned out badly for Guido Delfillo.

Regardless of the professor's corrupt behaviour, his humiliation and usurpation of the *professoressa*, case closed: presuming the court believed Melodia, Guido would be sent down for manslaughter. I imagined the commissario smugly crossing one more death off her 'to do' list.

And she would be right to feel smug.

I had crossed the traffic lights at the Viale, was walking down Via Fondazza when I thought: *the job*. The orchestra was due to perform soon and I had the whole team primed to break into the library. I called Dolores.

'Look, the Santa Cristina . . .'

'Everything's in hand,' she said. 'Alba's already ID'd them going in and got some excellent pics, so shouldn't take a minute to find the stuff once we're inside.'

I had arrived in front of the piazzetta outside the former convent. The crossroads was jammed with cars dropping people off.

'Where are you?' asked Dolores.

'Almost with you. Look . . .' The little piazza itself, however, was free of vehicles. Instead a group of young people due to perform in the *Commedia dell'Arte* troupe had raised a makeshift stage of wooden pallets and were messing about with hefty-looking, Shakespeare-era costumes, the men being assisted into dresses by the women, although even with those masks, their ubiquitous beards rather gave the game away.

And beyond them, standing in the gloom of the archway, dressed more sensibly in T-shirts and shorts, Melodia and Professor Gloria Penna, smoking, chatting. The *professoressa* made some remark. Melodia chuckled over her cigarette. Quite the cosy couple.

'Dan?'

'I'll call you back.'

A loose end, the Comandante had called Amanda Grimaldi, yet that suspicious behaviour of hers at the interval had apparently signified nothing – we had simply written it into the false narrative of Professor Bellario's poisoning.

Perhaps that thing in her hand *had* been chewing gum. Perhaps her tortured expression as she awaited the Bellarios had simply come from the requirement to socialise when she should have been preparing for the next act – she was 'a worrier', after all.

Perhaps she had just despised the professor for the bribe he had extracted and the bitter truth only they two knew.

Which was why she had, after all, killed herself.

I pictured her hanging by the neck from the mezzanine, the grey flap of her tongue, her shit-stained calves.

In the CCTV, the school photo, she had struck me, despite her anxious edges, as someone who very much wanted to live, possibly too much – who might be terrified by life's fragility but as a consequence seemed all the more concerned with clinging on to it. She just didn't seem like someone likely to let go. Yet according to the doctor, this was precisely what she had done – become another sad suicide.

And our corrupt Professor Bellario? He would leave behind only the whiff of impropriety, which would dissipate from one student intake to the next, and just another gold-stencilled name in the university entrance hall.

Real life was woven with such loose ends. Time moved forward, days passed, acquaintances forgot. Yes, parents and lovers silently mourned, but learned to carry on. That was the dull ache of it; the fact of death that truly frightened us – once we had gone, the world kept going.

I waited until the two women had returned inside before crossing the road into the piazza with its cross-dressing performers, among them, as I recalled from Angelo's lecture, Balanzone – the Bolognese professor – now a rather ample-chested young lady with bounteous auburn curls.

I slipped beneath the archway, made my way up the staircase to find Stella's Rooms.

I would not call Dolores back, or message the group to cancel. The operation would go ahead. Whatever science might say, it wasn't my imagination I was being followed or that Pasquale Grande had been squashed like a jam sandwich. Something was definitely amiss – I would trust my instincts.

I owed it to Amanda Grimaldi and all the other loose ends.

Chapter 27

Stella had created paths between an Aladdin's cave of junk in her first Room – piles of plates, boxes of cutlery, a dining chair with a ripped, wool-sprouting seat, candlesticks, photo albums, a broken bicycle, a rolled-up carpet, an old TV and a dial telephone.

Across the walls, those old paintings she had discovered: tower blocks drove into orange skies, skies swarmed with speeding bi-planes; platoons of pistons powered disembodied wheels – the very fabric of existence was about to shatter against the insistent strain of *the future*. An optimism that seemed terribly naive viewed from our jaded present. Hence, I supposed, the significance of the floor littered with articles that had also once signified pride and promise but now amounted to little more than trash.

I picked my way back out of the Room and into the still-bright day. Stella had entitled the Room, *When We Were Young*.

There was nothing in the next Room and I was about to pass it by, when I remembered that this was where I had helped her carry those plywood sheets. Noting the Room's title – *Hidden* – I looked closer.

Certainly, the Room appeared as I had first found it – defined by its beginnings as a nun's cell before it became a Carabinieri office and after that, who knew what. But the basic structure had remained, stripped clean and abandoned – the small shuttered window beneath a concave ceiling, the battered cream walls, a small, dead fireplace. Its thick walls made it larder-cool even in this heat, which also meant it must have been freezing in the winter. But not all the walls were brick thick, I realised: carefully painted to match the others, complete with grime and a graffiti tag, a false wall stood at an angle to the real one creating enough space for a narrow corridor alongside what was the actual wall, which in fact continued to another opening.

I had to step sideways to get inside – just as we had into Nonno's room in the Faidate *cantina* – but there was no need to turn on my torch because natural light was pouring through the 'real' doorway.

I entered another cell, this with its shutters open.

There were yet more plywood panels here. Pinned to them, in much the same way we had attached my daughter's sketches, only much larger, were life-size charcoal and crayon drawings of people. Not delicately done, but with broad strokes and masses of scribbles. Although apparently rapidly, roughly drawn, the pictures seemed alive. Perhaps it was their posture, perhaps their sad faces, their sloped or proud shoulders, or where they placed their hands. Their very urgency seemed to provide them with a sense of action, as if they might step out of the paper, start a conversation, or ask you to move out of the way.

Some were nude, others dressed in old-style clothes. One

man was holding a cat. There was an old woman with a bunch of flowers, a skinny boy with his foot resting upon a football. And against all that black and grey, a dash of red for lipstick, emerald green for the cat's eyes, straw yellow of a young woman's hair.

And each and every one was looking at you.

Stella Amore rose from a corner as if she was, indeed, emerging from the picture. She had been crouched down, adding a few more lines to the round eyes of what I was sure was one of Chiara's French bulldogs, although I couldn't tell whether it was Jules or Jim.

'It's . . .' I took it all in. 'Extraordinary. Moving, disturbing.' With her black hair and white dress, that dash of red lipstick and freshly-painted absinthe fingernails, she seemed all the more like one of her figures. 'But aren't you worried about people not noticing? Passing by?'

'Then it works, doesn't it?' She looked around. 'We're in hiding, after all. From the *incurious*.' She took my face in her hands and kissed me. She wrapped her arms around my neck and hung back like a kid, gazing at the crowd of spectators.

Although she was dolled up for the opening, the Artist's giveaway: her face was smeared with charcoal.

She let me go to attend to a plump man who, following a series of dark slashes, had a couple of kilos added to his circumference, which now appeared to bulge out of the picture.

'Have you seen Rose?'

'I think she went off with Paolo and Nadia. Try the next Room.'

The Room of Infinite Histories, by Stella Amore and Rose

Maria Leicester, was two along, the cell beside it having been closed to accommodate the hidden part of *Hidden*. It was shuttered, but a series of photographers' lamps spot-lit the closed chest, looking remarkably as we had found it, with the hole Massima had drilled concealed by a bit of dirt and, I knew because Rose had told me, 'joke shop cobwebs'. On the walls around the chest were a series of sketches up-lit from lamps along the floor. There were a dozen, with Rose's trio lined up directly behind the chest. Pole position.

Stella's appeared to be drawn in black ink, the untouched blank space describing the shape of a severed hand, a tangle of old spectacles, a pair of entwined lovers, as if they had been picked out by the light of the moon. Yes, I could recognise the work of the established professional next to that of my daughter, the *dilettante*, but only by a narrow margin.

'The artist, Rose Maria Leicester?' She turned around. If with Stella I had felt as if I was holding a child, here I was again reminded that my fifteen-year-old, flanked by a pair of strangers, was becoming a woman. She was wearing one of her mother's cotton summer dresses that Lucia had bought from a church sale, probably dating from the sixties, with a daisy pattern upon a muted yellow background. It had always seemed a little long on Lucia, who was barely over five feet, but fitted Rose perfectly. In fact it was only the presence of the couple – a man and a woman on either side of her, unusually tall for Italians – that made her seem childlike at all.

'Dad,' said Rose. 'These are Antonello Ghezzi!' The pair looked a little embarrassed. The woman extended her hand.

'Nadia.'

'Antonello,' said Rose.

'Paolo.' I took the man's.

'Ghezzi,' said Rose.

'I've actually heard of you,' I said. 'I'm sorry, that probably didn't come out right. What I mean is, you're the artists – the door that opens with a smile, right?'

'That's us,' said Nadia.

'I tried it at the church at the end of Zamboni. How did you do that?'

'The holy spirit,' said Paolo.

'Actually, a camera,' said Nadia. 'We got some boffins that specialise in facial recognition at the university to programme it.'

'Stella went to your opening at the MAMBO after we'd just met. I saw a mirror of yours once, too, I think – *Guardami ancora* – look at me again.'

'Guilty,' said Paolo. 'And you're the fabled "English Detective".'

'Stella calls me that?'

'*Everyone* calls you that, Dad,' said Rose. 'Would you like to see theirs?'

We stepped into the corridor that looked down onto the quad. Through the open windows I could see the orchestra, although not yet changed into their costumes, was beginning to tune up. Caterers were arranging glasses upon tables set up inside the cloister and filling ice buckets. Large cold boxes, that required a person on either side to carry, were being brought in. Things were moving ahead – timing would be fluid, as ever in Italy – but I knew my people were ready.

Was it really, though, worth the risk?

This would be the final event before the summer, and by

far our best opportunity. Within a fortnight, pretty much the entire city would have packed up and left for the beach. The tragedy of Amanda, even Ilario Bellario, would remain rooted in that distant era before the holidays.

Vesuvio, having returned from the Caribbean and no doubt focusing on his next project, would put aside guilty whims, or simply not require the excuse to stay in Bologna. The case would close. Life would move on. Ilario Bellario and Amanda Grimaldi would be consigned to La Certosa, the city cemetery. Guido Delfillo would serve his time.

No – it was now or never.

We followed Antonello Ghezzi to the far end of the balcony and a room which still bore the somewhat unprepossessing moniker *WC*. In fact, it was an *ex*-WC: the stools had been dismantled and toilets and urinals removed, along with the sinks. All that remained were exposed rusty pipes, distressed white tiles and a line of tarnished mirrors along the walls.

But in the middle, one mirror stood out – literally, it was perhaps a centimetre more prominent than the others, and appeared new. The four of us stood facing it.

'What do you think?' asked Nadia. I glanced at Rose. I didn't want to embarrass her in front of her 'peers'.

Then I noticed the mirror begin to mist up. Either that, or I was experiencing a sudden onset of cataracts. 'Um, is it supposed to do that?'

'Write something,' instructed Rose. 'You know, with your finger as if you were in the bathroom.'

'Can I?' Nadia nodded encouragingly.

I wrote, unoriginally, in a shaky script: *Ciao!*

The mist began to clear, and with it, my writing. I was

about to make a complimentary remark when the mirror began to fog up again. This time with a set of words that appeared to have been written by an invisible finger: *Tu sei libero.*

You are free.

'We're schooled to think you can see the bad guys coming,' said Paolo. 'But they're not that obvious, they don't turn up in uniforms any more. It's more insidious than that. We're lost in a fog of algorithms, fake news, "bubbles" that obscure reality. Real life could pass us by while we're scrolling through Facebook. But we're saying it's possible to see through the fog, to write your own truth.'

'Or simply wipe clean the mist and view things as they truly are,' said Nadia. 'Isn't that like your job, English Detective?'

The orchestra was well into its rehearsal. Time was moving on.

'Yeah,' I said. 'Something like that.'

Chapter 28

I remained up there, keeping an eye on the orchestra and messaging the team once the musicians began to file out to change in the library building. Rose had been joined by Stefania and some other school friends, while Stella was chatting to Paolo and other art folk. I made my way back past the Rooms, down the stone staircase, and outside onto the piazzetta.

The 'gender fluid' production by the student *Commedia dell'Arte* troupe was already underway and attracting quite a crowd. The team was sat across the road outside the bar. Apart from the Comandante, who I had decided was better left out of this in case we had to move quickly – and we needed at least one person walking free to pull some strings if things went south – everyone was present. Alba would monitor the performance and alert us if it ended early. Jacopo would be positioned at the foot of the stairs leading up to the library with a fake pass around his neck to inform anyone wandering about that the area was off-limits and give us an early warning if someone came our way. Claudio would get through the locks, then Dolores and I would search the belongings with Claudio ready to copy the SIMs.

Seeing the team sat there, my stomach lurched. If this did go wrong, even with the Comandante on the outside, it could still create a world of trouble.

'Everything okay?' asked Dolores.

I pulled up a stool. 'Look – I'm thinking . . . Dolores, maybe you could hang back.'

'Why?'

'If we get caught, well, the shit could hit the fan. In fact, you, too, Claudio – you know you shouldn't feel obliged to do this.'

He chuckled. 'If I don't do it, will you still pay me?'

'Well . . .'

'I'm in.'

'But Dolores, maybe . . .'

'Same as Claudio.'

'Of course *you'll* get paid.'

'But it's my job, Dan.'

'Look everyone, what if I was to tell you that it's possible the professor wasn't poisoned. I've just heard from the coroner and he can't find anything. This whole operation may be a wild-goose chase. There might be no murder at all.' They looked, understandably, stunned.

Alba was the first to speak: 'Then why are we doing this?'

'Because . . . Well, because I'm just not satisfied. There's too much *wrong* for this to be right. The professor's corrupt activities, Amanda's suspicious behaviour and supposed suicide – the deleted SpeakSafe account. What happened to Pasquale Grande . . . and I'm sure I'm being followed.'

'Followed?' said Dolores. 'Who by?'

'I've no idea. But,' I confessed, 'well, I've nothing solid.'

There was a yell from the piazzetta, followed by a round of applause.

'I'll do it,' said Dolores. The others looked at each other, nodded.

'Anyway,' said Jacopo, 'we're not going to get caught!'

'Don't you go jinxing it,' said Alba. She leant over and kissed Claudio with a passion I think took us all off-guard, Claudio included, before she left.

Alba would 'count them all out' of the library. In the meantime, the rest of us sat in silence, watching/not watching the performance on the piazzetta through breaks in the crowd.

The plot, such as it was, appeared to revolve around the *dottore* doing his best to thwart a pair of young, cross-dressed lovers, only, as the sun dipped behind the spire of the church of Santa Cristina, for the performance to climax with a twist – just as we thought the lovers had finally succeeded in slaying the cunning and malevolent *professore*, now lying face down in the piazza, the bearded lady's lover turned to face him sporting the mask . . . of Balanzone.

My phone vibrated – a message from Alba. She had counted them out.

The audience didn't seem keen to hang around after the finale of the play, especially when it was announced there would be free *gelato* inside – enough to get any mob on the move, especially a Bolognese one – so we found ourselves caught in the press of people heading into the old convent.

Not only was the passage to the cloisters blocked, when we turned off down the hallway to access the stairs to the library, we attracted a following of audience members believing they had found a shortcut.

Jacopo meanwhile was stuck behind, so we continued along the corridor to lead them away from the library and out onto the quad. It turned out that this diversion *had* actually provided our followers with a shortcut, so they were able to get to the ice cream being doled out from those big cold boxes into little cardboard cups, before the rest. But not before Rose, I noticed, standing across the quad with Stella, cups of *gelato* in hand.

The pair hadn't appeared to notice me, and I let the crowd file past, their eyes on the prize. I took a final fond look at artists Stella Amore and Rose Maria Leicester, and returned inside.

The corridor was now clear, the fire door at the end closed. We walked quickly back along to where Jac was sat in the stairwell, lanyard around his neck. 'Good work,' I said.

Leaving him stationed at the foot of the stairs, the three of us headed up the two flights of stairs, through the double doors, then down the corridor to the room at the end – the library, its floor-to-ceiling bookshelves visible through the door. Claudio knelt beside the lock, pulling out a gleaming metal device shaped like a door knob from his shoulder bag along with a piece of wire which he inserted into the lock. He then flicked up a spike from the round end of the 'knob' and slid it in beside it. He flicked a switch. The device shrieked like a dentist's drill. I looked nervously back along the corridor.

Claudio switched it off.

'It's based on vibration,' he said. 'See?' He tried the door. It opened.

We walked quickly between the bookshelves to the glass-windowed office at the far end. The women's bags were piled up in the corner beside the desk. This time, the 'knob' barely let out a yelp before the door clicked open. We went in and Dolores and I made for the bags.

'Don't worry too much about where they're placed,' I said. 'No one will remember.'

I had tried to be thorough, to think it through: Dolores would locate the bags, and once she had got hold of the first, I would search it while she looked for the second. And it seemed to work: she found Melodia's quickly, a bottle-green Piquadro shoulder bag, and I managed to find the phone equally rapidly, tucked in the front pocket. I passed it to Claudio, who expertly plucked the tray out and, despite his beefy fingers, slid the SIM into the reader. Dolores meanwhile continued to root through the pile.

Claudio snapped the SIM out of the reader and back into the phone. He handed it to me. I tucked it inside Melodia's bag, looking expectantly at Dolores who was still working through the pile.

'Problem?'

'It doesn't seem to be here. Can you see it?'

'A North Face bag, right?'

'Right.' I couldn't see it. Then I received the message. PEOPLE COMING it read.

'People coming!' I whispered. Dolores swivelled around.

'But I haven't found it!'

'Never mind that.'

She threw the bags back onto the pile. I began to open the office door when Claudio caught my shoulder.

'You hear that?' We ducked behind the partition. Despite the distance, the closed library door, we could hear a commotion in the corridor.

So much for thinking it through: this was happening far faster than I had calculated – there would be no time to make it out.

'The door,' I said. I meant the office one, which I'd left open. Claudio shuffled over on his hands and knees, reached out and pulled it closed.

Just in time – the library door opened and half-a-dozen of the *Commedia* performers burst in, bouncing about in a post-performance high.

'Oh Jesus Christ.' I peered over the window. 'You don't think they've also stashed their stuff here?'

Dolores looked desperately around. 'I don't . . . think so. But it's all bags, who's to say?'

The kids were as loud as drunks. They began to tear off their heavy costumes at the entrance, gasping with relief as they shed the weighty gear.

'What do we say?' whispered Dolores.

'They're kids,' I said. 'If they get any closer, I'll pretend to be a librarian. Say what the hell are you doing making such a commotion. Offence is the best form of defence. You see those books there?' I meant the pile stacked by the side of a set of filing cabinets. 'Share them out between the two of you and spread them over the floor as if you're sorting through them.' Dolores gave me a doubtful look.

'All right.'

I watched the performers strip to their undergarments, shining with sweat and adrenalin, before there was some kind of debate between the guys and girls.

I braced to do my angry librarian act when the girls began a chant and, laughing, the three boys reached behind a bookshelf and pulled out rucksacks. The troupe had obviously been given permission to store their stuff here, too, but fortunately not inside the office. The boys re-opened the library door and stepped back into the hallway. For a horrible moment, I thought they were planning to wait outside while the girls stripped fully off and instead of being caught as thieves we would be nabbed as peeping Toms, but the girls began to sort through the costumes.

'You two,' I said. Dolores and Claudio were sat plaintively within a circle of flimsy-looking educational booklets with covers featuring African and Asian women. 'In the meantime, see if you can find this other bag.' The pair crawled back to the pile while I peeked over the partition.

The girls had now finished separating the costumes and were stood chatting. The doors opened again and the boys came in – 'About time, *ragazzi*!' – freshened up in T-shirts and shorts. The girls filed out while the boys began to gather the costumes – *'Mamma mia, che puzza!'* – what a stink! Between them, they carried the lot out.

The door slammed behind them.

'Well?' I said.

Dolores looked forlorn: 'We've gone through them twice!'

I looked at my own phone to check the photo Alba had sent us of Professor Penna's bag. I surveyed the pile.

I called Alba.

'Yes?' I could hear the sound of the orchestra in the background.

'We can't find the *professoressa*'s bag.'

'They're one song off the interval,' Alba hissed.

'Has she got it with her?'

'I didn't see . . .'

Just check.'

'Hold on.' I remained upon my knees, my ear pressed to the phone, listening to the muffled murmur of the crowd, the jaunty melody, which seemed to be reaching a crescendo. Christ, we only had a few more minutes.

'No, really, Dan, I can't see anything anywhere. No one seems to be holding it for her. You'd better go.'

She was right. After the kids, I wasn't prepared to take any more risks.

I stood up. 'Let's clear this up and get the hell out of here.'

While I replaced the books, the others piled the bags back up. I opened the office door, was halfway to the exit, when I heard Dolores shout: 'Dan!'

She was stood by a reading desk holding up a North Face bag.

'It was underneath!'

'Go on, then.' The pair of them begun to rummage through the bag. I called Alba. I could still hear the music in the background.

'We've found it.'

'You should go, they're on the last one before the interval.'

'How much longer? You timed the rehearsal, right?'

'I think . . . five minutes. But hurry!'

'Keep on the line so I can listen.'

They had found the phone. Claudio cracked it open. He fiddled with the side tray. 'Damn it.'

'What is it?'

'It's stuck.' He handed the phone back to Dolores. 'I'd put my stuff away,' he muttered. He unzipped his shoulder bag and emptied the contents across the reading desk, sifting through the mess until he pulled out what looked like a bent paperclip. He snatched the phone back from Dolores and began digging it into the slot.

The orchestra played on. I checked my watch. 'We've got no more than two minutes,' I said.

'Got it!' The SIM shelf pinged across the room. Dolores squeaked, scrambling after it while Claudio was stood there, blinking with surprise. She plucked the little gold chip between her fingers, scurried over and pressed it into his big hands.

'I'll need the tray to put it back,' he said, loading the SIM into the reader.

'I'm looking!'

The orchestra was still going strong but we apparently only had a minute left.

'How long will it take, to read it?' Claudio ignored me.

'Have you found it?' he called to Dolores.

'Still looking!'

The music stopped, along with my heart. 'Guys . . .'

Incredibly, it began again.

'Got it!' Dolores appeared from beneath another reading desk set at an improbable angle from where Claudio stood. She scooted over to Claudio, who was in the process of removing the SIM from the reader. Without looking at her, he took the tray and slipped the SIM inside, then, after an excruciating pause during which the tray appeared to stick again, he managed to insert it back into the phone. He handed the phone to Dolores, who placed it back in the North Face bag, while he swept his own stuff up. They looked at me simultaneously.

'Okay.' I gave the room a final scan. Everything appeared in place.

We made for the exit and I opened the door.

But our path was blocked.

Chapter 29

Stella Amore stood open-mouthed in the doorway.

'*So it's true.*'

I shook my head, my ear still glued to the phone. 'Um . . . What are *you* doing here?' Then I saw him over her shoulder – Vesuvio.

'I couldn't believe it when Vesuvio told me.'

'I was going to mention . . .'

'You know these people invited me to show here, and now you're using the occasion to break in and rifle through their belongings? How does that make me look? They'll never forgive me if they think I was involved.'

This time the music appeared to have stopped for good. The earpiece crackled with applause and Alba hissing: 'Get out! Get out!'

'I . . . This has *absolutely nothing* to do with you, Stella.'

'Come on,' said Claudio behind me, holding his own phone. I realised Alba had hung up on me and was now yelling at him.

But Stella stood firm in the doorway.

'Why didn't you tell me, Daniel? Why did I have to find

out from him?' She thumbed at Vesuvio who looked like a scolded puppy.

'Look, they're coming – if you don't want us to get caught, you'd better bloody well move.'

Stella stepped back, swearing. We dashed past her and down the corridor. I looked over my shoulder – she and Vesuvio were bringing up the rear. I pushed through the fire doors and headed down the stairs.

We had only made it down one flight when I heard women's voices below.

I turned to the others. 'Take it calmly. Act like nothing's going on.' There were just a couple of them – presumably most of the orchestra was taking a break among the audience, but it was inevitable some would break off to use the toilet or check their phones.

We passed them without incident, arriving at the ground floor where Jacopo was waiting anxiously with Alba. Dolores gave them a thumbs-up.

'You did great,' I said. 'Meet at the bar on the piazzetta? Drinks on me.' Alba bustled them quickly away.

Stella, with Vesuvio beside her, remained.

'I can't believe you did that,' said Stella. 'I mean, I *can* believe you did it, but without telling me?'

'It didn't occur to me,' I confessed. 'I'm sorry.'

'It didn't occur to him, either, until just now.' She strode a little way up the corridor pulling at her hair. I was going to go after her but Vesuvio took my shoulder. Stella stopped, apparently holding a heated conversation with herself, before turning around. Her face was perfectly composed. 'Well,' she said. 'I suppose it is partly my fault.'

'No,' I said. 'Don't say that – I get it. It was wrong of me. I genuinely didn't think about how you were connected, when it was . . . obvious, I guess?'

'What I mean is,' said Stella, 'I suppose I didn't make a big deal about the event because I've been putting off telling you – the women's library was also one of my sponsors for the Baltic Prize.'

'Baltic Prize?'

'Well, a sub-category – to encourage cultural exchange between north and south Europe. I won.'

'Congratulations! But why didn't you mention . . .'

'Because it means I'm leaving, Daniel. It's a year's residency at the University of Helsinki, followed by a show at the modern art museum.'

'Did you know?' I asked Vesuvio. I thought back to the time at the bar. *Is that it? Why you said we were both in the same boat?*

'Wasn't for me to say, *mite.*'

'And when? When are you going?'

'When I've packed up here.'

'Before August?'

'I'll have a lot to do. Look.' She reached out but I drew back. 'I wanted to tell you but . . . it was *nice.* I thought – why overshadow the time we had with this?'

'Nice?'

'More than nice.'

'When did you find out?'

'About a month ago.'

'A month,' I repeated. 'I suppose . . .' I was going to say – *we can keep in touch, I can come and visit, a year's not so long,*

Helsinki's not so far, but I could see her eyes were begging me not to. Not to force her to utter empty assurances, impractical promises. Maybe we would see each other, maybe we would not, but most of all, I understood that Stella Amore needed to be free.

'I'm sorry,' she began but I stopped her.

'That makes us even, then. We're both sorry, and not sorry. Maybe we have more in common than you think, *cara*. Well, I'll tell you someone who's going to be disappointed – Rose. *Hold on* – she doesn't . . .?'

'No. I mean, don't get me wrong, I was going to, just not right now.'

'Okay.' I was rolling with the punches. 'If you'll excuse me, I'll just . . .'

'Daniel, stay.'

Now it was me walking stiffly down the corridor. 'I'd better have that drink with the team,' I said.

I pushed through the doors without looking back.

But I didn't go to the team. That was just words, and words, said or unsaid, made no difference.

Instead I went to lose myself in the crowd. The cloister was now rammed with spectators. Beyond them on the quad, the orchestra was beginning to tune up for the second half.

I gravitated back towards where I had seen Stella and Rose tucking into their ice cream. I felt light-headed, which I put down more to the heat and adrenalin-comedown than getting emotionally kicked in the testicles, but who knew – in any case, I could do with some water or juice. The booze could wait until I was alone or with a pal. I didn't want to make a fool of myself in front of Rose or the team.

The tables were littered with spent plastic beakers and there were two plastic garbage bins filled with empty *gelato* cups, but no sign of drinks, soft or otherwise.

'You're too late,' announced Angelo, shadowed as ever by Roberto, whose crazy white hair made him look even more like Einstein, despite sporting a pair of incongruous wrap-around black shades. 'But, hey, I don't want to be greedy.' He held his half-melted pistachio and vanilla ice cream up to me. 'Hmm?'

'Thanks, I'm fine.'

'You don't look fine,' said Angelo. 'In fact, you look decidedly red. Like an Englishman who got caught in the sun.'

'Well, I suppose I am.'

'Have you met Alberto?' He meant the third member of their group, and the only one dressed age-appropriately – in contrast to Angelo and Roberto in shorts and T-shirts that barely contained their bulging bellies, Alberto was trim and clean-shaven in expensive jeans and a smart, pale-blue cotton shirt with a pair of trendy pink-rimmed reading glasses hanging on a gold chain around his neck.

'I haven't had the pleasure,' I said. He raised his own cup of ice cream.

'Better not to shake,' he said. 'I'm a bit sticky.'

'Alberto is curating the event,' said Angelo. 'A big responsibility!'

'Ah, yes,' I said. 'I've seen you on television.'

'But as I was saying to Angelo,' said Alberto, 'these commentary programmes just hire you to fill up the airtime, they're ephemeral. On the other hand a creation like Duke Magnesio will be enjoyed by generations of kids for years to come.'

'Indeed!' said Roberto. The old boys looked sufficiently pleased with themselves.

'You guys haven't seen Rose around, have you?'

'Oh?' said Angelo. 'Rose is here?'

'She has a joint exhibit with Stella – *The Room of Infinite History*; it includes some of her drawings.' Then I remembered who I was with – Alberto Fini was head of the Accademia delle Belle Arti, a 'big' who might have a say over whether Rose would be admitted to the art school in the not-too-distant future. 'That's my daughter *Rose Maria Leicester*,' I said. 'She's only fifteen.' I was pleased she hadn't been there to hear me say that.

'And she's exhibiting with Stella Amore?' asked Fini, plainly impressed.

'Hers are the three sketches behind the chest in *The Room of Infinite Histories*.'

'I haven't had a chance to visit Stella's Rooms yet, but I'll be sure to take a look. *Rose Maria Leicester*, you say?'

Mission accomplished, I continued to make my way around the cloisters.

Night had fallen and the heat too had acquired a kind of gravity – my shirt clung to my back and shoulders, the air lumbered around my lungs. The audience seemed somniferous. Even the music had become *adagio*-slow as if opening a requiem for the sisters of Santa Cristina who in the languor of those shadowy cloisters might have been mingling among us.

I rested against a wall and let the spirit-shadows ripple around me.

Only one shadow stayed put. 'Relieved, Daniel?'

It was the Comandante. 'You've congratulated the artist?'
I asked.

'I have seen her work, yes.' I looked at him.

'It's pretty bloody good.'

'It's . . . somewhat dark.'

'She's an artist,' I said.

'She's a fifteen-year-old.'

'Fifteen-year-olds are more grown-up these days, Giovanni.'

'But they remain fifteen years old,' said the Comandante.
'Something all too easy for them and, it seems, their parents,
to forget.'

'Is there a problem?' I asked.

The Comandante continued to face the orchestra, his profile as patrician as a Roman senator.

'I have always trusted your judgement, Daniel,' he said.
'Or, rather, I have placed my trust in your judgement, and I
am pleased to say, up until now, this faith has been rewarded.'

'If you're talking about Stella being a bad influence on
Rose. Teenagers . . .'

The Comandante glanced at me, then back at the orchestra.

'But I fear I have given you too much liberty,' he said. 'I
am getting older, thinking too much about holidays and not
enough about the well-being of our family. I apologise.'

'Now I've really no idea what you're talking about. Rose's
pictures really aren't a big deal, and as for Stella . . .'

'What were you thinking, Daniel, breaking into the office
when you knew there was now no longer anything to be
gained?'

'Ah,' I said. 'You spoke to Doctor Mattani. Well, it's over
now. No harm done.'

'No harm done?' He said it so loudly a couple in the audience turned around. The woman raised a finger to her lips. 'If you had been caught, you could have been arrested. You could have been convicted for breaking and entering. You could have lost your licence, and that of Dolores.'

'Come on, Comandante,' I said. 'That was always a risk. A risk we take every day.'

'*With good reason.* The coroner had confirmed poison was no longer involved, something which changed the whole nature of the investigation, and yet you pressed ahead.'

'I did inform the team. They were behind me.'

'Of course they were – they're loyal. But as their leader, it was your responsibility, your call, and you recklessly placed them, and yourself, at risk.'

'You're right, Comandante, it was my call, and I decided there was still *good reason* to take a calculated risk. Hell, you were forcing your gun on me the other night, so you're hardly one to talk about over-reacting.'

'That was different – we didn't know then what we know now.'

'And what I'm worried about, is what we still don't know.'

'Oh!' He threw up his hands. 'Always with the glib response.' He stepped across the portico to join the rest of the audience.

The evening was going from bad to worse. I set off along the cloister and up the stairs in search of a friendly face.

Rose was not in *The Room of Infinite Histories*, although there were a handful of visitors, a pair of whom were clearly admiring my daughter's 'smothered child'. This was surely the one that had triggered the Comandante. Who knew? In his career he may have seen the real thing, and I could understand how disquieting it might have been to come across a picture by his granddaughter, but hey – it hadn't been me who had planted the idea in the first place.

'It's so beautiful, moving,' said the woman in front of the picture.

'But there's no idea of price,' said the man. 'No catalogue available . . .'

'I can always ask,' I said, hovering behind them. 'Er, they're by my daughter.'

They looked surprised. 'Not Stella Amore?' said the woman.

'Rose Maria Leicester. It's a joint exhibit.'

The couple nodded thoughtfully and moved on. I felt like a shop assistant who'd scared off a customer.

I left the Room and stepped into the corridor. The music rolled enchantingly around the cloister. At least something was working out this evening.

I found Rose in the next Room along – *Hidden.* Her two friends were crouched in the far corner beside her in skimpy dresses, heels and make-up like a scene from Newcastle on a Saturday night. Rose was sat flat on the floor against the wall, her legs outstretched, head back, breathing laboured.

'Girls!' I said. 'What the hell's going on? Has she been drinking?'

'No, Signor Leicester,' said Stefania, looking desperate. 'I promise.'

'I'm serious, Stefi. You won't get into trouble – no booze, drugs?'

'Truly,' said Stefania. 'Truly, on my heart.'

'Rose, look at me.' Her gaze swung in my direction. Her mouth was slightly parted, sucking in shallow breaths. I felt her forehead: clammy. 'Have you taken anything? Tell me.'

'Nothing,' she panted. 'I swear, Dad.'

'It's for the doctors, so we know what to treat you with. I promise you won't get in trouble, you know I don't care about that.'

'No, nothing . . .'

I heard a clatter behind me. Stefania screamed. Their friend, who I didn't recognise, had just dropped to the floor. Blood began to seep from her hairline.

'Rose,' I held her face. 'Seriously?'

'Seriously.'

'Stefi,' I said. 'Call the ambulance – emergency. *Now.*'

'Christ, what's going on?' It was Vesuvio. He knelt beside the fallen girl and took off his jacket, laying it beneath her head.

'The girls,' I said. 'I think they must have drunk something, drugs . . .'

'I told you, *signore,*' said Stefi. 'Hello? We need an ambulance . . .'

Vesuvio came over to Rose.

'Look at me, *cara.*' Her eyes swivelled towards him. He felt her cheek, held her wrist.

'Doesn't look like drugs to me. Drink?'

'They say no.'

I gave Rose another searching look. Her eyes were beginning to roll backwards, her breathing shallower. I felt it. I knew it – I was losing her.

'Rose!' I shouted. She seemed to rouse. *'Don't sleep.* Vesuvio – you take the other one.'

'Should we move them? Where are we going?'

'We're taking them to the hospital,' I said. 'Right now.'

Chapter 30

I didn't wait for a reply. I scooped Rose up and began running.

'Keep talking to me, darling, keep talking.'

'Dad?' she said. 'Dad?' Then something that chilled me: 'Mum?'

We were down the stairs, into the spectators crowding the portico – this stretch was particularly dense because it led directly to the exit and was attracting passers-by.

With Rose cradled in my arms, I pushed my way through – *'Permesso, permesso'* – above the ebb and flow of the music.

At first the crowd resisted, but, when they realised what was happening, swept aside.

I approached the exit. There – beneath the arch, Stella's landlady Chiara sunk upon the flagstones, her head bowed, encircled by her billowing red dress like a great puddle of blood. But I didn't have time to stop: I ran into the quiet piazzetta.

Across the way, the rest of the team were having a celebratory drink. Claudio rose to his feet.

'Dan! What's happening?'

'Hospital,' I shouted. I ran down the middle of the road, mercifully traffic-free. At the end was the Viale and, on the other side of that, Sant'Orsola.

'Stay with me, darling,' I was saying. 'Just stay with me.' Rose mouthed something, her lips speckled with foam, eyelids fluttering. 'Keep your eyes open. Stay awake.'

Footsteps behind me – Vesuvio with the other girl.

I ducked between a pair of parked cars and ran along the final stretch of portico before reaching the Viale.

The traffic had halted at the lights, so the near lane was empty and the far one stationary. I sprinted across the first, then wove between the queued traffic, a scooter screeching to a halt before I reached the far pavement.

The side exit of the hospital – another stone archway – stood opposite. I passed beneath it and onto the campus, running down the main road bisecting the site.

'*Pronto Soccorso!*' The pedestrians along either side of the road began shouting, gesturing – that way, that way – straight on, it's not far – as if they were spectators at the finale of a marathon.

'Vesuvio!' someone called.

Another: 'Is it a video?'

Straight on . . . it's not far . . . my daughter draped like a rag doll in my arms.

'Daniel!'

Doctor Mattani at the top of the slope, a suitcase stood beside him.

'*Pronto Soccorso!*' But I was stumbling, falling forward yet somehow managing to keep upright with Rose across my arms.

An officer of the Polizia rushed past carrying the other girl. I looked around –Vesuvio was flat on his front amid a crowd. He pulled himself up onto his elbows, gulping for breath. He waved me onwards.

Doctor Mattani peeled back Rose's eyelids, then waved at a pair of white-clad orderlies. 'You two! Over here – get her to the emergency room. Never mind the formalities – straight through to *Resuscitazione*. My authority. I'll be right there.'

Rose was floating upwards, out of my grasp, being hurried away by the pair of burly men. The doctor helped me to my feet.

'What the hell has happened?'

We began to follow the orderlies as they disappeared into a huge modern building. I finally began to recover enough breath to form a sentence.

'They insist it's not alcohol, drugs . . .'

The doctor gave me a sceptical look.

'She was breathless, had palpitations . . .'

We went up the steps and past reception, through swing doors into the emergency room, then another set into *Resuscitazione* where a team of doctors and nurses had both girls on gurneys. Rose was flat on her back, gasping for air while a doctor shone a light into her eyes. The other girl had regained consciousness and was trying to sit up. She vomited into her hands.

The medical staff looked at the pair of us in surprise. Dr Mattani took the torch and checked her eyes for himself, then pressed the tips of his fingers against her chest. He looked suddenly grave. 'It seems like some kind of pulmonary paralysis which may trigger myocardial infarction,' he said. 'Treat with charcoal to reduce absorption, dantrolene to relax the muscles. Get the ventilator ready, but first see if you can't induce vomit or flush her out.'

'Do you know what she's taken?' asked the young doctor.

'Honestly, *giovanotto*, I've no damn idea.'

Chapter 31

'We must give them room to work.' Doctor Mattani led me out.

Although Rose's eyes were closed, she was still breathing. I would hold on to that – I would breathe for her; for every one of her breaths, I would breathe with her.

The seating area was relatively empty, the waiting times at Bologna's various hospitals – from one to four hours for the least serious ailments – helpfully displayed on the video screen.

Gradually the seats began to fill up, principally, it seemed, with friends and relatives of other victims of what was already being discussed among them as some kind of food poisoning – 'a bad batch of that *gelato*,' one man said confidently. 'They freeze and refreeze – bacteria gets in. It happens.'

Among the newcomers was Roberto, who in those black wraparounds now seemed less like an Einstein and more a Phil Spector – as if instead of *Pronto Soccorso* the addled, ageing rock star had wandered into a hotel lobby looking for the bar. He finally sat himself down opposite me, apparently without recognition.

'Roberto?' I asked. I had to repeat it twice. Finally, he lowered the shades down the bridge of his nose and looked, startled, at me.

'Who is it? Angelo?' He blinked, once, twice.

'Indeed,' he said.

'What happened?' He blinked in rapid succession, as if trying to signal Morse Code.

'His heart.'

'I also saw a friend,' I said. 'Chiara. An elderly lady. Did you see what happened to her?' He stared blankly back at me, then shook his head. He tilted his sunglasses back over his eyes.

I called Stella for the third time. No answer. Straight to voicemail. I left another message, struggling to keep the irritation out of my voice – I had told her Rose was in hospital, after all. 'Look, can you just call or message me so I know you're okay? Thanks.'

I turned to Vesuvio. 'You know, you don't have to stay here?'

'I want to find out what happened to the one I brought in, anyway. Frankly, after that sprint I'm surprised I'm not in a bed myself.'

The Comandante was sat on my other side staring straight ahead. He was a man of few words, but I had never seen him quite so silent. He suddenly looked all of his years, and ravaged by that stretch of time.

The double doors of the emergency department opened. Doctor Mattani stepped out as they swung closed behind him. He searched the room, gestured us over. He looked as if he was carefully considering what to say.

Chapter 32

'Rose has stabilised,' he told me. 'She is breathing unassisted. You did well, *giovanotto*, to get her here so quickly. I believe we have been able to either absorb or flush most of it out.'

'So she'll be all right?'

'She's weak. Her body's essentially suffered a violent internal assault. But she's young, she's strong.' He nodded, as if weighing it carefully. 'I should say so, yes. Although without knowing precisely what the poison is, it's obviously difficult to provide any cast-iron guarantees.'

'Poison? You mean "food poisoning". I was hearing about bacteria . . .'

Now Doctor Mattani looked at all three of us. 'Perhaps we should step outside for a moment.'

We followed the doctor down the steps and over to the grass. He pulled a pack of cigarettes out of his white jacket and offered them around. The Italians – Vesuvio and the Comandante – took them. The Englishman declined.

'So you were saying about food poisoning,' I said. 'There was talk about a bad batch of *gelato* . . .'

'In short, Daniel, and I may yet be proved wrong, but the symptoms do not appear consistent with E. coli, listeria, salmonella, whatever. And it's not just Rose.'

'How is the other one, by the way,' said Vesuvio, 'that I brought in?'

'Oh, actually, all right. I can't say for certain if she was actually affected – she may have fainted and simply hit her head. In any case, the poor girl was given the same treatment, and she's recovered, which is more than can be said for some. We've had half-a-dozen with similar serious reactions and one fatality.'

'Who?' I thought – Angelo? Chiara?

'Well, I shouldn't say,' said the doctor, 'as the relations haven't been informed.' He paused. 'But it is Alberto Fini.'

'I'm sorry?'

'The TV guy?' said Vesuvio.

'I met him,' I said. 'He's dead?'

'The heart. Another couple of older people also suffered from cardio-vascular issues. And there were some milder reactions.'

'But what are you saying, then, if it wasn't food poisoning?' The doctor sighed. 'What?' I repeated.

'Well, it is consistent with strychnine poisoning.'

'*Strychnine?*'

'If it is strychnine,' said the doctor, 'at least that will be easy enough to confirm.'

'*But . . .*' said the Comandante.

'It does seem a bit of a coincidence. What I mean is, this mystery poison we were looking for that allegedly struck Professor Bellario – which I was convinced was some kind of phantom, at least until now – well, it would have stimulated precisely the same kind of response.'

'But that *wasn't* strychnine,' I said.

'No,' the doctor said testily. 'Clearly not.'

'So just to be clear, *dottore*, what you're suggesting is that this could be *the same thing* that was used on Bellario? And, obviously therefore, Bellario probably *was* poisoned, after all.' Mattani shrugged. *'Doctor . . .'* I pressed.

'It's definitely a concern.'

'Presuming it's not strychnine, do you think you will be able to find out what it is this time?'

'Obviously we will analyse the excretions of the patients, stomach content, and so on. This will provide us with a lot more material than we had before.'

'But haven't you already run all the tests?'

'We did, and we'll do so again – perhaps there was something we missed.'

'And if these come up with nothing? You're not seriously going to argue these people were struck by another act of God.'

'Honestly, Daniel, I may have made light of it at the time, but the Milan lab tested for all the poisons on the toxicology list.'

'But do "all the poisons on the toxicology list" actually include all poisons?'

'That would be impossible. There are thousands of compounds, millions of poisonous chemicals. But it tests for all the poisons commonly, and uncommonly, used. They run a gas chromatograph, which is a highly sensitive analytical tool, to detect the presence of metals or other subtle compounds. It's the best instrument available.'

'Yet clearly it can't detect everything.'

'Each chromatograph test alone costs over two thousand euros. It's not like in the movies, Daniel – you can't just press a button and get a result. Human judgement comes into play, budgets . . .'

'Budgets,' I echoed.

'There always has to be an end point. Previously, it had seemed a reasonable place to call a halt, not least because failing that, well . . .'

'Well what?'

'It becomes a question of guesswork . . . of individualised, highly-targeted spectrometry. But we would have to know what we were looking for before we even began. It could take forever.'

'Okay,' I said. 'But doesn't the fact it mimics strychnine give you a clue?'

'I . . .' The *dottore* looked at a loss, although whether it was to do with my ignorance or sheer exhaustion, I could not say. He turned back to the Comandante, apparently for support, but Giovanni just looked straight back at him. 'I will certainly begin thinking,' he said. 'I promise you.'

'How long will these tests take?'

'We will speak to the labs in Milan and Rome first thing tomorrow morning.'

I checked my watch. It was coming on for eleven. 'You couldn't call someone tonight?'

'There are things we need to prepare, Daniel.'

'Then can we see her?' The *dottore* nodded.

We were about to head inside, when Vesuvio caught the doctor's arm.

'Stella Amore,' he said. 'A woman in her thirties. She was at the event but we can't find her.'

'I don't recall seeing anyone fitting that profile,' he said. 'But I'll ask around.'

Rose's long, rust-coloured hair nested a face as pale as a Pre-Raphaelite, the trail of freckles across the bridge of her nose apparently all that remained of her healthy, outdoors tan.

But she stirred as we entered, that English face made Italian by those dark eyes – her mother's eyes. She gave a weak smile.

'*Dad. Nonno.*' She raised a hand to her throat – down which they had probably just thrust a tube.

'Don't talk,' I said. 'Try to relax.' I took one clammy hand, the Comandante, *Nonno*, the other. We two 'excepted' men, stood sentinels by her bedside.

'What happened?' she whispered.

'You were poisoned,' I said. 'But you're going to be all right.'

'Valentina?'

'Who's that? Your friend?' She nodded.

'She's okay. Apparently she just fainted, then knocked her head. I'm sorry.' Rose frowned. 'For doubting you. Thinking it was drink, drugs . . .'

The corners of her eyes crinkled. Another weak smile – '*Magari*' – and I knew then that she would be okay.

Chapter 33

We stepped out of the lift and headed back to the waiting room. On the way, we passed a line of people sitting outside the drawn curtains of *Pronto Soccorso*, among them Melodia di Battista and beside her, in a wheelchair with a foil sheet across her legs, a drip in her arm, her head tilted back against the wall, her orchestral colleague with the mauve hair.

We stopped. 'How is she doing?'

Melodia blinked up at me. There didn't appear to be any recognition, or at least aggression, in her eyes.

'They've given her charcoal medicine,' she said. 'She has to stay under observation.'

'And you,' I said. 'How are you?'

'Me?' Melodia looked surprised. 'I'm all right, but I didn't have the ice cream. Someone was talking about food poisoning. Have you any idea what happened?'

She looked as ingenuous as any innocent person.

'They may have been poisoned.'

She finally clocked me. 'Hold on. You're him – the man, the private detective who was asking questions with that girl.

What are you doing here?' She looked appalled. 'You haven't come to track me down to here . . .'

'*No,*' I said. 'Not at all – my daughter has been admitted.' I nodded to her friend. 'With the same thing as her.'

'How is she? I hope . . .'

'She'll be all right, fingers-crossed.' I hesitated, my gaze lingering on the pair of them.

A tug on my elbow. The Comandante shook his head.

'Wishing your friend a speedy recovery,' I said and we moved on.

The team were gathered at the entrance.

'How is she?' asked Alba.

'Poorly but she seems to be recovering.'

She crossed herself. *'Grazie a Dio.'*

'Is there anything we can do?' asked Dolores.

'There is. We can damn well find the source of this mysterious poison.'

'Isn't that the job of the doctors?' said Jacopo.

'They've no idea what it is, and it could take them days, possibly weeks to work it out, presuming it's the same thing used on Bellario. We need to go back over what we've discovered so far, what we may have missed. Anything that might provide us with a clue to what it is and where it comes from.'

'The police.' The Comandante spoke for the first time. 'This is now, clearly, a matter for the police. We should turn everything over to them.'

'I've no problem with that,' I said. 'Sure, the cops might get to it. After the medics have conclusively ruled out it *wasn't* food poisoning. And how long is that going to take?

It's not their little girl in hospital. But . . . okay. Alba, speak to Commissario Miranda – she's a hard-ass but she's a reliable hard ass, she'll give you a fair hearing, and at least she won't be able to complain about being left in the dark.' I turned to Vesuvio. 'Any news on Stella?'

'I caught a taxi to her place while you were up there, but no answer. I also asked around Santa Cristina. Nothing.'

'They may have taken her to Maggiore?'

'I called – no record.'

'Presumably she hasn't already buggered off to Helsinki,' I muttered.

'Helsinki?' said Alba.

'Never mind. All right. I guess all we can do is keep trying.'

'What about me?' asked Dolores.

'Be ready for whatever legwork is required tomorrow morning.'

'And you?' said Alba.

'I need some time to think.'

Chapter 34

I could hear Rufus barking as the Residence gates yawned open. The poor mutt must have been wondering where the hell we had got to.

As we arrived at the *piano nobile*, the Comandante took my arm. 'I apologise,' he said.

'For what?'

'Earlier . . . for being annoyed. Evidently, there was some truth to your suspicions.'

I thought back to Melodia and her friend at the hospital. 'I don't know about the women. Frankly, after today it seems unlikely they had anything to do with it, but we'll check.'

'Your "hunch" was right, that the case was far from resolved.'

'Much good it did us.'

'Still, in other circumstances . . .' He shook his head.

I took him in my arms. Then Giovanni Faidate, the Comandante, *Nonno*, went to his apartment without another word.

Rufus jumped up at me the moment I opened the door and only calmed down when I went to the kitchen sink to run my head beneath the cold tap, although I could still feel his bulky body bouncing against my legs.

I finally removed my head from the lukewarm water and, in the absence of anything else, grabbed a dirty tea towel to dry my hair, much to the disgust, I imagined, of Rose.

My legs went.

I grabbed hold of the side of the sink but continued down, onto my knees. I bent forward with my forehead pressed against the kitchen unit.

'Dad . . . *Mum.*'

Were you still with us, Lucy? Were you really there while this shit was going on, looking down on us? Were you really waiting for her?

Are you waiting for me?

Rose's brave smile, her little joke: *'Magari.'*

I wish.

The dog's nose wet against my ear, his tongue. I straightened a fraction. Poor Rufus, comprehending only emotions, moment by moment. *Lucky* Rufus . . . I reached out, brought him towards me, buried my face in his woolly, springy coat, felt his rapid beating heart.

'Rufus, mate. *Rufus.*' I pressed my forehead against his.

It was no good just sitting here. 'Come on.' I got to my feet, reached for his lead.

I was closing the front door when I remembered.

I went back into the kitchen and pulled out a chair from beneath the table. I pushed it against the cupboard and stepped up.

I reached out and took hold of the Comandante's Beretta.

***

We drifted up towards San Mamolo. The streets were cinder-red, the city tossing and turning – we were certainly not alone.

Although the families had, for the most part, taken in their chairs and were now trying to sleep with the fans on full, there were still pensioners alone or in couples sat in the darkness or along benches, fanning themselves with a rolled-up newspaper or dealing out *Scopa* playing cards. Groups of kids roamed the streets in search of that mythical late-night bar or *festa* or simply a place to carry on partying. When we arrived at the park of San Michele in Bosco, there were at least two drunken picnics taking place upon the hill overlooking the city.

I had let Rufus off the leash when we entered the park, but he had had no inclination to leave my side, seemed happy to accompany me as we took the winding path up to the church through the woods.

'So it *was* poison,' I was saying. 'There *is* a murderer: Bellario, Amanda. Pasquale Grande?' I looked around. 'Or is it *me* they're after? What have I discovered that might lead them to make an attempt?

'And if I'm being followed . . .' A droplet of sweat dripped between the small of my back and the gun barrel. 'And I'm pretty sure I *am*, what does it signify? Are there more than one of them – is it a group, an organisation?' I shook my head. 'Jesus, this is Italy. Anything's possible . . .'

Something shifted in the undergrowth. I pulled out the Beretta, switched on the phone, scanned the foliage.

The thing, whatever it was – a bird or a rat or a cat – shivered deeper into the wood. I lowered the gun, returned it to my waistband.

I was in shock – dehydrated, tired, scared. I was a danger

to myself, and others. But in a sense that was fitting. Because if I wanted to take on whoever was behind this, I needed to be dangerous.

'The event.' I forced myself to recall the scene in *Hidden* – Rose sprawled on the floor, her eyelids fluttering. '*500 Years of Resistance*. This *cultural event* . . . Bologna's great and good . . . Alberto Fini . . .

'But a violinist was poisoned, too. *Melodia*? Might she have somehow wanted to throw us off the trail? To move the focus away from Bellario, Amanda? But could she really be such a monstrous psychopath?' Thinking of her in casualty with her friend, I found it hard to believe.

Rufus finally tired of my musings and ran ahead, along the path that led to the top of the hill.

The glow of the Red City, *La Rossa*, flickered between the trees. With it the faces of Bellario. Amanda. Alberto Fini.

'Better not to shake, I'm a bit sticky.'

Rose and Stella – standing across the portico with their cups of *gelato*.

I felt like throwing up.

I emerged from the woods onto the path beneath San Michele where Pasquale and Laura had embraced, where I had betrayed their secret.

I went to the bench where I had filmed the two lovers, Rufus snuffling around my feet, perhaps searching for the scent of his playmates. On the slope below, groups of picnicking kids. Beyond them, the great disc of the city, keeping its counsel, mute witness to centuries of drama – earthquakes, sieges, invasion. Bombing raids, riots, terrorist attacks.

Doomed love stories, notorious murders.

How many young people must have sat beneath this church over the centuries, cloaked as much by their own obscurity as the night? Instead of being 'Copernicus', 'Cervantes' or 'Mozart' – who, after all, had simply been a gifted prodigy when Father Martini fixed his exam – as anonymous as any of those kids now sitting below, drawing only the attention of dogs like Rufus, who had relocated to the fringes of their group hoping to be thrown some scraps.

No matter how grand we might become, we were all just minor characters in the great drama of Bologna, absorbed in the minutiae of our sub-plots.

So what was the main story? What did the city see that I was missing? What had the poisoning at Santa Cristina revealed that I had been too wrapped up in my own conspiracies and emergencies to consider?

One of the kids got to his feet, presumably to nip to the woods for a pee. Rufus decided to accompany him. The others laughed.

I called the dog to heel. The kid gave me a grateful wave. I waited for him to do his business and on the way back called: '*Mirko.*'

It took him a moment to focus, perhaps on account of the booze, the gloom, both. I made my way down the hill. 'Mirko, it's Dan from the university library. Dolores' friend.'

He perked up. 'Dolores is here?'

'I'm afraid not. Look, when we were in the foyer of Palazzo Gotti you said it hadn't been a great year for the academic staff, meaning the other ones on the plaque. How did they die?'

'I'm sorry?'

'Of death!' one of his friends called. 'I hear it's fatal.'

'Do you guys know? It seems UniBo's *professori* have suffered quite a lot of fatalities recently. Can anyone tell me more?'

'Well, there was Bellario . . .'

'I know about him.'

'And Dauni . . . Didn't he die in his sleep?'

'Well, he *was* a hundred and three!'

'That's not true – he was born looking old. But he must have been in his seventies.'

'Lepori.'

'I know about Lepori,' I said. 'He drowned in his bathtub, didn't he?'

'That's it.'

'Canova.'

'Fell under a bus.'

'Conte.'

'Stroke.'

'No, that was the heart, I think.'

'And the other one . . . Manni? Magni?'

'Didn't she drop dead as well? Weak heart, too, I think – but that was a funny one, a bit of a *Giallo* – a mystery. Didn't they find her dead in Naples? She had been on the Milan train to Bologna, but never got off. They only found her when they were cleaning the carriages; they thought she was asleep. She was only fifty-something.'

'Old enough.'

'And there was no investigation?' I said. 'Nothing?' Blank looks all around.

'Why would there be?'

I looked at the kids sprawled across the grass. Why indeed?
'Thanks.' I put the dog back on his lead.
'And . . . *dottore*,' called Mirko. 'If you see Dolores . . .'
'I'll tell her you said hi. Come on, Rufus.'

We began to make our way down the hill and back into the
blood-hot city, my mind swimming with possibilities: what if
the killing of Bellario had been the *symptom*, not the disease?

What if this had never been about the discipline – music –
but the profession – professor?

What if a serial killer was at work in the oldest university
in the world?

Chapter 35

It shook me awake, but the tremor had stopped before I had opened my eyes.

I reached out for Stella, something I never usually did in my own bed, but half-asleep/half-awake was perhaps the state I most associated with her – following a restless night of lovemaking, perhaps a little too much to drink, there we would be, drifting upon the raft of her bed with those spidery frescoed clouds above.

I bolted upright. Rufus, who usually spent the night with Rose, stirred at my feet.

It was light, the shutters were open, and so were the windows. I would have been feasted upon by mosquitoes.

I checked the clock – six-thirty. I had slept for no more than two hours. I was surprised I had slept at all.

I called the hospital about Rose. A grumpy nurse told me simply: 'No change,' and put the receiver down. I called Stella again – straight to voicemail. Sent her another message, noted the others had gone unopened. I wrote to Alba: *Can you track down Stella? Vesuvio has tried her home, etc, but no joy. Liaise with him.*

I went for a shower, stood beneath that cold-warm water, my palms flat against the tiles.

Got out, dried off. Messaged Dolores: *I want as much as you can get on the professors who died this year.*

She replied immediately: *On it chief.*

I was at Ospedale Sant'Orsola by seven-thirty. I knew visiting wasn't until nine, but thought I would chance my arm and see if I could slip into the ward. However, when I arrived, I found the entrance to the ward locked and when a nurse – probably the same one who had put the phone down – spotted me loitering outside, she irritably waved me away.

I retreated outside to a bench on the grass facing *Pronto Soccorso*. I thought of Rose in there, Stella . . . *somewhere.* The killer, or killers, no doubt well pleased at having crossed another professor off their list, this time Alberto Fini. Never mind the 'collateral damage'.

Rose's eyelids fluttering as she slipped out of consciousness.

Some sick fuck, who clearly thought they had out-smarted everyone. And they had, if my hypothesis was correct, because no one else had yet appeared to notice.

I thought back to Amanda – once again permitted to poison Professor Bellario – well, the police would be all over that soon. But how could Amanda's actions relate to a much wider plot to eliminate university professors? How was she involved? Could she be the link that tied it all together?

The morning mocked me with its beauty, even as I sat in the grounds of a hospital: the chirruping of cicadas, the fresh, pine-infused air, Italy's inability to design even utilitarian medical facilities without a touch of finesse. The sign in front of me was written in appropriately Italicised script: *MEDICINA 1, CARDIOLOGIA, TRAUMATOLOGIA, REPARTO LUDOVISI, REPARTO MARATI, ORTOPEDIA.*

It was an aesthetic that continually reminded me I was a foreigner, having grown up in a country where a sensibility to beauty was considered frankly effeminate, frivolous, weak; even somehow morally deficient. Anglo Saxons were of the Word, not the Image, substance, not appearance. But just as the English-speaking world was certainly not immune to words without substance, so it was an error to consider the Italian aesthetic only skin deep. On the contrary, in the Italian language, beauty had a moral dimension.

And Santa Cristina had certainly been a beautiful setting for murder.

What if totting up dead professors on a plaque hadn't been enough – what if you wanted to get noticed?

500 Years of Resistance? You would show them resistance!

'How's Rose?' It was Dolores in a khaki T-shirt and cargo shorts. With her cropped hair and those mirrored sunglasses, she could have been a photojournalist in Vietnam circa 1970.

'No news . . . is good news.'

'Stella?'

'Nothing, but Alba's on it, so something should turn up.'

'I've found what I could on the dead professors.'

Dolores had managed to get hold of four addresses, most importantly that of Professor Manni, who had died under mysterious circumstances on the Naples train. We agreed that, after visiting Rose, I would see what more I could find out about her while Dolores would follow up Canova – if 'fell under a bus' didn't sound like a euphemism, I don't know what did.

'So Manni was in the Statistics department,' I said. 'Canova?'

'Archaeology. I never had him as a lecturer, but he was well-respected.'

'Old?'

'He . . . *seemed* old, yeah.'

'Well, statistics and archaeology . . . they certainly don't seem to have much in common.'

'The only thing I can think of is they're both in Via delle Belle Arti – practically next door.'

'But Bellario's DAMS department is in Via Zamboni.'

'They run parallel, though,' said Dolores. 'I mean, Lepori, Bellario's predecessor, was also based there. Although Conte was an economics professor – and that department literally straddles Zamboni and Belle Arti. Meanwhile, the Art School where Alberto Fini was based is of course in—'

'Belle Arti. All the departments, basically, occupy the same two streets.'

'And a few others nearby.'

'Okay, we'll proceed as discussed and ask the rest of the team to look into the background of the other professors.' I nodded towards the Comandante, Jacopo and Alba approaching. 'They can feed us additional info we need as we go.' My hand was gripped around the arm of the bench. Dolores gave it a squeeze.

'We're not going to let them get away with this,' she said. 'I promise.'

Rose had been moved along the corridor to an ordinary two-bed room. An elderly lady with her arm in a splint was propped up beside her, looking on approvingly while the entire Faidate clan gathered around my daughter's bed. She still appeared drained and was hooked up to a drip, but the sparkle was clearly returning to her eyes.

'A miraculous recovery.' I stood at the foot of the bed. She smiled weakly, my little girl, and I moved around to hug her. She smelled of iodine.

'Did you find the poison?'

'Not yet, I'm afraid. But most importantly – how are you feeling?'

'Hungover.'

'How would you know what a hangover feels like?'

'I've seen you often enough.' I kissed her on the forehead.

'I can tell you're on the mend.' We hugged again.

'Oh!' said Rose.

'What is it?'

'This tube . . .'

While the others eventually drifted their separate ways, I remained with my daughter until she dropped off. And so did I, it appeared.

The rattle of the trolley woke us both, Rose's hand still in mine. She let go and reached for some water, sat herself up.

'Great,' she said. 'I'm famished.'

'Even for hospital food? Are you sure you're not still sick? Hang on, what time is it?' It was half-past eleven.

'Late for something?' asked Rose.

'Well . . .'

'As long as it's about getting the bastard who put me in here,' said Rose. 'Go.'

Chapter 36

It took me almost as much time to find a parking space in the zone around the Giardini Margherita as it did to drive there from Sant'Orsola, which was just down the road. The address I had for the late *Professoressa* Manni was among the affluent roads that bordered Bologna's most up-market park in the south of the city, home not only of ornamental lakes packed with turtles and carp, but also, behind impenetrable hedges, its exclusive tennis club to which, despite all our contacts, I had never even bothered trying to attain membership. In this regard, at least, the Faidate retained their traditional status as 'tradesmen' among the successors to 'the Hundred'.

I finally found a parking space close enough to the club to hear the *thwok* of tennis balls. The Liberty-style houses along these quiet roads were set back a little, with ample gardens behind high iron railings and, not uncommonly, a couple of dogs waiting for an opportunity to run up and have a jolly good bark.

These streets would have been laid out during the early twentieth century as the rapidly industrialising city expanded – north beyond the railway lines to accommodate the workers in Bolognina, and over here in the more fashionable and elevated south for the new bourgeoisie. Although technically charming, these large houses had always struck me as a little sinister – they brought to mind the kind of places fascist-era secret police might bring prisoners, their screams reverberating around the empty streets and going unremarked upon by frightened neighbours.

I got out of the car then remembered the Beretta. I leant back in and flipped open the glove box. I tucked it into my waistband, where it was practically invisible beneath my navy polo shirt.

I looked up and down the street. There was no sign of anything suspicious and, frankly, with all my driving along the narrow streets, it would have been pretty hard to have kept a low profile.

The late Professor Manni had lived in an apartment in one of the mansions. Her name was still on the bell beneath that of her partner – evidently Caprese. Both had *Prof* before their names, which I thought even in Italy was a little excessive. I checked my watch. It was twelve. I pressed the Manni-Caprese bell.

It did not take long to be answered – a teenage boy by the sound of things, who seemed disappointed when I explained I had come to see his father. I heard him shout – *Dad, it's for you* – before disappearing off somewhere.

'Hello?'

'Professor? My name is Daniel Leicester. I'm a private investigator looking into the background of your wife's death. May I have a word?'

'You're . . . excuse me, what?' I told him again – I didn't

have the time or inclination to play games. 'I . . . still don't understand.'

'If you let me in, I'll explain.' The gate buzzed. I walked across the gravel path to the front door, which was also unlocked, stepping into a spacious entrance, sunlight pouring in through a large window on the landing. These 'Liberty' villas were the Italian equivalent to Britain's 'Arts & Crafts' style buildings, combining medievalism with nineteenth-century modernity, hence the smart floral floor tiles and winding, carved oak staircase. There was the sound of a door opening above.

'Up here,' called the professor.

Professor Caprese was in his late middle-age although lean and healthy-looking with it. He reminded me a little of Bellario in that he was also bald, although the professor had simply shaved his sideburns and not bothered with a hairpiece. He was dressed smartly in a pale-blue shirt and Chinos. He looked set for work.

'I'm sorry to disturb you, Professor.' He gave me a penetrating look far removed from the jaded acceptance of Signor Delfillo. Here was a man entirely unaccustomed to dealing with the likes of me. 'As I said, I'm looking into the death of your late wife, Professor Manni.'

'So you said – why? And who's paying you?'

'I'll be honest with you, signore, it's complicated, but it is part of a far broader investigation into a number of suspicious deaths, your wife's among them.'

'This is nonsense, there was nothing suspicious about Mariella's death, it was simply . . .' There was the sound of someone coming down the stairs; the son materialised behind his father. 'Really, this is absurd.'

'Is this about Mum?' said the boy.

'You had better come in,' said the professor. 'It's nothing, Davide – have you got your beach stuff like I asked?'

'Locked and loaded.'

Professor Caprese sighed. 'I've told you not to use those video game expressions.' He ushered me along a book-lined corridor. We entered what I presumed to be his 'studio', or office. He closed the door.

'You're a mathematician yourself, Professor?'

'I *am* a mathematician. My late wife was a statistician. But, well . . . numbers. Now what has any of this got to do with Mariella?'

'It's a line of enquiry we're pursuing – that her death may somehow be connected to others at the university. I realise it might seem like a bit of a long shot, but we discovered a possible link to a recent poisoning – of a Professor Bellario, Illario Bellario. Did you know him?'

'No, I'm afraid not.'

'He was a musicologist.'

'Sorry – we're not, we were not, very keen on music.'

'Can you tell me a little about your wife? She was in the statistics department, in fact the head of the department. Had she been in the post long?'

'Not that long – around five years.'

'And during that time, did she have any run-ins with students? Other lecturers?'

'Oh! If you knew the world of academia, Signor Leicester, you wouldn't ask me that. But someone angry or crazy enough to kill her? Well, that's something else entirely. She was just a statistics professor, for heaven's sake.'

'She caught a train, I understand, from Milan. She was returning to Bologna.'

'From a conference, yes.'

'But she didn't come home and was discovered passed away in Naples. The cause of death was given as . . .'

'Heart failure, yes. To answer your question – it did come as a shock. It's true, her father had died of a heart attack in his early sixties, and she suffered from arrhythmia during her pregnancy, but that was years ago, and otherwise she was in good health. She didn't smoke, drink, at least not to excess. She was not overweight – we belong, belonged to a running club. The autopsy took place in Naples . . .' He paused. 'Because, of course, that was where she was discovered, but the medical examiner and coroner seemed thorough. You speak of poison, but they did run a toxicology test and it came back negative. They concluded it was a freak event. Apparently, it happens. Sudden arrhythmic death syndrome.'

'They undoubtedly had no reason to think it could be anything other than natural causes,' I said. 'Your wife's replacement as head of department . . .'

'Ernesto Farnese.'

'Excuse me, Professor, but why the sour face?'

'Oh. Ernesto. Well, look – I don't for a moment think he's a murderer. He couldn't organise his teaching schedule let alone an assassination. That was always the problem – his opinion of his genius fell far short of his ability as an educa- tor. He was the bane of Mariella's life – she was always having to fill in for him or make excuses. He would have been better in some kind of research institute, but now he's department head with, no doubt, everyone else having to run around and make things work while he lords it in his ivory tower. In a sense, he's your classic Italian university professor, although I've heard it said he always claimed that my wife only got the job because she was a woman. Nonsense.' Professor Caprese's jaw clamped shut with indignation.

Dolores messaged me as I was walking back to the car.

Canova's done. Call me. I did so.

'Tell me.'

She let out a long sigh. 'Well, it was pretty hard going. It turned out the prof's widow has Alzheimer's. He was caring for her – I mean, he was in his early seventies – but after he died, she had to go into a home. When I got there, I met the daughter-in-law who was with an estate agent. They were trying to sell off the property. It was pretty sad. Anyway, she wasn't able to tell me much more than we know already. He was on his way to work on a slippery February morning, waiting at a bus stop and the next thing anyone knew he was under the bus.'

'You say "anyone". There was quite a crowd waiting then?'

'Yes, I asked – there were plenty of witnesses. No one saw anything suspicious.'

'Although – would they? Unless they had been looking for it? Alba wrote Canova was a tenured professor. I mean, he wasn't head of department like Bellario or Manni.'

'No,' said Dolores. 'But tenure . . . a job for life. It's still quite a prize and once one professor drops off his perch, there's always room for another. I'm actually outside the economics faculty now to find out who got it.'

'Good work. I'm heading the same way. Meet me at the entrance to the department of statistics.'

Chapter 37

It would be hard to find a drier subject to house opposite the Accademia delle Belle Arti than statistics and, sure enough, that morning the usual ragtag of scowling weirdoes sat in the shade of the art school portico smoking or sketching while, directly opposite them, a decidedly nerdish group was gathered outside the Department of Statistical Science chatting excitedly about their forthcoming vacations. It was easy to imagine that summer for the stats nerds represented a welcome break and chance to reacquaint themselves with their pals, while for the art students it meant quite the opposite – twelve weeks of parental approbation and small-town angst.

I was watching one of the staff hang a black ribbon from the entrance of the art school, presumably mourning the late Alberto Fini, when I spotted Dolores walking up Belle Arti from the economics department.

'So?'

'No luck, chief. Turns out they're still talking about it. There's some kind of competition and the winner won't be announced until the autumn.'

'More than one professor participating in this "competition", I presume?'

'Yeah, a whole bunch, although probably only a handful with a serious chance, two guys and a woman. I've got the names.'

'That doesn't tell us much. Excuse me,' I turned to the statistics students. 'We're looking for Professor Farnese. Do you know where we could find him?'

This caused much hilarity. 'If you do, let us know!'

But they did know where his office was. We made our way into the building, slipping past the receptionist who had her head down over her mobile phone.

The professor's office was along a corridor on the third floor. The door was closed. I knocked but there was no answer, tried the handle, it was locked. While Dolores stood guard, I picked it open.

'You're getting better at that,' she said. 'Remember the first time . . .'

'The first time,' I straightened up, 'like I always told you – it was rusted.'

Professor Farnese's office was a far cry from the likes of the dean of the conservatory or Professor Bellario's, although it remained a cut above that of the more junior lecturers in that it had a window, along with a small, round table that looked as if it could barely support the stacks of papers piled on top of it. But otherwise there was barely space for the professor's desk amid the piles of books and papers hoarder-high which created a single-lane pathway to and from it. A framed cartoon on the wall behind the desk seemed to make light of this, depicting a bespectacled man very much as I imagined

Professor Farnese, peering between stacks of papers at a student nervously perched on the edge of his seat, with a bubble appearing from the professor's mouth saying: 'Surprise me.'

I fanned the air. The room was a tinderbox.

'I don't suppose the professor is hiding behind all of this,' said Dolores.

'Always a possibility.'

'So, what now?'

'I'll see if I can track him down at home, or the beach.' Still flapping at the warm air, I led us back into the marginally cooler corridor. 'Who have you got?' She checked her phone.

'Alba recommends Dauni . . . He was head of Biological, Geological and Environmental Science. Quite a mouthful.'

'I heard that one may have *actually* died of old age. I was thinking,' I checked my own phone, 'instead of Conte, I might nip over the road to the art school.' The phone rang. 'Jacopo. Rose okay?'

'She's fine, well, not fine obviously, but no news. No, it's that I've got a lead on that car.'

'What car?'

'The one that hit Pasquale Grande and smeared him across Via San Mamolo? You asked me to check it out. Well, you were right – someone came back with CCTV asking for a reward. No wonder it flattened Grande – it was a silver or dark-grey Audi Q8, the thing's the size of a tank. I managed to blow up the image and pluck the number off the plate. Unfortunately, it turned out to be stolen.'

'The car or the plate?'

'The plate for sure. From a Nissan Qashqai in Pilastro.'

I sighed. 'Well, at least it tells us it was unlikely to be a simple hit and run, but equally it leaves us at a dead end – stolen plates. We'll never find the bugger now.'

'I thought so, too, but then I got to thinking – how many of the new model Audi Q8s can there be in Bologna?'

'Quite a lot, I would have thought.'

'It's only been out three months. Anyway, I managed to narrow the field even further. I was just staring at the image, you know – 3.0L GTI – then I realised there was more. The dealership had placed their emblem in chrome beside it: MAZZINI.'

'Fantastic. So, what next – can you hack their system?'

'I could . . . But we're in a hurry, right? Hacking people is simpler.'

'What do you mean?'

'We're there now – outside the dealership.'

'Who's "we"?'

'I'm waiting in the car – Alba's gone into the office. She said she looked more respectable, and let's face it, she's not wrong.'

'What's she doing in there?'

'I knocked up an ID for her.' He meant on the printer we had bought for precisely this purpose. 'She's an investigator for *L'Agenzia delle Entrate*. Remember when they raided Cortina this March to photo visitors' cars and check them against their tax declarations? She'll say it's something to do with that, but she left her notes at home and could they spare her the trip back and give her the details.'

'Do you think they'll buy it?'

'It's the *taxman*, Dan. They'll do anything to get her out of their hair ASAP, and they certainly won't want to piss her off.'

'And Alba was all right with this? You know she always hates this kind of thing.'

'She suggested it. I mean, in the circumstances . . . Hold on, here she comes.'

I heard the sound of the car door opening. By the weighty thud as it closed, I realised they must be in the Comandante's limo. An exclamation from Alba, then: 'What are you waiting for? Get us out of here!' The ropey turn of the engine – Jacopo should have known the aged Lancia was not the ideal getaway car.

'How did it go?' said Jacopo. 'I've got Dan on the line.'

'*Mio Dio*. Just get going, Jaco!' Another mechanical lurch, then a splutter. I imagined black smoke coughing from the exhaust. '*Finalmente!*'

'Hello?' I said. 'Hello?'

'Concentrate on the road! Give it to me.'

'Is everything all right?'

'*Mio Dio*. Never again. I thought I was going to faint! The way he looked at that ID, I thought he would never believe me. That he would call the police!'

'But he didn't. It went okay?'

'*Grazie a Dio*. Anyway! *Anyway* . . . I got it. The details – there was just the one silver and/or dark-grey, actually silver, Audi Q8. Leased to a company: EdificioBo SpA.'

'EdificioBo, you say?' I looked at Dolores. She did a double-take and began scrolling through her phone. She held up a photo of the property plan we had seen in Bellario's office – stamped with the logo *EdificioBo*.

'Do you want us to check it out?' asked Alba.

'You've done brilliantly,' I said. 'We can handle it from here.'

Chapter 38

The address provided for the car was north of the city near Funo, a rather dismal suburb at the beginning of the Po Plain. We drove along a thoroughfare lined with shabby residential blocks, light industrial units and fast food outlets, turning right at a petrol station to find ourselves in the countryside. On either side of the single lane road the parched plain stretched as flat as fens.

We passed a shuttered *osteria*, a lonely cemetery. A pair of stone gate-posts that had once, presumably, signalled the entrance to an estate but now stood like abandoned sentries. Ahead, the navigator informed us, we would reach our destination.

It was not easy to miss – it stood in a cypress square upon the burnt-brown landscape, set back from the side of the road.

I slowed the car. Through the trees: a handsome eighteenth-century *palazzo*, possibly once the seat of minor aristocracy or a hunting lodge for one of the more prominent families among 'the Hundred'. In any case, it was a building that would not look out of place in a brochure on posh Tuscan holidays, except it was on the fringes of an industrial estate in an outer Bologna suburb.

There was a smallish entrance with a black iron gate mid-way along, but I kept going along the road for around fifty metres before doing a U-turn and pulling in along the embankment. Two-metre-high spiked iron railings continued around the property, although I hadn't spotted any CCTV.

I reached across Dolores and pulled out the gun.

'Hold on,' she said. 'Where did you get that?'

'It's borrowed.'

'Do you even know how to use it?'

'Dolores, you're not my mother.' I opened the door. Dolores got out the other side. 'You stay here,' I said.

'You're joking.'

'It could be dangerous.'

'I'd say so – I'm most worried about you and that thing.'

'Just stay.' I crossed the road while Dolores stood disapprovingly by the car. I considered the railings. Although they hadn't seemed so high from across the road, looking at them now, I realised they wouldn't be such a cinch to scale, even with a foot on the horizontal bottom bar.

'Actually,' I called. 'Would you mind?' She came across. 'If you could give me a foot up . . .'

'You're going to impale yourself on those spikes.'

'Are you going to help?'

'Come on then.' Dolores was dressed like a war photographer and, it turned out, as tough as one: there was no give at all when I placed my foot in her cradled hands – instead a small grunt and I was elevated forcefully upwards. I managed to place my hands on the bar between the spikes, and push myself forwards, straightening my arms with the hope of swinging my legs over the top. Instead, I tilted too far forwards and was lucky not to fall on my face, hitting the earthen ground with my knees before being propelled onto my front.

'Jesus,' said Dolores. 'Are you all right? Did you mean to do that?'

'I'm . . . fine.' I brushed off the leaves, was about to get going when I felt for the gun. It was lying beside Dolores on the other side of the railings. She picked it up by the barrel. 'Dolores . . .'

She hesitated, then passed it through.

'If you don't hear from me within half-an-hour, call the Carabinieri.'

'And if I hear shooting?'

'I'm sure it will be fine.'

The trees were three or four deep around the house, which was a faded Bologna-red, its plaster façade crumbling, old brick visible behind a terracotta crust. The green wooden shutters were in need of a lick of paint and quite a few had slats missing.

The solid main doors at the top of a set of stone steps were chained together, and looked like they'd been for a long time. It didn't seem like the headquarters of a property development company, although perhaps this was simply a property in need of development.

I followed the tree-line around the side of the house where a white BMW SUV was parked. Beyond, an open door revealed a hallway, dimly lit by dated Murano chandeliers. There was no discernible sign of activity.

I continued tracing the trees around to the rear of the

property where I came across it: a car, covered in a black tarpaulin.

It was the size and shape of a large SUV and around ten metres from the tree-line, parked square to the rear of the house, so was completely invisible from the road. Beyond it, a set of steps led down to a *cantina*.

I crouched, trying to discern sound beyond the racket of the cicada, movement in the glare of the sun. The driver of that BMW had to be around here somewhere.

I decided to risk it – keeping low, I dashed across the grass.

First I tried the rear of the car with the hope of being able to lift up the tarpaulin and check for the dealership logo, but the sheeting was tight and there was no lifting it up unless I wanted to risk fully exposing myself to the side of the house. I was able to confirm one thing, however – the car was silver.

Keeping on the tree-side of the car, I began to make my way towards the front, peeling back the tarpaulin skirt as I went. I paused at the front wheel – it was an Audi. The hub was splashed with dark spots. I licked my finger and rubbed them – blood.

That was enough.

A siren approaching. Had Dolores called the cops, after all? It hardly mattered. I had enough evidence to call them myself.

It faded. The car had continued along the road.

I was beginning to back away towards the tree-line when I heard it.

'Help! Please, help me!' The woman's voice trailed off. She, too, must have realised the police car had passed by.

I pulled out the Beretta and moved towards the *cantina*.

Chapter 39

The *cantina* was not so different from ours – the strong smell of clay, the sweet hint of vermin; old brick arches, passages leading into darkness. And just like home, down among the building's bared roots, not much had changed: you could have substituted the light of my phone for an oil lamp, a cutlass for my pistol. Well, almost – plastic sheeting hung across one of the passages. A dusty transistor radio sat on a carpenter's bench. A patchwork of fresh concrete was smeared across some brickwork.

There was a light switch just inside the entrance, but I chose not to use it, at least not yet. Whoever I could hear sobbing in the darkness didn't know I was here. But neither, I hoped, did her captor.

'*Please*,' she was saying, although with none of her previous conviction. 'Please help me, someone . . .'

The sound seemed to be coming from the passage behind the sheeting. I pulled it warily back and shone my light along a corridor lined with storerooms set beneath brick arches. Each appeared closed by an old wooden door secured either by a heavy iron bolt, a padlock, or both.

I began to make my way along the passage.

Cobwebs brushed my face, a mouse darted out of the light of my phone.

'Hello?' I said softly. 'Can anyone hear me?'

'Here!' The woman's voice. 'I'm here!'

It appeared to be coming from the room at the end.

The bolt was secured by a padlock. 'Hold on,' I said. 'And quieter, please.'

'Hurry. *Please hurry.*'

I unrolled my picks. Ordinarily a standard combination padlock like this could be sprung in a matter of seconds, but I had to place my phone on the floor so it was shining upwards while the woman continued calling loudly for help, despite my pleas to keep it down.

The lock sprang. I snatched it off the bolt and picked my phone off the floor. The door scraped open. I shone the light inside. The room was piled with old furniture, suitcases, crates of empty bottles covered in grime.

'It's all right,' I said, imagining she was hiding behind something. 'You can come out.'

'Help,' she cried. 'Can't you hurry?'

I ventured more deeply inside. 'I can't see you. Where are you?' I stepped over a toppled stack of old cane chairs. Tracked the light around the room, which was little larger than a standard garage. Now it was me who was calling: 'Where are you?'

'I'm here! I'm inside here!' Her voice rose in panic. She began pounding against something. I followed the sound to a credenza stood against the wall. Thinking she might actually be inside, I opened the bottom doors, but the shelves were packed with old crockery.

'*Where the hell are you?*'

'Here!' The crockery rattled with each thud.

I reached behind the credenza. My hand came away damp, sticky with fresh concrete. I tucked my gun back inside my waistband and with some effort pulled the credenza aside.

Behind, there was a messy patch of concrete the size and shape of a doorway. I scraped at it. Beneath was breezeblock.

'You're in there?'

'Yes, help me!' I could clearly see the wall tremble with each thud.

'Who are you?'

'Laura. Laura Guerrera. Who are you?'

It took a moment to register: '*Laura Guerrera?* The lover of Pasquale Grande?'

'Arturo said he would kill him.'

'First, let's get you out of there.' I pushed the block but it wouldn't shift. I dragged the credenza further back and began scraping away the wet concrete with my hands. Meanwhile, Laura was talking, gibbering really, already half-crazed by her captivity.

'He said he would wall me in, like they used to with witches, unfaithful women. He said he would do the work on the house and no one would know any better, that they would find me hundreds of years from now, a skeleton. That I'd have gnawed off my own foot. He . . .'

I began to kick at the breezeblock. Finally, I felt some movement. 'Get back,' I called, preparing to give the wall an almighty boot.

Then the lights came on.

Chapter 40

Light filled the storeroom but there was no source as such inside – instead it was bright enough in the corridor to illuminate the room through the open door.

'Why have you stopped?'

'Someone's coming.'

'It must be my husband, Arturo, he . . .'

'Be quiet. *Quiet.*' I drew my gun, waited. There was little doubt he was coming my way. I could hear his heavy footsteps along the corridor. And with that wide-open doorway, he would clearly know where to look.

I heard Arturo pause, the click of a torch. Was he armed? This was a man who had knocked down his wife's lover then walled the wife up in a cellar, so I wasn't going to take any chances.

'You may as well show yourself.' I heard him step inside the room. 'Look – there's nothing of value here. If you show yourself, I'll let you take what you can carry. I was going to clear it out anyway.' The light flashed lazily around the room. 'And if you don't show yourself, I'll simply lock you inside here and then what will you do?' The scuff of steps nearby.

The light fixed on a spot at a right angle from my hiding place.

A phone began to ring.

My phone.

I looked down: Vesuvio.

'*Gotcha*.' But Arturo's voice was no longer distant. It was in my ear. I swivelled around. My face was burning.

And I was blind.

I remember screaming with the shock of it, cringing against that concrete-wet wall thinking my face had burst into flames and trying to beat them out. But it wasn't that – it was pepper spray. As I had stood with my gun at the ready facing the door, he had somehow managed to creep up behind me and shoot a jet straight into my face.

The blows were coming quick, sharp, heavy. Kicks to my legs, my gut, my head, anything exposed.

Forcing open my chilli-flooded eyes I caught sight of a phantom, a hellish creature bearing down on me through my screams, her screams.

A heel hammered my head, cracking it against the stone floor.

I raised my arms to protect it, and received a sharp stamp in the ribs. There was a definite, wood-like crack.

'Please . . . stop.' But this wasn't going to stop. I knew it – the kicks just kept coming, delivered in deliberating silence. I would twist one way then another and he would choose his mark. He was going to keep at it for as long as it took; until I was unable to move at all. And still, he would keep going.

Which was when I felt it – unyielding against my spine – the rigidity of gunmetal.

I had to risk it – I withdrew my arms from my head, reached out.

As he raised a heel above my face, I gripped the Beretta and swung it upward.

Did he waver then? Did his arms begin to rise in a sign of surrender?

I pulled the trigger. Once, twice.

The Beretta bucked in my hand; the sound hammered around the room. But still I heard it – the dead weight of a human body.

'What happened? Hello? *Hello?*'

I lay there, pointing the gun into the empty space.

My gaze finally drifted downward, chilli tears burning my cheeks. Blurred, veiled by blue-grey gunsmoke – a body.

I began to achieve some definition: a round-faced middle-aged man with cropped grey hair and matching bristles. One of my bullets had entered his head just beneath the right eyebrow, puncturing his skull and popping his eyeball.

Strung from its tendons, it rested on the bridge of his nose pointing incuriously at the floor.

And beyond the post-percussive ring, Laura Guerrera calling:

'Anyone? *Anyone?*'

My throat caught with the cordite.

'It's all right,' I said.

Continuing to train the gun at the body, I stretched out a foot, gave it a prod.

It didn't stir.

'Dan! Where are you? Dan!' I heard Dolores come in.

'Christ! What happened? Dan, put the gun down. *Put the fucking gun down, Dan.* Fuck. Are you all right?'

'Does it look like it?'

'Shit! Who is he?'

'Arturo – husband of Laura Guerrera. The guy who flattened Pasquale Grande.'

'*Jesus*, what happened to your face?' Dolores picked up a palm-sized aerosol. 'Sabre,' she said. 'Super-strong. He zapped you? I passed a sink on the way in, let's see if the tap works.'

'Please!' The banging resumed.

'What's that?'

The tap was working and although my eyes remained swollen into slits, they began to recover serviceable, if imperfect, vision.

'You're bleeding.'

'Where?'

Dolores reached up to touch my cheek, then traced her finger up to the side of my head. She winced. It came away smeared with blood.

'Bad?'

'You might need a couple of stitches.'

I wiped my face with the front of my shirt. I could hear sirens. This time they weren't drifting away.

'When I heard the gunfire . . .'

'You did well,' I said. 'Could you go outside, meet them? We don't want any more shooting.'

'Yeah,' she said, 'best avoided.'

'And Dolores?'

'What?'

'Thank you.'

I waited until she had disappeared back up the steps before going to the carpentry bench. I emptied an old plastic bag containing screws. I placed a hand inside and picked up a claw hammer.

I went back along the corridor, into the gloomy storeroom where, my vision being what it was, I walked straight into the chairs.

'Is anyone there?'

'Help is coming, Laura,' I called. 'Don't worry – it's going to be all right.' I turned Arturo's corpse over with my foot. There was the shot that had hit him in the face – that eyeball flopped onto his cheekbone – and another stain spread across his chest. Not bad, I thought, for an amateur.

I picked up the hammer and pressed its flat face against my bloody cheek. I closed his right hand around the handle and set it beside him.

I stood up, satisfied with my handiwork. I pocketed the plastic bag.

'Are you still there?' asked the woman.

'Still here.' I pushed the credenza further back and began to kick at the wall. A block shifted. I gave it a further three kicks until I was finally able to push it inwards, leaving a rectangular hole. A pale face instantly appeared against it.

'Please.' She coughed. 'Just get me out.'

'Now what's all this mess?' said a voice I had grown to know too well.

Chapter 41

'I'm sorry, Dan,' said Dolores. 'Honestly, I called the Carabinieri.'

'Oh, you know those plods.' Commissario Miranda stepped over the scattered chairs, shone a Maglite onto the corpse of Arturo. 'Well, well, well. You did him good and proper. An eye for an eye, eh? Where's the gun?'

I pointed to the floor by the wall. She swung the light towards it, then at Laura Guerrera.

'*Mamma mia*. I thought you were having me on! But, signora! I've never seen such a thing!'

'Please help me,' said Laura. She looked as if she was about to pass out.

A pair of uniformed cops entered, one carrying a sledge-hammer.

'Signora,' said the commissario. 'You'd better stand back.'

Laura disappeared into the darkness. The police pushed the credenza fully aside. It toppled in a crash of crockery.

A cop swung the sledgehammer against the wall. The breeze block shot through like a Jenjo piece.

Another thump, another block gone. 'Hold on,' said the

other one. 'I think we can do the rest by hand.'

We watched as they dismantled the rest of the wall. The stink of human faeces began to mix with the lingering edge of gunpowder.

A crude man-size hole was made. Holding his torch up to his chest, the first officer ducked inside.

'I'm going to need those bolt cutters,' he called.

While the other cop went back out, we ducked into the cell.

Laura Guerrera was sat on the floor barefoot in a filthy flannel dressing gown, her ankle chained in a rudimentary but effective manacle to the wall. The commissario went to crouch by her, took her grubby hand. 'You're safe now,' she said. 'He won't hurt you any more.' Nevertheless, Laura eyed the hole as if expecting Arturo to reappear at any moment. She flinched as the officer bearing the bolt cutters made his entrance.

I ducked back out to give them some room.

A snap, a sob. Laura Guerrera finally emerged through the hole.

'Take the signora into the fresh air,' said the commissario. 'And call an ambulance.' Cradling Laura between them, the cops carried her away.

The commissario put on a pair of gloves and reached down to bag the Beretta. She straightened up, came to join me by the body.

'Arturo, her husband,' I said. 'He found out about her affair.'

'You know, back in 1980, when I started out in the force, this kind of thing was considered legal. Well,' the commissario shrugged. 'Maybe not *this* – even then they might have considered this a little . . . *excessive*. But "honour killing"? "Crimes of passion", we used to call them then, and let the fellow off with a slap on the wrist. Just to remind us women of our place.' She gave the corpse a kick. 'You're not going to deny this one, I hope?' I shook my head. 'You'll claim "legitimate self-defence"?'

'I would say so, wouldn't you?'

'So, your story is . . . he sprayed you, then came at you with the hammer?'

'Something like that. It was pretty confused.'

'Hence that nasty cut on your head. And look – there's some blood on the hammer, too. You poor boy. You should go to the hospital, get checked out.'

'I was on my way.'

'Get them to photo you for my report.' She held up the bag. 'The gun isn't yours, I presume?'

'The Comandante's.'

'You're lucky it's cut and dried, then.' We stood facing each other. 'Well, what are you waiting for? Get yourself stitched up before you bleed all over my crime scene.'

Chapter 42

We were back at the car when I returned Vesuvio's call.

'What happened?' he said. 'Did I disturb you?'

'Just tell me.'

'I've found her. Stella.'

'Where? How is she?'

'She's . . . okay, but turns out she was also affected. She's actually at Sant'Orsola – Ludovisi Ward.'

'We're on our way.' I started up the car.

'Are you sure you're okay to drive?' said Dolores. 'Your eyes . . .'

'They're better now.'

'If you've got a fractured skull . . .' She pointed tentatively to my forehead, which had been rather inexpertly patched by the cops with a gauze and blue tape.

'I'm fine.' I checked the mirror before pulling out, wincing from the pain in my ribs. Cracked? Broken? Well, I was still breathing.

'Imagine that,' said Dolores. 'Being walled up, left to starve in the dark. It's the stuff of nightmares.'

'Or fantasies,' I said. 'It takes imagination to come up with something that cruel. I'd like to think enough imagination to hatch our plot, but I don't see it. This was only ever about Pasquale, Laura and Arturo – their toxic little triangle. It had nothing to do with me, or the professors.'

Dolores looked at me. 'You don't feel bad about it, then? Killing Arturo?'

'He was trying to kill me. I just . . . did what I had to.' I thought about it. It left me cold, frankly. 'I'll worry about it later.'

'You put the hammer there, didn't you. That's why you stayed behind in the *cantina*.'

We passed the shuttered *osteria*, the gateposts. I took a left at the petrol station onto the main road.

Seeing that she wasn't going to get a response, Dolores continued: 'You'd better have those photos done, though. Like the commissario told you.'

'How the hell did she happen to turn up, anyway? You called the Carabinieri, right?'

'Yup. Maybe they had some arrangement – they divvy up areas sometimes for emergency calls.'

'Last time I checked, the commissario wasn't a first responder.'

We drove on to the Viale, began to circumnavigate the city.

'Look,' said Dolores. Outside a turn-of-the-century mansion, veiled by scaffolding, hung a banner: *IN VENDITA. EdificioBo SpA.*

'Small world,' I said.

'Worlds within worlds,' said Dolores. 'Bellario was looking for somewhere to stash his ill-gotten gains from the taxman, and probably from his wife, too. So who did he find? Birds of a feather . . .'

'Crap together.'

Chapter 43

'Ward' did not do Reparto Ludovisi justice. Set back from the main thoroughfare of the hospital campus and hidden behind a modern ten-storey building, what the building lacked in height, it made up for in scale – we crossed a cobbled car park towards a classic Bolognese building of the late Renaissance.

Handsome porticoes fronted the two-storey structure that must have stretched for a hundred metres either side of its steps, the entrance topped by a functioning clock tower.

We stepped into an atrium more like that of a small town hall or museum, busy with statues, plaques and paintings of benefactors – mainly, by the look of things, cardinals. At the marble reception desk we were told to go right.

'Do we need a room number?' I asked. The receptionist shook his head.

'Just go in the first door along.'

The long portico was empty except for a line of white wooden benches facing a barren courtyard. The sunlight hurt my still-sensitive eyes. It was unforgivingly hot, lifeless.

Dolores pushed open the door.

***

I was accustomed to modern Italian hospitals, which tended to eschew large wards for two- or four-bed rooms. But here we had travelled back in time. I followed Dolores into a wood-beamed building the size of a church.

The ecclesiastical effect was heightened by the clear-glass cathedral windows set at either end of the building, constituting the only natural light. Running high along the sides of the otherwise whitewashed walls were biblical scenes, faded with age, while here at the entrance we faced a man-sized wooden crucifix, the stencilled gothic script above reading *Domine non sum dignus ut intres sub tectum meum* and below, *sed tantum dic verbo et sanabitur anima mea.*

'Lord, I am not worthy that you should enter under my roof,' said Dolores, 'but only say the word and my soul shall be healed.'

A dozen beds ran down either side of the ward, spaced to modern requirements and with the usual hospital apparatus between. Strip lighting hung low on wires attached to the ancient beams, but otherwise little must have changed since those words had been inscribed.

It was almost as hushed inside the ward as out. We crossed the scrubbed flagstones to the nursing station.

'Stella Amore?' The nurse checked the computer.

'Bed twenty.'

We walked along the aisle, the beds on either side of us numbered. Stella's would be near the end.

A set of blue blinds were placed mid-way between her bed and that of her neighbour, an old man laid on his back like a cadaver, so it wasn't until we were almost there that I saw her: that fine profile tilted to the side. It now turned towards me.

'I was just saying,' she said softly. 'You'll do anything to keep me here.' She smiled weakly as she began to sit herself up. Vesuvio was in the chair beside her.

'Man.' He stood up. 'What the hell happened to you?'

'It's nothing.'

'You look like you've been hit by a truck.'

'Are you all right?' asked Stella.

'Really, it's nothing.'

'If that's nothing, I'd hate to see something.'

'The important thing is that you're all right. But what happened to you? We were trying to call . . .'

'The phone's lost somewhere,' she said. 'Must have been when I was with Chiara. It actually happened when I got her into the ambulance, that I began to feel ill myself, as if I was having some kind of migraine.'

'And how is Chiara?'

'Not so good. Suspected stroke. She's in the ICU. They think it was food poisoning.' Stella caught my glance at Vesuvio – obviously he hadn't told her what had really happened.

'What is it, Daniel?'

Vesuvio's phone rang. 'I'm sorry,' he said. 'I have to take this.' Dolores also took the opportunity to disappear.

I took the vacated seat. 'It may be connected with the case I've been investigating.'

'Your dead music professor?'

'They think it may be the same poison.'

'Poison? Not *food* poisoning? But *why* would they target the show?'

'That's the big question, although another professor was among the victims – Alberto Fini.'

'*Alberto*, oh.' Stella looked as if she had suffered a blow. 'And he's . . .'

'Dead. I'm sorry.' Now I realised why Vesuvio had kept mum. Tears toppled down Stella's cheeks.

'He was one of my greatest champions – he was my tutor at the Accademia, and helped organise my first show. It was he who pressured me to enter the Baltic, put in a word with the organisers . . .'

I handed her some tissues. 'You don't know anyone, then, who might have wanted to harm him?'

'Why would anyone want to hurt him? He was the nicest . . . It just doesn't make sense.'

'Revenge? Ambition? Someone certainly seems to have it in for Bologna's academics.'

'I just can't believe he's gone.'

I sat there as it sank in. Finally, she looked at me above the tissues. 'I'm sorry, Daniel. I should have told you about the prize. I'd planned to, I could just never find the right time. And I didn't want all that . . . *shittiness* to hang over us in the short time we had together.'

'We can stay in touch,' I said. 'I can come and visit.'

'Yes, that would be nice.'

Now sweet nothings didn't seem to matter so much. I raised Stella's hand to my lips like a count in a Russian novel. We talked for a little of trivial things, before I made my excuses and said goodbye.

Chapter 44

Dolores was sitting alone on a bench in the atrium opposite a bronze bust of a stern-looking cardinal. I lowered myself carefully down beside her.

'Vesuvio?' I asked.

'It was from his wife. He told her he was at the studio.'

'Not for the first time, I suspect.'

'You should get those photos done, Dan. Get checked out.'

I felt a sharp twinge in my side. 'Maybe I should. In the meantime, you follow up with our missing stats professor, Farese. See if you can't smoke him out. When I'm done here, I'll head back to the Accademia delle Belle Arti and sniff around. Strike while the iron's hot.'

As we were standing up to leave, Dolores muttered: 'Well, at least one mystery's solved.'

'I'm sorry?'

'The bloke.' She meant the bust. *Ludovico Ludovisi, Archbishop of Bologna, 1595-1632.*

'The one who persecuted the nuns,' I said. 'But what's "solved"?'

'Remember when we were trying to work out what might

have happened in 1632 for the Faidate to hide all that stuff away in the *cantina*? Nothing stood out, but here's something – the death of the *archbishop*, although heaven knows if it's really related.'

I looked at the bust. With his 'cavalier' moustache and beard, Ludovico Ludovisi didn't look so very different from Guido Delfillo, if somewhat better fed.

'Have you noticed,' I said. 'He was only thirty-seven when he died. Young even for those days. Any idea what of?'

'Hold on,' Dolores checked her phone. 'It says here: "after a prolonged battle with gout, his heart stopped". Can gout kill you?'

'I don't believe so,' I said.

'Hold on. It says here, "no".'

'Do you remember that list you showed me in the university library? The order written in Latin from the infirmary at Santa Cristina? I don't suppose you took a photo of it, did you?'

'As it happens . . .' She brought it up on her phone.

'Can you send it to me.'

I took a closer look at the yellowed list. It still meant nothing. 'Call Doctor Mattani,' I said. Dolores frowned but dialled the coroner's number.

'What am I supposed to say? Oh, hello, Doctor. Did I wake you? I'm sorry, it's just that Daniel Leicester wanted me to call you.' She winced.

'I'd like a word.'

'He'd like a word.' I took Dolores' phone.

'I'm sorry, Doctor, but Dolores is about to read you a list of items that were procured from the Botanical Gardens . . .

No, please. Please just listen, this is serious.' I passed Dolores back her phone, then held up my own.

'Go on,' I said.

She put it on speaker. 'At the top it says: Officinalis.'

'That simply means natural medicine,' the doctor said.

'Rosmarinus officinalis.'

'Rosemary.'

'Salvia, oh,' said Dolores. 'That's sage.'

'Correct. What is this? A damn recipe?'

'Cinchona?'

'Quinine.'

'Euphrasia.'

'Another plant, I think it was also known as Eyebright. It's for treating rashes.'

'Melissa.'

'Lemon balm. Fantastic. You know, I've just worked for twenty hours solid. I only got to bed four hours ago . . .'

'Paeonia, that would be peony,' said Dolores. 'Zingiber, ginger. Taraxacum?'

'Damned dandelion!'

'Gelsemium.'

There was a pause. *'Gelsemium?'*

'That's right.'

There was another long silence. 'What is it, Doctor?' I said.

'It's a creeper from China. It's exceedingly rare. And ordered from the Botanical Gardens, you say? By whom?'

Dolores looked questioningly at me. I shook my head. 'What is it about this Gelsemium, Doctor?' A long sigh.

'All right – there was an accusation that it was used in the death of a Russian dissident in the UK a decade or so ago, but they conducted very stringent tests which came back negative. I also remember reading a paper about traces in the stomach of a poisoned Chinese businessman, but it is so rare as to be . . .'

'Did you test for it?' I asked.

'Honestly, Daniel – it wouldn't have even occurred to us, it's such an immensely rare plant and would entail an entirely independent process of . . .'

'Then check, please,' I said. 'Straight away.' I signalled Dolores to end the call. 'Remind me,' I said to her. 'Before I asked you to follow up with Farnese, who was the next dead professor on your list?'

'Dauni. Biological, Geological and Environmental Science.'

'Where was he?'

'He lived in San Lazzaro.'

'I don't mean that,' I said. 'Where is the department of Biological, Geological and Environmental Science?'

She scrolled through her phone. 'Er, well, it's spread all over. There's mineralogy in Zamboni, Geology, too. Biology in Via Selmi. Botany in Via Irnerio.' She looked at me. 'Hold on, Via Inerio. That must mean the Botanical Gardens.'

'And Dauni was?' I didn't really need to hear the answer.

'A botanist,' said Dolores.

Chapter 45

We drove along Via Irnerio, a busy boulevard running parallel to Belle Arti.

Dolores fed me information thick and fast: 'So, apparently Gelsemium is also known as "heartbreak glass" and its use dates back to China in the seventh century. It's a yellow creeper but it actually looks quite like daffodils. Pretty, no?'

'I can't look now, I'm driving.'

'It's super-deadly but also extremely hard to detect. Actually the doctor got it around the wrong way, the British police decided that even though this Russian dissident was young and fit he had simply died of natural causes – drum roll – a heart attack. It was only *three years later* during the inquest, that "a special test by toxicology experts at Royal Kew Botanical Gardens" found traces of *Gelsemium elegans*. They linked it to a case of a Chinese man who had a heart attack after a contract killer had put it in his – get this – cat stew! Well, I supposed he deserved what he got! It says here: "just a few drops in the bloodstream can trigger cardiac arrest, making it appear that the victim suffered a heart attack".'

'Let's not get too excited,' I said. 'We don't even know if the plant's there, yet.'

'You always sound strangely calm when you're the opposite.'

'This garden,' I said. 'I've only been there once . . .'

Dolores looked back at her phone. 'Founded in 1568,' she said. 'Imagine – the same plants used by the nuns still there to this day.'

Now I looked at her.

'I would stick to the Latin and Greek.'

'What's that meant to mean?'

'Well, the seeds certainly might have survived, making them the great-great-grandchildren of the origi— Hold on.' I pulled into a space outside the black railings marking the border of the gardens. Further along, near the entrance, was a police car and, standing beside it, Commissario Rita Miranda and a uniformed police officer.

We walked towards them. The uniformed officer looked familiar. She asked the commissario something, and took off her hat. Although her dark hair was pulled tightly back, I realised it was the woman who had been following me.

'That's right,' the commissario told me. 'We have "trainees", too. Constable Zen still has something to learn, but then we all have to start somewhere, and let's face it, Sherlock, you're hardly the toughest target, especially with that big blue plaster on your noggin. Didn't I tell you to get stitched up?' She nodded at Dolores. 'Have you ever considered a career with the Polizia di Stato, young lady? I've been impressed so far.'

'I've been on the wrong end of your batons too often.'

'And precisely how long have you been listening in on us?' I asked.

'You really thought it was just a coincidence you bumped into Guido Delfillo in the holding cell? It was wired for sound, young man, and we've been keeping a tab on you ever since. I know I may seem a little bit impatient at times but I have another characteristic, too – I learn.'

'So you want to claim credit for this one all on your own?'

'Does it really matter to you?'

'Not at all.'

We began to make our way along the gravel path towards the two-storey botany building with Dolores and Constable Zen bringing up the rear.

'Have you let Guido out yet?'

'To be honest, with all this running around, I had quite forgotten about him. There's no hurry, is there? After all, he's safe and sound in *La Dozza*.'

'And Amanda's parents – will you inform them there was more to it than suicide?'

'Let's see where this leads first, shall we? After all, that poor young girl is certainly not going anywhere.'

Set amid its gardens, the botany building had the feeling of an Emilian country villa. We went up the steps onto the porch. There was no one at the reception desk, but when we asked for the director's office, a pair of students sat smoking on the steps directed us upstairs.

Another quiet corridor. It was as if the entire department had already left for the beach, or perhaps in their case, the rain forest. The shabby walls were lined with framed antique prints of plants, roots and all. At the far end of the corridor was an open door and, visible through the large windows, a view of treetops.

The office of the director was also empty – of human life, at least. The shelves were lined not with books but plants. The furnishing occupied a pair of spaces between archipelagos of large-leafed greenery – one a trio of armchairs and a coffee table, another the large Victorian oak desk, backed by the same set of flags I had seen in the office of the dean at the conservatory.

'Can I help you?' A middle-aged lady stood at the doorway.

'Excuse me,' I said. 'Are you the director?'

'Cinghiale? Oh no,' she said.

'And they are . . .?'

'Oh, he's not here?' She peered around as if expecting to find him behind a monumental palm. 'I only left him a few moments ago. Perhaps he just popped out. And you are?' We told her. 'Oh! I see – well, if you could just wait, I'm sure he will be along in a minute.' She headed back along the corridor.

The view from the office, I realised, looked down not just upon the garden but upon the gravel pathway along which we had arrived at the building.

'He could have seen us coming.'

'That's quite a leap,' said the commissario. 'I grant you, as a possible source of the poison, this is of interest.'

'Along with the fact that someone appears to have been murdering university professors, and Cinghiale is one of those who would have benefited.'

'It's an interesting theory,' she said. 'And you were right to have thought it would have taken us some time to get around to. Certainly, before the event at Santa Cristina I would have taken some persuading. But it remains a theory, Signor

Leicester. My principal reason for being here is to speak to the prof and establish whether the poisoner could have gained access to this substance, or anything else obscure enough to avoid the toxicology apparatus.' She checked her watch. 'But I haven't got all day.' We both looked at the secretary clacking back towards us along the corridor.

'He hasn't reappeared yet?'

'Could you try calling him?' said the commissario.

'Oh, the professor doesn't possess a telephone.' She smiled apologetically. 'He can be a little eccentric. *Academics*.'

'Where else could we find him, then?'

'Well, if he's not here, he could be anywhere. '

'Where would you look if you had to find him in a hurry?' I asked.

'I suppose, if I had to try anywhere, it would be the gardens.'

The sun was high in the sky, it must have reached forty degrees, and the high pitch of the cicadas sounded like a warning.

We heeded it, lingering in the shade of the portico.

Rita Miranda turned to the two 'trainees'. 'Zen,' she said, 'you go left. Signorina,' she meant Dolores, 'you—'

'I don't take orders from you.'

'Why don't you head off to the right,' I said. 'But don't approach the professor. Call me if you spot him.'

'How do I know what he looks like?' She held up her phone. 'I couldn't find anything on here.'

'I suspect you'll know when you see him. He'll look . . . *professory*.'

'And what about you?'

'I'm going to have a quick nose around inside,' I said. 'And you?' I asked the commissario.

'I'll do the important work of guarding the perimeter.' She pointed to a bench along the path. 'And make sure he doesn't escape. Or catch him when he comes back from his coffee.'

'Privileges of seniority,' I said. 'Okay, we'll report back, boss.'

'That's the spirit.'

I returned to the building and, looking back to check the commissario was actually where she said she would be (she was scrolling through her phone), I slipped up the stairs. I found the secretary in a room adjacent to the director's office.

'Tell me,' I said. 'There must be a greenhouse where the poisonous plants are kept – where is it?'

'In the secure area around the back – there's a fence. You have to access it from inside this building, but he won't be there.'

'Why not?'

'Because,' she pointed at a rack, 'he didn't take the key.'

'Where can I find it?'

'Like I said . . .'

'*Signora*, humour me.'

The entrance to the greenhouse was via a laboratory on the ground floor that seemed more like a vegetarian kitchen with its long, dark wooden benches crowded with plant life. Glass flasks and cylinders were dotted between the foliage, some suspended on metal stands above the greenery and connected by yellow rubber tubing, but the containers were all empty, as was the laboratory.

It was clear enough where the secure greenhouse was – above a set of double swing doors a red and black sign read DANGER.

I pushed them open into a white, canvas-walled tunnel, its wooden platform sloping gently downwards to a metal door. As I made my way towards it, my steps sounded my approach.

The door appeared closed, but I discovered it had simply been pulled to. As I suspected – there had been another set of keys.

I took hold of the handle and, gently, began to pull.

Chapter 46

I dodged leering green leaves weighed down by the humidity. The scratch of my feet on the sandy path amplified that jungle silence – the sense I was far from alone, that all other animate life had settled down to wait for the tiger to pounce.

While outside it was full day, the greenhouse seemed set to perpetual dusk: the metal blinds running the length of the long glass roof were closed.

The only natural light entered through side windows largely obscured by flora set on broad metal tables – a riot of colour ranging from innocent-looking daisy-like flowers to more sophisticated stems sprouting sinister purple petals and hostile, blood-red buds. The glass behind them was crisscrossed with toughening wire as if it were some kind of plant prison.

This outer path skirted a clump of larger plants in ancient terracotta pots and tubs. I reached the end of the greenhouse and followed it around, doing my best to avoid the touch of the leaves on my exposed skin. But it wasn't only big plants along this trail. There were what I imagined were even more exotic species – yellow and purple monsters rising out of the turf, vines of alluring, but also certainly deadly, red and black berries; pretty yellow daffodil-like blossoms wound around ordinary-looking trees I couldn't help feeling were being silently throttled.

A whisper of smoke emerged from behind one such trunk.

'You found me then. Indeed you did.'

He was sat on a brown metal heater in a little alcove that had been created between the plants, puffing at his pipe.

'Roberto,' I said. 'So this is where you get to when you're not in Comix.'

There was a puff of grey that might have been a chuckle.

'I apologise for the warmth, but my children are quite particular about the temperature – we have to shield most of them from direct sunlight, especially during the summer, hence the roof blinds. We actually need these things,' he drummed upon the heater, 'to maintain the correct tempera-ture. I've been asking for a proper electrical system for some time instead of these old paraffin stoves, but it was not to be. And in the end I suppose they served their purpose.' He took a couple more puffs. 'Indeed they did.'

'How's Angelo, by the way? When we met in *Pronto Soccorso* you said something about his heart.'

'Better. Not too happy. Not at all, no.'

I gave him a long look. 'I wanted to ask you about a plant, Gelsemium. We thought it might be linked to the poisoning at Santa Cristina. Come to think of it, if the poison was, as we suspect, contained in a batch of ice cream, you were digging into it along with Angelo and the late Professor Fini. How did . . .?'

'Acquired immunity! I forgot about that – the effect I

mean, on the others. Over-calculated!' He plucked off a yellow blossom and popped it in his mouth. 'See? No effect. Force of habit, self-medication – ancient cure for migraine, and extremely powerful painkiller – so powerful, in fact, that it will kill you as effectively as it does the pain. Your Arthur Conan Doyle famously experimented with it on himself, but had to give up when he almost died. But, you know, dainty *Gelsemium elegans* here is hardly alone, oh no. You see this one?' He stroked a quite lovely-looking flower with lilac petals. 'Anyone can purchase it, plant it. And why wouldn't you? Isn't it rather lovely? Yet all parts of dear oleander are packed full of cardiac glycosides, quite deadly. People have even fallen ill from its honey! Or this,' he stroked a green pod lined with red beans, 'the humble rosary pea – it's named because its seeds are commonly used to produce rosary brace-lets. Yet a single seed contains enough abrin to shut down a man's organs in four days.'

Roberto seemed to be enjoying what we both knew would be his final lecture. I reached behind for my Beretta, but of course, I had surrendered it to the commissario. Little mind: unless he was armed himself, I couldn't see him getting past me, and if he tried, I would take great pleasure in seeing how many of those yellow plants or red seeds I could stuff down his throat, acquired immunity or no.

'But they're not all poisonous in here, of course,' he con-tinued. 'That is usually just a by-product of their struggle to get noticed, you see? The real plants with murder on their mind are not deadly to humans at all, like *Drosera rotun-difolia* here.' He pointed to a fragile little magenta-coloured plant shaped like a sombrero, its hairs sparkling with dew.

'She uses her sticky sugar to trap bugs before consuming them. Or this lovely *Nepenthes truncata* specimen,' he nodded to a fleshy, upright plant the size and shape of a small vase, 'who invites small rodents inside only to trap them – they're unable to climb up her slippery walls. She dissolves them in her digestive enzymes. We drop a mouse in on her birthday, just to keep her happy. Which reminds me.' He dug out a set of keys from his pocket and clicked a plastic fob. I heard the metal door clunk closed. He winked. 'Have to keep the heat in.'

'But why did you do it, Roberto?' I said. 'I understand why you might have wanted to get rid of your boss, but the other professors? What on earth did you have against them?'

Roberto's jaw worked around the stem of the pipe as if he was chewing upon it. 'It's simply the law of the jungle,' he said. 'Indeed it is.'

'What the hell are you talking about?'

'Here you are, young man, confronted by it, but you don't see it – why? Because of their stillness, their silence. One talks about the jungle, but they *are* the jungle. My children are struggling as much as any jaguar or tiger, bed bug or bacteria, plumber or university professor – to get to the top, to thrive.' He frowned at his pipe. It had gone out.

'You're talking in riddles.'

'The late Professor Dauni, my predecessor, was a very mediocre scholar. All show, despite the dirt beneath his fingernails, which you can be certain he made sure no one missed. Alberto Fini? Utterly undeserving. Anyone could see that. No great loss to the world of academia.'

'And the others – you didn't always use poison, did you?

Sometimes you resorted to your bare hands. That's right, isn't it?'

'As I said, sometimes the most deadly plants aren't poisonous at all. Others use more direct methods.'

'But why did you do it, Roberto?' I repeated. 'Poison the other people at the event?'

He lit a match, drew in the smoke. 'Isn't it obvious? For the garden to thrive, it is sometimes necessary to prune back flowers as well as pull up weeds.'

The flame of the match had almost reached his fingertips.

He dropped it.

Chapter 47

Roberto ignited. The heat of the fire forced me back through the plants. I fell hard onto my back. The man must have soaked himself in paraffin.

Yet, as the flames flared, he stayed sitting there, his hand clenched around the bowl of the pipe, as unmoving as one of his plants, his face impassive, his gaze fixed curiously upon me.

I looked for a fire extinguisher but there was nothing. I certainly couldn't get any closer. I was forced to look on as his clothes blackened, a blue halo consuming his white hair. And yet, even as the fire came to utterly engulf him, Professor Roberto Cinghiale continued to sit erect, his gaze remaining set upon me.

A little voice whispered: *'Better keep the heat in.'*

Because it wasn't just Roberto. Fire was tearing through the rest of the greenhouse, blocking my exit. He must have doused the whole place with paraffin. He was going up with his children, and planning to take me with them.

I scrambled on top of a bench and pushed away the plants, sat so my feet faced the toughened glass. I began to kick at the window as the smoke closed in.

It finally shattered.

It bent.

But it damn well wouldn't break.

I was in darkness. The fumes forced my eyes closed, began to find their way up my nose and down the back of my throat.

I kept kicking, kicking . . . Only it wasn't the window, but the table that finally gave. Listed like a boat upset by waves, tilted . . .

I was tipped onto the floor, the table collapsing on top of me.

The very ground was shaking. There was an almighty crack and the roof collapsed, glass smashing against the table top and exploding around me.

I was in the darkness. I wasn't breathing. I wasn't thinking. Yet somehow I continued to kick. A reflex action, a silent protest – I would not go gently into this night.

Something gave.

By then I was too far gone to know what, only that I was being wrenched from death's black mouth; that I was scrambling away, pursued by its billowing, noxious breath.

I was on my knees coughing my guts up beside Dolores and the commissario, their legs outstretched as if this was a picnic, or a concert in the park. The stage: a fire raging from those glass ruins, a black plume smearing the blue.

Alarm bells. Sirens.

'Earthquake,' someone said, and so it was: leaves were still floating from the trees. I watched a chimney collapse, brickwork slaloming down the roof of the botany building to crash through another glass ceiling.

But I kept returning to that blackened figure sat in the middle of it all even as it turned to cinders; still casting curious, hollow eyes upon me.

Chapter 48

They discharged us together – once Gelsemium had been confirmed as the cause of the poisoning it was simply a question of monitoring Rose, while I had been taken in for smoke inhalation along with superficial cuts and burns and the pain in my side which did turn out to be a pair of cracked ribs. There was little they could actually do about them – they would have to heal themselves.

The Comandante proposed whisking us straight down to Cesenatico for our 'convalescence' but neither of us was in the mood to be rushed. We needed time to come to terms with everything that had happened, and so did our city: following the earthquake, Bologna had seemed as bruised and battered as I had, although, like me, most of the damage had been superficial. They were still sweeping up shattered terracotta tiles, stray bricks and plant pots as we returned to the Faidate Residence. Having said that, standing in the courtyard, even I could make out the additional tilt to the roofline. We would need Vesuvio's cash to literally help shore us up.

'Have you seen this?' Angelo held up the front page of the

Carlino. Although he had been admitted to hospital, he had grown bored and discharged himself. 'They're talking about prosecuting the seismologists for getting it wrong – it says here they were calling them "aftershocks" when they were actually "foreshocks"! Poor bastards! What were they supposed to do? Consult the earthquake god Poseidon?'

'It does seem a little harsh,' I said.

We were sat in the portico outside Comix, sipping *caffè shakerato.* It felt a bit mad dogs and Englishmen in this heat, but I had spotted Angelo when I came to meet Rose, who was working on a graphic novel idea with some friends inside. I had asked him about Roberto but he hadn't had much to say. Behind that bushy beard, his mouth tightened, his eyes dipped. I thought I understood – it had to be hard to mourn a friend who had almost killed you.

'I didn't know him so well, in truth. In fact,' he glanced up at me, 'well, obviously, it turns out, hardly at all. Roberto came here from the botany department, I came here to work. We were both on our own. I suppose he sort of latched on to me. There seemed no harm. He seemed,' Angelo shrugged, '*innocuous.*'

There was banging on the window. It was one of the girls. Valentina, the one who had fainted at the show, was to be the writer of the girls' 'novel', which would depict the vicissitudes of the nuns of Santa Cristina, culminating in their poisoning of Archbishop Ludovico Ludovisi. It seemed a pretty ambitious project, but hell, I would buy a copy.

'Okay! I'm coming!' Angelo rolled his eyes and got to his feet. He had agreed to help them on their storyboard.

I followed him inside where it was cool, and sat at a table, checking out the crowded bookshelf. Included among the volumes of *Dylan Dog*, *Topolino*, and *Corto Maltese*, I noticed a hardbound copy of Duke Magnesio stories. I pulled it down and flicked through. I was reasonably familiar with the eponymous hero, especially since Angelo had sold the rights and the Duke had begun to crop up on T-shirts, rucksacks and baseball caps, but apart from glancing occasionally at his strips syndicated in *Internazionale*, I had never bothered reading any of the stories he was best known for.

The hardback contained half-a-dozen Duke Magnesio tales, each around twenty pages long and featuring Ignazio, the owner of a bar in the small, fictitious Sicilian town of Rombulo, who serves up endless coffees while his clients share their problems with him, or each other. With his long, pendulous nose, drooping bushy black eyebrows and chocolate-drop eyes, Ignazio rarely reacts to their tales of woe, which are usually connected to some peculiarly-Italian challenge like a permit being blocked by a jobsworth at the town hall, trouble finding work, or an overbearing mother-in-law, with little more than an '*Ma insomma*', '*Meno male*', or '*Magari*' – 'really?', 'thankfully', or 'here's hoping'. But when the customer has left, he hangs up the bar's 'closed' sign, pops a magnesium supplement and puts on his Duke Magnesio costume – a rather poor approximation of a superhero get-up fashioned out of an Italian flag – and sets about righting the wrong.

Judging by the strips, I had always envisaged Duke Magnesio as a principally lightweight, if sardonic, superhero whose cynical barbs were usually aimed at the latest populist politician. In this sense, we were all Duke Magnesio, but, reading the stories that had made Angelo's name, I realised that in fact Duke Magnesio had originally been a more developed character. And there was a dark undertone to the stories absent from the magazine strips. In *Down in the Dumps* for example, about a corrupt recycler who takes the town's rubbish then tips it down a ravine, Duke Magnesio climbs into the man's truck while it unloads and, after battling the culprit, puts the lorry in reverse so it goes over the edge with the man in it. In *Baby and Bathwater*, a venal old man who rules tyrannically over his family is drawing a bath when Duke Magnesio creeps up and drowns him in it. And in *One Way Only*, a particularly obstructive local government official is found dead on a train returning from Palermo to Rombulo and everyone in the carriage turns out to be a suspect, only the true culprit is the Duke, who had coated her papers with poison before she set off.

I put down the book, picked up my phone and scanned the files Jacopo had forwarded after we had copied the SIMs.

I was not surprised to discover that there had been no evidence of the SpeakSafe app on either Professor Penna's or Melodia's phones, or any other conspiratorial evidence from their messages.

But now I opened Melodia's folder and searched for Angelo's name. Nothing. Then I tried Professor Gloria Penna's. There were two results.

From: Gloria.Penna@unibo.it

To: AngeloPittore@gmail.com

Dear cousin, as far as I know, Alberto will be arriving a little early, around 1800, to be talked through the running order. If

you would like to catch him then, that would probably be the
best time. Glad to hear you've finally patched it up after all these
years!

   X Gloria

To: Gloria.Penna@unibo.it

From: AngeloPittore@gmail.com

Dearest Gloria, I'm so looking forward to your concert! I hear
Alberto Fini will be the Master of Ceremonies. We are always
talking about catching up but we keep missing each other! I won-
dered if you could let me know when he is scheduled to arrive?
Maybe we'll have more luck!

   Huge hugs,

   Angelo

So Angelo had reached out to his cousin to arrange a meeting
with the late Alberto Fini, at the very event where the head of
the Accademia had been fed the poisoned *gelato* by his friend
Roberto.

   His cousin, who had been placed in pole position for the
top job at her department twice, thanks to the demise of her
immediate superiors, one of whom had previously humiliated
her in debate.

   Meanwhile his creation, Duke Magnesio, had used very
similar methods to eliminate his victims years before they
had been brought to fruition in real life.

   And yet . . . Angelo had also fallen foul of the poison, con-
veniently removing him from suspicion.

How was he? I had asked Roberto.

'Not too happy. Not at all.'

Had Roberto simply followed the Duke Magnesio rule-book? Or was he actually following the lead of the one who wrote the rules?

Chapter 49

'She's got a sure hand, your young lady.' Angelo sat down in front of me.

I placed my phone face down on the table. 'Stella really helped,' I said.

'Ah yes,' said Angelo. 'Of course, of course.' He frowned. 'And how is she?'

'Better.'

'*Grazie Dio.*'

'I've been flicking through your old work.' I held up the book. 'It didn't occur to me until now, but speaking of a sure hand, I realised I had seen your work around Bologna. Not just the Duke . . .'

'Ah yes. They want him to feature on a range of aprons now. Can't think why, but it'll be good for the pension!'

'I mean – in people's offices and homes. Not the Duke, but definitely your style. For example, I saw one in Professor Ernesto Farnese's office featuring a prof hidden behind a pile of papers.'

'Ah yes, Ernie, he comes in here every now and again. I knocked it out for nothing – old joke, though. Not mine.'

'And there was a cellist, too. Some cartoons featuring an orchestra. She was with the *Teatro*. With the opera house being just down the Guasto, I suppose musicians come here often.'

'It's a veritable melting pot, this place. As you may have noticed.'

'Just like the Duke, I suppose – you simply have to keep your ears open. You must hear all the gossip.'

Angelo chuckled. Rather mirthlessly, I thought. 'True.'

'You never mentioned how you knew Alberto Fini.'

'I didn't? Oh, we used to work together.'

'On graphic novels?'

'No, we were at the university.'

'Students?'

'We were in the same department.'

'Lecturing, you mean? At the Accademia? You were a professor yourself? I thought you had always been a cartoonist.'

'I turned to that when I left the Accademia.'

'I suppose there would be room for you now Alberto's gone.'

He frowned. 'Oh, that time has long passed.'

'Was there some kind of rivalry between you two back then?' He didn't respond. 'Roberto didn't offer to do you a favour, I take it?'

'Poor Roberto! What was he thinking? But as I said, in truth, I was never really sure about him – quite the Sphinx!'

I looked around. Rose was still sat around the corner with her friends. Otherwise Comix was empty except for me and Angelo, and Eros and Marco behind the bar. 'Now I remember the name of that cellist. You know – the one you did those cartoons for: Amanda Grimaldi.'

I laid my palms down on the table and looked calmly into Angelo's ice-blue eyes. 'So, how did it work? You won Amanda's confidence, then used the information you'd over-heard about her *bustarella* for Bellario to blackmail her into delivering the poison?'

Angelo didn't blink. 'Oh come on,' I said. 'You must be bursting to tell someone now Roberto's gone. Although admittedly, as a partner-in-crime, he could never have been much of a conversationalist.'

Angelo glanced down at my phone, flipped it over. It was displaying a recording app. 'Testing, testing,' he said. He placed it back upon the table, face up. 'Did you really expect me to fall for that?'

'*Dai,*' I held up the book. 'You're the *author*, Angelo. Don't you want to receive some credit? It never really added up: someone like Roberto wouldn't have had the *imagination* for a project like this, the *ambition.*

'I admit, he played it well in the end, was apparently happy to cover for you – out of a kind of misplaced gratitude, or debt? – for getting rid of his boss. Or because he simply con-sidered you a friend?

'But the truth is you used him like you used Amanda Grimaldi. You really were quite the puppet master – and the event at Santa Cristina, your *capolavoro,*' I smiled. '*Pièce de résistance.* But tell me – was it by accident or design Alberto Fini was the only actual fatality?'

Angelo's face seemed to contract behind his beard as if disappearing into the forest, and then expand, like a hunter coming in for the kill. I had the keen sense I was glimps-ing the true man, the murderer hidden behind the convivial cartoonist. He glanced over my shoulder at the portico. Was he calculating whether he could get around me? He was welcome to try – he wasn't the only killer at the table.

'Turn it off,' he said. I pressed the red stop button on the voice recorder. 'I mean the phone. Do you think I'm an utter fool?'

He watched me shut it down. Took a careful look around. The girls were far removed, absorbed in their project; Eros and Marco were preparing lunch in the kitchen.

Angelo's chest swelled.

'Roberto was a scientist,' he said. 'Not a pharmacist. The intention was to cover our tracks, given that Fini was rather too closely connected to me, by spreading the effect a little, but he apparently misjudged the quantities, or got carried away with the salt shaker. I sincerely apologise for your daughter and Stella. It was never meant to turn out that way; it was only supposed to have caused a few upset tummies, headaches.' Alberto's death would have simply been put down to an unfortunate reaction to a bad batch of *gelato*, when his heart gave out . . . It wouldn't have been the first time.

'If the authorities had even bothered to investigate, it was unlikely they would have come up with the cause, and even if they had, he would have simply been the most unfortunate among the victims. Safety in numbers, so to speak.'

'And Amanda? Were you always planning to kill her?'

His smile hardened. 'I didn't have much sympathy for the privileged little bitch, if that's what you mean. She was a part of the problem – a prime example of the dead wood stifling the prospects of more talented folk – although admittedly, I didn't think that far ahead at first. I had told her the drug was simply to put Bellario out of action for a few days, give him a nasty case of the shits as payback for a friend. Considering what she knew about the real man, that certainly can't have seemed too unlikely. But when she panicked after reading the newspaper, well, she had to go. It was pretty straightforward, to be honest, a spur of the minute thing. I just picked up the luggage strap, looped it over her head and hey presto. I think she was too surprised to react, at least until it was too late.'

'And the rest? The other professors?'

'Oh, you know – like you say, you hear things, especially here. The Bolognese love to talk about "resistance", but do they really mean it? Of course not! The great and good who came to celebrate the nuns' spirit of resistance would have once been their jailers, the jokers who now raise a toast to the partisans would have been among the first to turn them in.

'The university, hell, the country, is run by mediocrities. You get to the top by crushing talent, not rewarding it. So I decided to even things out a little, just like the Duke.

'After a while of going solo, I ran into Roberto, realised he had an entire armoury at his disposal: I just had to do him a little favour. And you know, Daniel – *it has been tremendous fun*. Happy to be of service! After all, who truly cares about a few bed-blockers? And the beauty of it is, providing you take rudimentary precautions, doing away with absolute strangers is a piece of cake. Of course, it becomes a little trickier when there's something to link you to them, which is why I took my time to come to my, um, "nemesis", so to speak.'

'Alberto Fini, President of the Accademia of Fine Arts and TV personality. The fame and prestige that should have been yours.'

'Something like that. Did you hear him? That false modesty: "My television appearances are ephemeral but your cartoons will endure, for children".'

'So what happened?' I said. 'He got the job you were after so you were forced to turn to cartoons?'

'They fell for it, all his flimflam. I couldn't bear to stay in the same building as that fraud.'

'Did it ever occur to you, Angelo, that maybe you just weren't good enough?' He sat back. Clearly it hadn't.

'That you may have had the artistic ability,' I continued. 'You may even have had some good ideas. But perhaps you couldn't teach as well, manage staff. I don't know, maybe even Alberto Fini was better than you at everything?'

Angelo blew a raspberry.

'Did it ever occur to you,' I leant forward, 'that you just had an obscenely inflated opinion of your own abilities and were in thrall to a malignant narcissism?'

But he wasn't listening to me. Of course he wasn't: 'I only wish I had actually been there to see the bugger croak.'

I heard the door open behind me, the heavy boots of the Polizia di Stato, followed by the click-clack of a commissario's heels.

After the drama of Angelo's arrest, the girls rather lost interest in their work. Stefi and Valentina headed off to sunbathe in the Giardini Margherita while Rose chose to accompany me home.

We stepped from air-conditioned Comix into the Bologna heat.

'But I don't get it,' said Rose. 'You say Angelo confessed,

but you had turned your phone off, so when it comes to being questioned by the police, he could just keep his mouth shut. It's his word against yours.'

'He might never have 'fessed up if he hadn't thought he had out-smarted me. But once he thought he was safe, he couldn't help himself. That was what this was ultimately all about, after all: his ego.'

'*So?*'

'Remember I mentioned Rita Miranda was bugging our phones?'

'Is she going to stop that, by the way?' Rose looked genuinely concerned.

'I'm sure – and I'm also pretty sure she wasn't listening in on you and your friends' secrets, anyway.'

'Why not?' Now Rose looked offended.

'Because you were not a part of our investigative team, honorary member that you are. Anyway – it turns out we weren't the only people the police eavesdropped on.'

It took Rose a moment to grasp: 'You mean – Comix?'

'Wired for sound. It makes sense, if you think about it. University favourite, hotbed of activism. Keep that to yourself, though, all right?'

We were passing Palazzo Bentivoglio. The derelict was laid on his back along the ancient stone ledge, snoring in the shade. He was naked save for a pair of pale-blue briefs, the rest of his clothes providing a pillow for his head.

Beyond it, inside a small ceramic bowl with a delicate filigree band, were a handful of coins. I opened my wallet and slipped a twenty euro note beneath it.

'That's a bit generous, isn't it?' said my daughter.

'I'm feeling generous. Speaking of which, do you fancy a *gelato*? You've not gone off ice cream after everything that happened?'

She looked at me as if I was mad.

Chapter 50

Here, *il vento della sera* blows like a balm upon our burnt skin. Here, the air is sweet with rosemary, cistus, myrtle and the pine of beachside brush. Here, from the front garden of our house – more an old bourgeois villa, to be honest, draped with purple bougainvillea and large enough to be divided into spacious apartments for the three families that have bought it – we have an unbroken view across the sand to the glistening sea, the gentle sunset.

All right, the distant beat of eighties Italian disco is audible further along the beach where the ubiquitous clubs begin with their Ballardian ranks of parasols and sunbeds, and yes, the beach is 'public', so during the day kids and families set up in front, but it is far enough from the town to discourage all but the most determined sun-seekers and far enough from the beach clubs to keep the music to a murmur.

Of an evening I typically walk, barefoot, sneakers in hand, along the shore until the beach reaches the causeway, then up to the quayside towards the centre of Cesantico where I meet Rose and Stefi – who is spending the summer in her family's summer home in nearby Cervia – along with her parents, for dinner. Occasionally the Comandante accompanies me, or Alba and Claudio, but this evening Giovanni is happy to play cards with his friends, while the young-*ish* couple are meeting pals in Rimini, a little further down the coast, so this evening I am alone as my toes dig into the wet sand and the warm sea slops over my feet.

Not for the first time, I think of Stella, picture her strolling along some Baltic beach. I shudder at the thought of the icy water. *Ice-cold veins?* Had I been more 'hot-blooded', might she have stayed? *Who am I kidding?* Stella's decision had nothing to do with me. She had a ticket to ride, while my train had already carried me home.

Mid-way along the shore, I notice a group of young people spread out upon the warm sand with an icebox of beers. At their centre sits the ubiquitous lad with his guitar, and knelt beside him a skinny beach-brown blonde. It somehow moves me – how, despite all the gadgets and gizmos of the twenty-first century, a guitar, a few beers, and a sunset remain enough for Italian youth, just as they were for their parents, and their grandparents. And then the boy begins to pluck his guitar, the girl sings, and I am drawn towards them – close enough to see it is Guido Delfillo on guitar and the voice of Melodia di Battista; to hear the unmistakable lament of a song by Lucrezia Orsina Vizzana, praising God while praying for a kind of release.

I am close enough for them to recognise me – and in fact, despite everything, Melodia has asked us to track down her late husband's secreted assets – but I remain, for all intents and purposes, invisible. The kids are too caught up in the moment, and quite right too.

I walk on, the fragile Latin lyrics fading upon the breeze. Then laughter, a smattering of applause.

I leave the sand and round the corner to the canal-side, the opening of a great network of waterways originally surveyed by Leonardo da Vinci.

Fishing boats line the quay, their burnt orange or marine blue nets hanging up to dry or wound tightly around winches, the pungent legacy of the day's catch still present, even if it has now been transported a few metres across the road to the restaurants.

I sit outside the appointed place and order a sparkling white Pignoletto while I wait for Stefi's mum and dad. I trust my daughter and her friend to materialise at the appropriate time – they are Italian, after all, and it would be unthinkable to miss the evening meal – and watch the beginning of Cesenatico's *passeggiata* when the youngest families emerge before turning in early to catch the morning beach. I remember those days with Lucia and Rose, of acquiescing to the daily routines – day merging into day, our time at the beach as much a rite as the evening meal. When I had once proposed something different – perhaps a trip further afield, hell, maybe even abroad? – Lucia had looked at me as if I was mad. *'But where will we find the time?'* I realised then that this was not so much a 'break' as a *continuation* of Italian life – just as work merges with family, so the holiday is not a symbol of freedom but comes with its own obligations and responsibilities.

I hear foreign voices. A little family at the next table. Judging by their patchy, hurried tans, broad-boned bodies, they're plainly not Latins. Northern European – a husband

and wife, pre-teen brother and sister. In fact, I realise, once I have finally tuned in – they are speaking English.

The two kids dubiously eye the un-translated menus. The boy lowers the card.

'Can I have Spaghetti Bolognese?'

'This is a fish restaurant,' says the father, trying to make sense of his own menu by the use of some mobile app. 'There's only fish.'

'A pizza, then?'

The wife inspects both sides of the card. 'There's no pizza, Simon.'

'No pizza,' the boy mutters, looking blankly back at the menu.

The dad gestures to a waiter. 'Menu in Inglese? *English?*'

'No,' the waiter says apologetically. 'No English.' The wife shoots her husband a look that says – *you wanted authentic. You got it.*

'Can I help?' I wave my own menu.

'Oh, brilliant!' says the man. *'Thank you very much.'*

I talk them through the options, and even order, in fact, *taglietelle al ragu*, which isn't written down but every Italian parent knows that even fish restaurants will usually rustle up for children, providing one knows to ask.

'Thank you,' says the man. 'That's so kind. And your English is excellent, by the way. *Complimenti!'*

I am about to correct him, but then spot Stefi's parents with the two girls in tow, so simply wish them *buon appetito.*

Both Cristina and her husband, Rocco – a corporate lawyer – are deep-tanned after a month of sun, and outfitted like a pair of hippies.

Very wealthy hippies.

After the usual salutations, we take our seats.

'I've been thinking.' I look around the table. 'It may be time.'

'Time for what?'

'To apply for citizenship,' I say. 'To become officially Italian.'

'Finally!' says Rose.

'Well,' says Rocco. 'That certainly deserves a toast.' The girls join us in raising a glass.

'*E' viva!*' they cry.

'Drink up,' says Rocco. 'You're going to need it.'

Over at the next table, the British couple convivially lift their own glasses, while along the Leonardo canal the last fishing boats cut through the ink-dark water, their rigging lit up like fairground lights.

Author's Note

Although I have done my best to be true to the geography of Bologna, by fictional necessity I have had to make a few things up.

Although situated on the map, you will search in vain for Vesuvio's 'Studio Fontanelle', christened after a grimly fascinating ossuary in Naples, and be hard-pressed to find the offices of Faidate Investigations, should you wish to track down a missing spouse, or a 'supertaster', for that matter, although if you visit Via Mirasole, the inspiration for the family home should be clear enough.

Another location you will be hard-pressed to find is the Osteria della Luna, for much the same reason as Vesuvio saved it from gentrification. However, an *osteria* resembling Daniel's preferred watering hole is not too far away, and if you happen to see the English Detective there he probably wouldn't decline the offer of a glass of Sangiovese.

Afterword

Fittingly, part of my inspiration for *Requiem in La Rossa* came with a visit to Bologna's International Music Museum and Library organised by Susanna Tassinari of the local International Women's Forum. On this occasion, the men folk were invited to accompany the members, and guide Enrico Tabellini pointed out the instruments used by the sisters of Santa Cristina as he recounted their story.

I was touched by the plight of the nuns. While it is all too true 'the past is another country' the desire for freedom is largely ahistorical. One nun from a Bolognese convent wrote to the pope:

> 'Notwithstanding that their relatives shut most of them in here against their wills ... and at a time when they have been tormented with various statutes and orders that they no longer have the strength to endure it. Most recently ... nobody except their father and mother can see or speak to them ... Wherefore, we feel that, deprived with such strictures and abandoned by everyone, we have only hell in this world and the next.'[1]

1 Craig A. Monson, *The Crannied Wall: Women, Religion and the Arts in Early Modern Europe.* University of Michigan Press, 1992

As Craig A. Monson explains in *Divas in the Convent: Music and Defiance in Seventeenth-Century Italy*, which became my principal reference source, by the time the papal authorities laid siege to the convent, 13.8 per cent of Bologna's *total* female population of around 30,000 were nuns. This percentage would have been considerably higher among the noble and aristocratic class.

Alongside the work of Professor Monson, who has been exploring the Bologna archives since 1986, Bologna-based professors Candace Smith and Vera Fortunati should also be acknowledged for helping bring this formerly hidden history into the light.

I hope introducing Santa Cristina into my narrative will whet the appetite of readers to discover more about Bologna's hidden musical history both by turning to Professor Monson's books and visiting *Museo internazionale e biblioteca della musica di Bologna*, the real home of Father Martini's corrected exam of the young Mozart.

In the meantime, I have provided the nuns of Santa Cristina with a little of the justice in fiction they were denied in real life, although who knows? Their tormentor Archbishop Ludovico Ludovisi *did* die at thirty-seven from a heart attack believed to have been brought about by gout, which has to work very, very hard indeed to kill you! It is also true that the botanical gardens were well established by that time and 'heartbreak glass' was known in the West, so almost certainly in one of its foremost seats of learning. As Dolores Pugliese might remark: *causa latet, vis est notissima*. The cause is hidden, but the result is well known.

Commissario Miranda's remark about so-called 'honour

killings' was spot on – the law granting laxity to perpetrators was only repealed in 1981, while well into the 1970s in some Italian regions rape victims could be expected or forced to marry their rapists under a legal statute (Article 544) which classed rape as a crime 'against public morality' that could be 'expunged' if the victim agreed to marry the perpetrator.

While the infamous Article 544 was repealed along with the protection for honour killings in 1981, sexual violence only became a crime against the person (as opposed to 'public morality') in 1996.

Inevitably, writing about Bologna, I returned to the university, which I visited first in *A Quiet Death in Italy*, and now again in *Requiem in La Rossa*. Once more I have my friend Paolo Ghezzi to thank, this time for introducing me to a senior member of the administration when I first began thinking about the setting.

Although it is more of an issue south of Rome, favouritism is a notorious problem in Italian academia as within other professions. A statistical analysis[2] from University of Chicago researcher Stefano Allesina, PhD, found 'widespread nepotism'. 'In Italy, there is an enormous brain drain,' he said. 'I think these kind of hiring practices contribute a lot to . . . the fact that Italian universities are not ranked very high internationally.'

As the husband of an Italian academic who moved abroad to further her career, the issue seemed particularly germane, and speaking as a newly-minted Italian citizen, it is infuriating

2 Measuring nepotism through shared last names: the case of Italian academia, PLoS ONE, August 2011

to see so many of the nation's brightest and best *buttati via* – thrown away – like this.

But while it is true the cynicism of the Italian system can seep into every aspect of life, one should always remember that the opposite also applies – from the campaigning magistrates who take on the mafia in the certain knowledge it will end their lives to the overwhelming majority of scrupulously honest Italians – there is plenty to fight for.

Avid readers may have noticed a passing reference to art collective Antonello Ghezzi in *A Quiet Death*, Stella Amore's visit to their private view in *The Hunting Season*, and now their appearance in person in *Requiem in La Rossa*.

Given *Requiem in La Rossa* featured an exhibition, I thought it only fitting to commission the real-life collective, so *500 Hundred Years of Resistance* boasts a unique exhibit they created especially for the fictional event, arguably the ultimate work of conceptual art, and all yours for the price of this book . . .

If you are interested in further work by the multi-award winning, internationally-renowned duo, go to antonelloghezzi.com

I would like to thank friend and fellow author Giovanni De Feo, who is an authority on, well, everything I am not, from *fumetti* to fantasy, and especially Italian folklore, carnival and Commedia dell' Arte, and who suggested I usher Balanzone onto stage.

Then there are my pals Glauco, Marco and Antonio who have phlegmatically put up with my weekly monologues about things literary, at least when we have been able to meet outside lockdown, as well as Prue and others among the British community in Bologna, especially Dave and Berni, whose culinary spectaculars have helped make up for the lack of open restaurants.

I would also like to thank my weekly Zoom mates, Gordon, Keith, Chris, Mark, Pete, and even, on occasion, Scott, Ian and Anouk whose meet-ups have helped keep me sane and even, now we are spread across Europe, managed to bring us closer together.

Speaking of sanity, I'm not sure where I would have been without that Friday-evening Zoom with my fellow D20 authors. Our tight-knit group of writers who debuted during the first Covid lockdown has provided mutual advice and support throughout a difficult year and, I hope, will continue to do so long into the future.

I would particularly like to thank Emma Christie, MW Craven, Gregory Dowling, Philippa East, Philip Gwynne Jones, Louise Hare, Harriet Tyce and Trevor Wood who were all kind enough to read my previous novel, *The Hunting Season*, at proof stage and provide supportive quotations. The kindness and solidarity of the writing community has been one of the unexpected joys of the past year.

Needless to say, I am immensely grateful for the continued and enthusiastic support of Krystyna Green and Hannah Wann at Constable, not only for their confidence in me but helping bring out the best in my writing, and my agent Bill Goodall for having the level head that I may, on rare occasions, have misplaced. *Grazie mille* to ever-patient Amanda Keats for steering me through the editorial process, along with copy-editor Colin Murray and proofreader Joan Deitch, along with publicist Clara Diaz for garnering those all-important reviews.

I would like to close by, as ever, thanking my family. One person who has been overlooked in previous acknowledgements is my mother, Marion, which is an appalling oversight, but – what can I say? – typical of children. She has been with me, albeit usually over the phone, throughout the entire process – one of my very first and avid readers, and naturally my number one fan.

Then there's my family here in Bologna, my sister-in-law Silvia and her children Simone, Luigi, Massimo and Elena, as well as my parents-in-law in Puglia, Ida and Luigi, and the Sienna contingent – Rosanna, Giuseppe and Giulia. Of course, there is the ever-present Louis-Ferdinand, our Chartreux cat, who continues to fulfil his vocation as *enfant terrible*.

This novel is dedicated to my wife, Lea, who came an awfully long way from her small southern Italian town to win a scholarship to New York's Columbia University. Alongside her brilliance and hard work she was indubitably standing on the shoulders of generations of women who had struggled for equal rights. I'm sure the sisters of Santa Cristina would have been proud.

Tom Benjamin
Bologna, March 2021

*Keep reading to see where the adventures began for
Daniel Leicester with a sneak peek at book one in the series,
A Quiet Death in Italy.*

Chapter 1

Like much else in a city that had once been governed by the Catholic Church, the old morgue was a muddle of the sacred and profane. The brick-domed room with its crucifix above the doorway felt as reverent as any crypt, the corpses were stacked on marble shelves in white body bags that could have passed as shrouds. The strip lights suspended from the ceiling and capital-lettered ordinances of the secular authority reminded us that God had since died and we would all end up in this place or somewhere like it one day, tagged and bagged in white if we were lucky and no suspicious circumstances were associated with our passing.

But we weren't stopping here. Doctor Mattani unlocked the door to the autopsy room and paused. 'Better that we allow a moment,' he said, opening it halfway. He meant to acclimatise. Not a hint of the macho humour that usually bludgeoned you in places like this – if one of us threw up, the doctor would probably have to dispose of the mess himself. This was not an official visit, after all.

'They found him attached to some fencing,' said the doctor. 'Apparently, that was what alerted the authorities in the first place – some kind of blockage in the canal system. He went missing two weeks before, and the state of decay would be consistent with this timeframe.'

That peculiar hybrid smell – from the butchering and the pickling – exited the doorway. Not so disagreeable until your imagination got to work. That was when your stomach would begin to tighten and you were glad you had had a light breakfast. But it wasn't the anatomy that really troubled me, it was the entropy. The toll time took on an abandoned body; the reminder that death was not only an event but a process, and a progressively ugly one.

Standing outside that room alongside my boss, the Comandante, and our friend the doctor, I began to sense its presence: insinuating itself behind the blood and chemicals like the base note to a particularly sickly perfume.

The doctor opened the door fully and we stepped in. This room was like a smaller version of the 'crypt', only white-washed and with a pair of gleaming stainless-steel tables plumbed to sinks. Lying flat on the first was a black body bag zipped to the top.

The extractor fan came on and a weary rattle began to escape from the vent. I turned to the Comandante. 'A black bag,' I said. 'Didn't our guy at the Questura confirm it wasn't being treated as suspicious?'

The Comandante shrugged. Doctor Mattani shook his head. 'I don't know anything about that.' He stepped forward and positioned himself beside the corpse. 'If you wouldn't mind closing the door.'

I felt it click behind me. The doctor took hold of the large plastic zip and, walking the length of the table, opened the bag from head to toe. Despite having adjusted to the stink, the accumulated gasses caused us to step back and place our hands across our faces. We stood observing the corpse for some time, each, I think, unwilling to make the necessary effort to speak until our senses had sufficiently recovered and the ventilation system had played its part.

Death had utterly claimed Signor Solitudine, who was unrecognisable from the photo I had stored on my phone – the sinewy, clean-shaven older man with windswept hair and bright eyes marching behind a protest banner – unless, that is, you were looking for the Man on the Moon. A fortnight in the river that ran beneath the centre of Bologna had done its damnedest to swell his features to comic proportions. He had assumed a flattened, almost two-dimensional appearance, bolstered by the silver-grey patina that always came with corpses that had spent too long in dirty water. His eyelids and mouth were bloated closed, his fingers swollen together like fins, and from his collarbone to his pelvis there were broad post-mortem stitches, as if he'd been sewn up in a hurry.

'There was evidence of trauma to the cranium,' said the doctor, 'but we are unable to say whether this took place before or after he was submerged, or what caused it. There is water in the lungs—'

'River water?' I said. The doctor smiled.

'Yes, Daniel, river water – he was not drowned in his bathtub and dumped, I can tell you that at least.'

'The bang on the head, though,' I said, looking at the Comandante, 'baton?'

'It certainly could have come from human agency,' said

the Comandante, 'but equally a boat or even the debris in the current . . . isn't that so, Matteo?'

'In those conditions,' said the doctor, 'it would be impossible to say for sure.'

'Anything else?' said the Comandante.

'We scraped his fingernails and so on but nothing.'

'River water . . .' said the Comandante. The doctor nodded.

'Remarkably corrosive. I always say that if I was to commit a murder, that would be how I would dispose of my victims. River water doesn't just wash any evidence away, it scrubs the corpse clean.'

'And you'd be the perfect murderer too,' I said, 'being the one to examine the bodies.'

'If we are ever asked to hunt an elusive serial killer,' added the Comandante, 'who dumps his victims in the Reno, we will know where to come.'

The smell had now almost disappeared, although that had as much to do with mankind's faculty to adapt to new odours, no matter how unpleasant, as the efficacy of the ventilation system, and we found ourselves smiling over the mouldering corpse. Looking back down at it sobered us up.

'Done?' said Doctor Mattani. The Comandante looked at me. I took in Paolo Solitudine's body one last time. Thought of the handsome older man he had been, of the woman who had sent us here.

'Done,' I said.

NEWPORT COMMUNITY
LEARNING & LIBRARIES